# Praise for

# shannon stacey

"Books like this are why I read romance."
—*Smart Bitches, Trashy Books* on *Exclusively Yours*

"Shannon Stacey's books deliver exactly what we need in
contemporary romances.... I feel safe that every time
I pick up a Stacey book I'm going to read
something funny, sexy and loving."
—Jane Litte of *Dear Author* on *All He Ever Needed*

"I'm madly in love with the Kowalskis!"
—*New York Times* bestselling author Nalini Singh

"*Yours to Keep* was a wonderful,
sexy and witty installment in this series....
This was a truly magical book."
—*The Bookpushers*

"This contemporary romance is filled with charm, wit,
sophistication, and is anything but predictable."
—*Heart to Heart, BN.com,* on *Yours to Keep*

"One of those books
that simply makes you feel good and happy."
—*Smitten with Reading* on *Yours to Keep*

D0190905

**Also available from
Shannon Stacey
and Harlequin HQN**

*Exclusively Yours*
*Undeniably Yours*
*Yours to Keep*
*All He Ever Needed*
*Alone With You* (*Be Mine* anthology)

**And coming soon**

*All He Ever Dreamed*

**Also available from
Shannon Stacey
and Carina Press**

*Holiday Sparks*
*Mistletoe and Margaritas*
*Slow Summer Kisses*

# shannon stacey

# all he ever *desired*

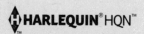
HARLEQUIN® HQN™

If you purchased this book without a cover you should be aware
that this book is stolen property. It was reported as "unsold and
destroyed" to the publisher, and neither the author nor the
publisher has received any payment for this "stripped book."

Recycling programs
for this product may
not exist in your area.

ISBN-13: 978-0-373-77756-3

ALL HE EVER DESIRED

Copyright © 2012 by Shannon Stacey

All rights reserved. Except for use in any review, the reproduction or
utilization of this work in whole or in part in any form by any electronic,
mechanical or other means, now known or hereafter invented, including
xerography, photocopying and recording, or in any information storage
or retrieval system, is forbidden without the written permission of the
publisher, Harlequin HQN, 225 Duncan Mill Road, Don Mills, Ontario
M3B 3K9, Canada.

This is a work of fiction. Names, characters, places and incidents are
either the product of the author's imagination or are used fictitiously,
and any resemblance to actual persons, living or dead, business
establishments, events or locales is entirely coincidental.

This edition published by arrangement with Harlequin Books S.A.

For questions and comments about the quality of this book,
please contact us at CustomerService@Harlequin.com.

® and TM are trademarks of Harlequin Enterprises Limited or its
corporate affiliates. Trademarks indicated with ® are registered in the
United States Patent and Trademark Office, the Canadian Trade Marks
Office and in other countries.

Printed in U.S.A.

HARLEQUIN®
www.Harlequin.com

This one's for Leah.
You opened your heart to a thirteen-year-old girl
and have been one of my life's greatest blessings ever since.
Thank you for being a wonderful stepmother, an amazing
grammy to my sons and, most of all, for being my friend.
I love you.

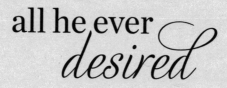

all he ever *desired*

# CHAPTER ONE

BECAUSE HECTIC MONDAY mornings didn't suck enough all on their own merits, Lauren Carpenter managed to miss her lashes and apply mascara straight to her eyeball. Cursing and blinking, she groped for a tissue.

She wasn't sure why she bothered making herself up anyway. Over her years working as the entire office staff for the only insurance agent in town, she'd seen communications swing from office visits to phone calls and faxes and then to email. Entire days could go by without anybody but her boss actually stepping foot in the place.

It was the principle, she decided as she mopped up the damage and tried again. She'd long ago given up on giving a crap what anybody thought of her, but it made her feel good to look good. There was a limit, though, and she smiled as she shoved her feet into the battered leather loafers that were even older than Nick. Her feet were usually under her desk anyway.

Thinking of Nick, she glanced at her alarm clock and sighed. Morning battle to commence in three…two…

"Ma!" The bellow made her cringe.

She'd asked him not to shout at her from across the house even more times than she'd asked him not to call her Ma. Ma made her think of calico dresses and aprons and churning butter. It also made her feel old, and being

the mother of a sixteen-year-old was reminder enough
of that, thank you very much.

Lauren left her bedroom and went down the hall,
purposely not glancing into the train wreck that was
her son's room, fastening small pearl earrings as she
walked. "Don't bellow, Nick."

"If I don't, you won't hear me."

He was in the kitchen, rummaging through his backpack at the table while a full bowl of cereal turned into
mush on the counter. "You planning to eat your breakfast?"

Shrugging, Nick pulled a crumpled ball of paper out
of his bag. "Yeah. You need to sign this."

"What is it?" She carried the bowl of cereal to the
table and traded it for the paper. "Eat. The bus comes
in five minutes."

When he kept his eyes down and shoved a heaping
mound of cereal in his mouth, Lauren's stomach sank.
Whatever the paper was, it wasn't good.

Physically, Nick took after Dean, her ex-husband.
Nick's hair was darker than her blond and his eyes were
a lighter brown. He'd gotten not only his dad's good
looks, but his struggles in school, too.

It was a detention notice, assigned due to missing
homework. "Nick, you've only had three weeks of
school and you're slipping already?"

"I don't like the teacher," he mumbled around a
mouthful of cereal.

"You don't have to like the teacher. You do have to
do your homework." He shrugged and the nonverbal
*whatever* was the straw that broke Monday morning's
back. "I know which form I *won't* be signing and that's
the driver's ed registration."

"But, Mom—"

"Save it. The bus is coming."

She signed the detention paper while he dumped his bowl in the sink, then watched him ball up the notice and shove it back in his pocket. The faint rumble of the bus came into earshot and he hefted his backpack.

"Walk straight home after detention," she said to the back of his head as he walked toward the front door. "And no video games."

"Uh-huh."

After the door closed behind him—he knew better than to slam it—Lauren leaned against the counter and blew out a breath. Something was going on with her son and she'd be damned if she could put her finger on what. He didn't get a pass because he was a teenager or because of that *boys-will-be-boys* crap, so it was time for an attitude adjustment. And that meant talking to Dean, because if they weren't on the same page when it came to Nick, she may as well find a brick wall to talk to.

Of course, talking to Dean Carpenter was always like talking to a brick wall. Communication wasn't his strong suit. Their son, though, was more receptive if his parents were giving him the same message. Usually.

She'd have to find a few minutes to talk to her ex when he picked up Nick on Friday evening, which meant having an idea what she was going to say before he showed up. And she'd worry about that some other time, because now she had less than ten minutes to get to work.

It took her twelve to drive across Whitford because she had to stop for gas, so Gary Demarest, insurance agent extraordinaire, was already in when she arrived. She'd worked for him since her divorce eight years before, when she'd been looking for a job in town with mother's hours. Demarest Insurance had mostly fit the bill, though Nick got out of school a couple of hours before she left work. When he was younger, the neighbor had kept an eye on him. Now he was mostly on his own, though in a town like Whitford, somebody was always watching.

"I left some notes on your desk," Gary said. He was in great shape for a man in his mid-sixties and prided himself on being a smart dresser, despite the fact that the majority of his clientele wore jeans and T-shirts. "Paige Sullivan's going to be renting out her mobile home, so she needs a price on adjusting the property insurance accordingly. I'll let you know when I get the numbers together, but you can get started on the paperwork if you get a chance."

"No problem." When Gary disappeared into his office, closing the door behind him, Lauren leaned back in her very nice office chair and sighed.

Paige Sullivan was going to rent out her mobile home because she was marrying Mitch Kowalski and they were going to buy a house together. And, of course, thinking of Mitch naturally led her to think of his brother.

Ryan Kowalski. Her *what-if* guy when she let herself indulge in ridiculous fantasy. *What if she'd said yes?*

He'd been in town a few times lately, she knew, helping his brothers straighten out the Northern Star, their family-owned snowmobile lodge. But, as in the past when he'd visited, he stayed close to home and they never got close enough to speak. She wasn't sure whether it was deliberate, but he'd managed not to run into her since he'd graduated from college.

The phone rang before Lauren could give in to the *what-if* fantasy, which was a good thing. With Nick needing an attitude adjustment and Dean to deal with, the last thing she needed was another guy with issues. Her ex-husband's ex—best friend could stay out of sight and out of mind where he belonged.

RYAN KOWALSKI MADE very few mistakes when it came to running his business, but trapping himself in a pickup with an idiot definitely counted as one. "Put the phone on vibrate."

Dill Brophy snorted, just as the phone in his hand sounded another incoming text with the grating, electronic sound of a duck call. For almost five freaking hours he'd been listening to Dill's phone quack, and if he had a shotgun he'd pull over and play an impromptu round of Duck Hunt. Not even a minute later, it quacked again.

Ryan jerked the wheel hard to the left and had the satisfaction of hearing Dill's head thump against the passenger window.

"Ow! What the hell, man?"

"Pothole."

"Matt wants to know if we're almost there yet." *Quack.* "Or if not, can we stop for lunch, because it's after lunchtime."

Ryan put on his blinker and pulled over onto the shoulder. Once Matt Russell had pulled in behind him, he turned to Dill. "Let me see your phone."

Rather than throw it out the window and run over it repeatedly, as he wanted to do, Ryan took it and powered it down. Then he got out of the truck, slamming the door with Kowalski Custom Builders painted down the side, and walked back to the identical vehicle Matt was driving. Well, not totally identical. Ryan's had heated leather seats and a custom sound system. It was nice to be the boss.

Matt lowered the window. "What's up?"

"Give me your phone." Since both guys carried company-provided cell phones, refusing wasn't an option. When he had it, Ryan gave the young carpenter a stern look. "You text while driving one of my trucks again, you're fired."

After he tossed both phones into his door pocket, they got back on the road and Ryan took a deep breath when, not long after, they passed the Welcome to Whitford, Maine sign. Home again. Dammit.

A while back, when his youngest brother, Josh, had busted his leg and the oldest, Mitch, had gone home to give him a hand, the shit had really hit the fan. The Northern Star Lodge—which had gone from gentleman's hunting lodge to snowmobiling lodge under the ownership of several generations of Kowalskis—was in bad shape, both financially and physically. Some rehab needed doing and, since Ryan was a builder, it was his turn to spend a little time in Whitford.

Because he'd be away from his business for who knew how long, he'd left his top guys and most experienced builders down in Massachusetts to keep the jobs going, which was how he'd ended up stuck with two young, less-experienced pinheads to work with.

That wasn't quite fair. They were good kids and they worked hard. If they weren't he wouldn't have them on his jobs. But his current feelings toward them were colored a bit by four and a half hours of the quacking duck and the twinkly chime that sounded when Dill's pregnant wife texted. And she texted a lot.

For a second, he regretted shutting Dill's phone off, but then he told himself that if there was an emergency, she'd call him or the office, looking for her husband. And when they got to the lodge, he'd give the phones back.

As eager as he was to get to the lodge, he didn't want to show up with two hungry guys looking to rummage through Rosie's kitchen, Ryan decided to stop at the Trailside Diner and let them eat before driving the last few minutes to the Northern Star.

Because it wasn't quite two yet, Paige Sullivan—his future sister-in-law—was behind the counter and she smiled when she saw him.

"Ryan! I didn't know you were coming in today."

He leaned across the counter to kiss her cheek. "It was kind of fluid. Had to wrap up some stuff and wait on a granite delivery, then I made a break for it today."

"Does Rosie know?"

"I called her when I hit the road this morning." Rose Davis was housekeeper at the Northern Star Lodge by title, but she'd helped raise the Kowalski kids after their mother died. Ryan knew better than to pop in without giving her enough advance notice to make his favorite dinner. Not that he expected her to, but Rosie liked to fuss. "Is Mitch at the lodge?"

"He's in Miami for a few days. I don't think he expected you until at least next week."

He realized the guys were hovering behind him, obviously waiting for an introduction, so he gestured to each in turn. "This is Dillon Brophy and Matt Russell. They work for me and they'll be helping out at the lodge. This is Paige Sullivan, my brother's fiancée."

Matt and Dill straightened up, smart enough to catch his cue that Paige was as good as a member of the boss's family. Both guys were in their early twenties, but the similarities ended there. Dill was tall—almost as tall as Ryan—and skinny, with sandy hair and an easy smile.

Matt was shorter, more muscular, and had the dark and serious thing going on. Ryan watched them each shake Paige's hand, both *very* respectful, before heading off to a table to look over the menu.

"Rosie's just going to eat them up," Paige said, her eyes filled with laughter. "She's always complaining she doesn't have enough people to fuss over anymore."

"They're employees, not grandchildren. She doesn't need to fuss over them and I'll kick their asses if they let her."

The look she gave him was pure skepticism, and he shook his head before joining the guys. They all had cheeseburgers and fries, and Ryan had to admit that, despite the fact he hadn't wanted to stop at the diner, the food hit the spot. The mood was good all around, especially when he told them they could retrieve their phones while he paid. They were out the door before he got all the words out.

"They're worse than kids," he muttered, handing the check and the company credit card to Paige.

"You took their cell phones away? Totally a dad-like move."

"I'm not *that* old." He signed his name to the slip she handed him, then took his card back. "If you talk to Mitch, let him know I'll be around for a while this time."

"I will."

As he turned to leave, he was aware of the door opening and he stopped walking so he wouldn't run into anybody while tucking his card back into his wallet. Then he looked up.

Dirty-blond hair. Dark-chocolate eyes. A body that time and some added pounds had molded into curves any man would take his time savoring. And a familiar face that hit him like one of his brother's wrecking balls.

LAUREN MIGHT HAVE forgotten how to breathe for a few seconds. God, he looked good. Even better than he had in her imagination. Since his brothers had aged well, she shouldn't have been surprised by the still-thick dark hair or the flat stomach and broad shoulders shown off by the Kowalski Custom Builders polo shirt. But part of her wished he'd gone downhill a little. Or a lot, actually.

She'd seen him a couple of times since Josh had broken his leg, but always at a distance. So she hadn't been able to see the blue eyes or the way the years had added character to his face, nor could she have smelled whatever delicious cologne or aftershave he was wearing.

And distance meant not having to do this awkward dance of not knowing what to do or say. They hadn't actually spoken since Nick was a baby, when Ryan had asked her a question that could have changed her life and she'd said no.

He was supposed to stay away. It was unspoken, but understood.

"Hi, Lauren." His voice was deeper. Stronger.

"How have you been?"

For a few seconds he looked like he was trying to figure out how to sum up fifteen or so years in a few words, but then he smiled. But it was the polite smile, not the full, devastating grin, for which she should probably be thankful. "I've been good."

"Good. And how are things at the lodge?"

"Good."

"And Josh's leg?"

"It's good."

"That's…good." Now that they'd established everything was *good*, she'd reached the end of her having-a-clue-what-to-say rope. "I don't have a long lunch break, so I should probably order."

"Of course." He stepped out of her way. "I'll see you…around."

He left before she could say anything else and that was fine, since all she could think to say was "good." And seeing him around would be anything but.

As she sat down, Lauren tried to shake off the nerves that being so close to him seemed to have set to quivering, only to find herself pinned by Paige's all-too-observant stare. She should have made the time to pack a lunch this morning.

"Coffee?"

Lauren pressed a hand to her stomach, cursing the butterflies. "I think I'll have decaf."

"They have that effect on women."

"Coffees?"

"Kowalskis."

Uh-oh. The last thing Lauren needed was the population of Whitford thinking she had a thing for Ryan. "Hectic morning. Nick didn't want to get out of the house and then things at the office were crazy. I've already had more than my fair share of the high-test stuff."

"Mmm-hmm. What are you eating?"

"Grilled cheese on wheat, I guess. With coleslaw instead of fries."

"So, the regular, in other words." Paige rolled her eyes and went to give the order to the cook, but she was gone only a few seconds. "Weren't your ex and Ryan best friends back in high school?"

It was to be expected, Lauren told herself. The woman was marrying a Kowalski, so it was natural people would fill her in on the family details. "Yeah, they were."

They weren't anymore. There hadn't been a fight between the guys, but Dean seemed to think Ryan had gone off to become a big shot and forgotten where he came from. There was some resentment on Dean's part, but it was misplaced. Lauren had never told her ex-husband about Ryan's visit, even though it had been a serious betrayal of the guys' friendship. Ryan had gone away, and every week, then month, and finally year he was gone made it easier to justify not telling Dean.

"And?"

She'd almost forgotten Paige was standing there, no doubt waiting to hear the rest of the story. "And Ryan got his degree and moved to Mass and that was that."

"Oh, come on. It's me!" Paige bent down and rested her forearms on the counter so they were at the same height. "Mitch thinks there's some kind of history between you two."

"Nope, sorry." It wasn't exactly a lie, but it wasn't exactly the truth, either. It was time to change the subject. "Speaking of Mitch, when are you guys getting married?"

Paige's face lit up and, almost by reflex, she put out her left hand to admire the sparkling ring on her finger. "It hasn't even been two weeks since he asked me."

"From what I've heard, Mitch is in a hurry and you'll be lucky if he doesn't have you kidnapped and put on a plane to Vegas."

"We want to get married at the lodge, but we don't want to do it during the sledding season and he doesn't want to wait until spring."

"That doesn't leave you a lot of time."

"We're thinking about Columbus Day weekend,"

Paige said. "It falls early this year, so maybe we'll still have some fall foliage."

"It's also not quite three weeks away."

"We don't want anything fancy. He's going to call everybody when he gets home and see if we can make it work. As long as his aunt Mary and uncle Leo can make it from New Hampshire, and his brother Sean and his wife, we'll probably go for it. But he'd like his sister to fly in from New Mexico, too."

"I haven't seen Liz in ages."

"I guess nobody has, except when Sean got out of the army. They had a party for him at Ryan's."

And back to Ryan again. Thankfully the bell dinged and Paige left to pick up Lauren's grilled cheese sandwich, because Lauren could feel the heat creeping into her face. She was going to have to come up with a way to stop doing that or wear more makeup or something. She couldn't blush every time somebody mentioned the man's name.

To make matters worse, it wasn't some leftover attraction to a young Ryan, which was more nostalgia than anything. It's not as if she'd been lusting after him while running around with his best friend. She'd loved Dean and, while she found Ryan attractive, it wasn't until later her subconscious mind had given him the starring role in her sexual fantasies. Probably because he was safely far away so fantasy couldn't intrude on reality.

But right now, grown-up Lauren's body, which hadn't been up against a naked man's in *way* too long, seemed to think the very grown-up Ryan was just the man for the job.

Paige set Lauren's lunch in front of her, then untied

her apron. "I hate to run out on you, but I have an appointment to look at a house."

Lauren had been so wrapped up in trying not to think about Ryan Kowalski, she hadn't even noticed that Ava, the second-shift waitress, had shown up. "I have to inhale this and get back anyway. When I step out for lunch, it's like Hurricane Gary passed over my desk during the half hour I was gone."

"Don't make any plans for Columbus Day weekend," Paige reminded her as she headed for the door. "I'm not planning on having bridesmaids, but you and Hailey *have* to be at my wedding."

"I wouldn't miss it," Lauren said, and she meant it. But as the door swung closed behind Paige, her undersexed mind coughed up a tantalizing image.

Ryan in a suit. Her in a sexy dress. A few drinks. A slow dance or two…

She shoved a forkful of coleslaw in her mouth and told herself to get over it. There was enough on her plate as it was and she already knew they had almost nothing to say to each other. He was as good as a stranger now and, no matter how her hormones felt about the matter, it was best he stay that way.

It seemed like he'd been avoiding her for years. Now it was time for her to avoid him. Simple as that.

## CHAPTER TWO

RYAN WASN'T SURPRISED at all that the first thing Rosie Davis did, after wrapping him in a suffocating hug, was try to feed Dill and Matt.

"They're here to work, Rosie, not be adopted." He knew any attempt to mark boundaries with the lodge's housekeeper was an act of futility, but it was a good reminder for the boys. "Besides, we stopped at the diner on the way in."

"Oh, did you see Paige?"

"Yup." Along with Lauren Carpenter, and seeing her had thrown him so far off balance he was still sideways.

As he always did when he thought of her, he remembered back to the day he'd asked her to leave her husband. He'd promised her he'd love her in a way Dean didn't seem capable of, and that he would raise Nick as if he was his own son. The memory of feeling like a humiliated, stupid ass as he'd driven out of Whitford alone was still almost as vivid as the reality.

Running into her so unexpectedly had brought out the stupid ass in him again, he thought as he grabbed his bag out of the backseat of the truck. He knew how to hold a conversation, for chrissake, but one look at Lauren and all he'd been able to say was "good." Everything was good. Life was good. She probably thought he was a total idiot, and maybe that was good, too.

Josh stepped out onto the porch, his hair still wet

from a shower. "You brought backup this time? Must be getting serious."

"I had to bring somebody who'd work instead of taking bubble baths halfway through the afternoon."

Josh grinned. "When you spend the day working on the insulation in the attic, you can take a bubble bath in the afternoon, too."

It was damn good to see his little brother smile. Ryan had been blown away by Josh's shitty attitude after being summoned home because Josh had busted his leg. His brother had been surly, drank enough to raise eyebrows and looked like hell.

It had taken a while, but Josh finally confessed he wanted out. Out of Whitford and away from the Northern Star. One by one, his brothers and sisters had left home until he was the only one left to help out. Then, after their dad passed away, he was stuck holding down the fort and it had never occurred to the others he didn't want to be there. Suddenly he was thirty and he'd never done a damn thing.

Now they had a plan and the first step was working together to get the lodge back on its feet financially. Then they'd put it on the market or hire somebody to run it. Either way, the old place needed some structural work and a face-lift, and that's why Ryan was there, along with Dill and Matt for the heavy lifting.

Rose gestured to the two carpenters. "I'll show you boys where you're sleeping and you can get settled."

"They can bunk at the end of the hall. The room with the double bunk beds." It was an overflow room, generally used for groups of guys who wanted to split the bill and keep costs down.

"We have plenty of rooms and you'll all be gone before the snow flies."

"They don't need to be mucking up two rooms."

She put her hands on her hips and gave him the look. "Did you come to pound nails or are you going to run the place now? I got some toilets that need scrubbing if you are."

He could be stubborn, too. Especially in front of guys who worked for him. "They're not paying guests."

When she just kept giving him the look, one eyebrow raised, he felt the heat creeping up the back of his neck. He hated when she did that. Had since he was a little kid. He couldn't remember how old he was when his parents had hired Rosie to help his mother around the lodge. But he was eleven when Sarah Kowalski died of an aneurism and, with help from his aunt Mary, who lived a state away, Rosie had stepped into the void she'd left. The housekeeper had done everything a mother would do for him as he'd grown up, including giving him that damn look.

"Fine. But they clean up after themselves."

"We're not kids, boss," Dill said, but then his phone quacked and Matt snickered.

"Go."

They followed Rose into the lodge, and Ryan dropped his bag onto the porch before sinking into one of the chairs. Josh took one beside him, stretching his legs out.

"How's the leg?"

Josh shrugged. "Good. Not a hundred percent yet, so I'm trying to take it easy, but it could've been worse. What's under the tarps?"

Ryan looked at the two company trucks, both of which had tarps covering the beds. "Windows. I noticed the living and dining room windows are fairly new, and the ones in the guest bedrooms, but we need to do the kitchen and the family rooms."

"I'd planned to do one a month, maybe, next summer. Pain in the ass getting the tools out and then putting them back, but updated windows would save on the fuel bill."

Ryan wanted to point out that he got a much better deal on windows than Josh could and he should have called him, but he kept his mouth shut. Pride and stubbornness had kept Josh working himself into the ground on a shoestring budget, rather than admitting to his siblings and co-owners that the lodge was in trouble. They'd already been through all that and there was no sense in rehashing it.

"I have to go see Dozer in a few," Josh said. "He was going to mix up the paint for the shutters this morning. Wanna take a ride?"

"It's going to take a while to unload those windows, even with Dill and Matt helping."

"No rush," Josh said. "I can give you a hand."

"I just got out of my truck. Don't really want to get back in it now." Mostly, he didn't want to go to the hardware store when he'd just run into Lauren.

Dozer owned Whitford Hardware. His name was Albert Dozynski, but when he'd bought the business in the nineteen-seventies, everybody had started just calling him Dozer. He was also Lauren Carpenter's dad.

Snorting, Ryan bit back a curse. Freaking small towns.

"What's the matter?"

"Nothing. Just remembering something I didn't do at the office," he lied.

"Did you hear Mitch and Paige want to get married Columbus Day weekend?"

"Isn't that like three weeks from now?"

Josh nodded. "Not quite three weeks. And they want to get married here."

"In less than three weeks."

"Mitch doesn't want to have a wedding with sledders roaming around the lodge and he doesn't want to wait for the snow to melt in the spring. But Paige wants to have it outside, so it needs to be soon. Like three weeks soon."

"I might not be done by then." He was almost sure he wouldn't be.

"I told Paige that. She said it was only going to be friends and family and, as long as there are a couple of spots to have pictures taken, she doesn't care."

She'd care. When the day came and there were sawhorses and power tools in the yard, she'd care. Ryan had been married once—he knew that a lot of women started out focusing on the love and family and friends, but as the big day drew near, they lost their freaking minds.

"Hopefully, whatever idiot's been vandalizing the place is bored with us now."

Somebody had been messing around on the property and they hadn't caught the little jerk yet. Stupid shit, like dumping paint buckets and pounding a dozen nails into a piece of lumber, but the money added up and it was a hell of a mess to clean up. "I'll wring his neck if I catch him."

Josh laughed. "What if it's a girl?"

"Then I'll sic Rosie on her." His mind turned back to their eldest brother's wedding. "Has Mitch called Aunt Mary yet? And Liz?"

"He's going to when he gets home from Miami. If they can make it, and Sean, we'll be having a wedding."

"I guess we'd better get to work, then." And work

was just what Ryan needed. Hard, sweaty work that left his mind and body too exhausted at the end of the day to miss having a woman in his bed.

It had been a while since he'd seriously dated, but once he was done here in Maine, it might be time to start going out again. He couldn't be happier that Sean and Mitch had found women they wanted to spend the rest of their lives with, but thinking about the upcoming wedding made him feel restless.

He was thirty-six. He wanted a wife and maybe some kids. Living alone in a house built for a family sucked, even though he'd built it himself, but he'd been so busy running his company that he'd stopped going out at night looking for opportunities to meet a woman he might like. Time to remedy that when he got home.

Right now, though, it was time to unload some windows.

On Wednesday, Lauren stopped at her dad's store on her way home from work. She kept forgetting to call and ask him to order new filters for her furnace, so she'd just drop in while she was thinking of it.

Whitford Hardware was like a second home to Lauren, with sights and sounds and smells as familiar to her as those of her parents' home. The jumble of displays near the front of the store that changed with the seasons. The mingling scents of lemon wood-polish, mechanical oils and lawn fertilizer.

Her dad was behind the counter as usual, a stout, dark-haired man whose broad shoulders and chest made up for his lack of height. And, as usual, his face lit up when he saw her.

"Lauren! How is my sunshine today?"

"I'm good, Dad." She was about to mention the filters when her mother walked out of the back room. As fair as her husband was dark, Pat Dozynski was still a head turner. "Hi, Mom. I didn't expect to see you here."

"CeeCee and I went to the yarn store and then she had to rush straight home to get her casserole in the oven. She dropped me off here, so I'll ride home with your father."

"Get anything good?" Lauren had never had the patience for knitting, but it was one of her mother's passions.

"They had a gorgeous pink cotton on clearance. Now I just need a baby girl to knit a sweater set for."

Lauren laughed and held up her hands. "Don't look at me. I gave you a grandson and, trust me, one is enough."

"How is Nicky doing?" her dad asked. "It's been quiet here without him."

Nick worked part-time at the hardware store during the summer, though it only earned him a little spending money because her dad was old-school and felt it was the natural way of things for his grandson to help out. Lauren had certainly done her time as a teenager. Once school started, however, not only did he want his grandson to focus on his studies, but there really wasn't much to do around the store besides gossip and make sure they kept up the stock of snow shovels.

"He had detention Monday," Lauren said, taking her usual seat on a wooden kitchen stool. She was pretty sure there was a conspiracy not to buy it so the men would have a place to sit when they visited Dozer. "Didn't do his homework."

Her mother made a *tsk* sound and shook her head. "Boys."

"Boys are just as capable of doing their homework as girls, Mom."

"I never had this trouble with you."

That was because she'd had big plans to get a full scholarship to some big, faraway college and have a fabulous career doing...something. But there had been no scholarship and no college. Instead she'd fallen in love with Dean. Then she'd accidentally gotten pregnant and, before she knew it, was married. Her dad hadn't literally brought out the shotgun, but the Dozynskis and the Carpenters had been very emphatically pro-marriage. And she *had* loved Dean.

"What are you going to do about it?" her dad asked.

"I emailed the teachers Monday, and every day Nick has to write down his homework assignments and they'll initial each one. No video games. If it happens again before midterms, he'll lose the iPod."

She didn't need to tell them that was probably the most dire punishment she could administer. Besides not letting him take driver's ed, of course.

"When are you coming over for dinner?" her mother asked.

Lauren knew she was looking for an in to give her grandson a lecture and hedged. "Soon, Mom. I'll call you and see if there's a good night."

The bell over the door rang and a couple of guys walked in. She didn't know the first man through the door. But the second one made her pulse quicken and she focused on not showing any reaction to Ryan Kowalski as he walked into the store. The last thing she wanted was for her mother to guess she was attracted to the man.

"Hey, Dozer," Ryan said, stepping around the other man. "This is Matt Russell. He works for me and so does another guy named Dillon Brophy. They might stop in from time to time, and the plastic they use will have my name on it."

"I'll make a note of it," her father said.

"Hi, Mrs. Dozynski. It's been a long time since I've seen you, but I swear you haven't aged a day."

Her mother was still preening over the compliment when he turned his head and saw Lauren. How her parents didn't feel the sizzle and pop when those blue eyes made contact with hers, she couldn't say, but she sure as hell felt it.

"Hi, Lauren."

So much for avoiding him. She might have guessed a builder doing renovations might spend some time at the local hardware store, but what were the chances they'd end up here at the same time? "Hi. Nice to see you again."

"Definitely." He smiled and she was glad she was sitting down, because her knees going weak while she was standing up surely would have attracted her mother's attention.

"Boss, you got the list?"

Ryan turned his attention back to the guy who'd come in with him, and Lauren let out a deep breath. She might have spontaneously combusted if he'd kept looking at her like that—which was also something her mother, who had told her on numerous occasions that it was past time to find a new husband, would notice.

She wasn't husband shopping. She wasn't even seriously boyfriend shopping. But there was something about the way Ryan looked at her that reminded her it had been a while since she'd had a man in her life and that certain parts of her body weren't quite as over-the-hill as she sometimes felt.

"You need to talk to your father."

Lauren blinked, belatedly realizing her mother was talking to her. Her dad had disappeared into some aisle or another with Ryan and Matt. "About what?"

"I want him to retire."

"He'll never sell this store, Mom. You know that." Even if he wanted to, he'd be lucky if he could find a buyer. Small-town hardware stores were an endangered species.

"These are golden years and I want to enjoy them."

"You're hardly in your golden years yet. Maybe things will get better soon and he can afford to hire somebody to work a few days a week."

"How much does that insurance company pay you?"

Oh, no. She'd been dodging this conversation with her mother for several years. "They pay me more than Dad could, and I get health insurance. Plus, remember when I was a teenager? Dad and I don't work together all that well."

Her mom sighed. "It seems like it's taking forever for Nicky to grow up."

Lauren opened her mouth and then closed it again. Nick wasn't going to take over Whitford Hardware when he graduated from high school. Not only did Lauren want him to go to college, but her father wanted more for his grandson and had made that clear over the years. It was only her mother who was convinced that if Nick stepped into his grandfather's shoes, it would make everybody happy.

She heard Ryan laugh and she lost her train of thought as the deep sound echoed through the store. The man was distracting as hell, and she only half-listened as her mom moved the conversation to preparations for winterizing her garden.

And when he turned the corner at the end of the

building-supplies aisle and looked at her again, she lost all interest in when a person should cut back her peonies.

The look in his eyes made her wonder if he was having the same kind of thoughts about her as she was having about him. And when he smiled at her, she had to become suddenly interested in untying and retying her shoelace to keep the heat that rushed through her from showing on her face for everybody to see.

"I'll need to borrow Nicky one day after school," her mother was saying. "It's almost time to yank the annuals out of the garden, and he can push the wheelbarrow to the mulch pile for me."

Lauren nodded and, for once, was thankful her mother's obsession with her garden gave her something to focus on. This was Lauren's real life, and she needed to keep her fantasies about Ryan out of it and firmly in her imagination where they belonged.

RYAN WAS DOING his best not to ogle Dozer's daughter right in front of the man—and her mother—but she drew his attention anyway. And, because he liked the way a little bit of pink colored her cheeks when he smiled at her, he did it again.

When she bent over to retie a shoe that didn't need retying, it took all his willpower not to chuckle at her. Luckily, Mrs. Dozynski was talking to her about something and didn't seem to notice that her daughter was blushing.

"You want this on the Northern Star account?"

Feeling guilty, even though he hadn't really done anything wrong, Ryan stepped up to the counter and turned his back on the corner where Lauren was perched on a stool. Dozer not only was the guy who controlled the building supplies in town, but he could probably break Ryan in half if he wanted to. "No, I'll throw it on my card."

He stood in silence while Dozer ran the transaction, trying to think of some small talk he could make. At the very least he should ask Mrs. Dozynski how she'd been or ask Lauren how Nick was doing, but he felt so awkward lusting after her while her parents were in the room—to say nothing of Matt, who was standing at his elbow—that he just waited to sign the credit slip and grabbed one of the bags from the counter.

"Have a good day," Dozer said, as he always did.

"You tell Rose I said hello," Mrs. Dozynski added.

"I will." He nodded at Lauren and fled, not even making sure Matt grabbed the other bag and followed him out.

"Pretty lady," Matt said on their way back to the lodge. "The one sitting on the stool, I mean."

"Yeah." That was an understatement. She'd only gotten more beautiful with age.

"I wonder if she's single."

Ryan's fingers tightened on the steering wheel. "Doesn't matter, since you're here to work, not socialize."

"Can't work all the time." Matt was looking out the window, so he most likely missed the boss's knuckles turning white. "I'll probably have to make trips to the hardware store. Maybe I'll run into her again."

"And maybe her father, who was the barrel-chested guy behind the counter, will bury your body in the woods."

"Dads always love me. I'm a solid guy, or so I'm told." Matt laughed. "Moms love me, too. My problem is finding a woman who loves me longer than a couple of months."

"Maybe you need to worry more about them and less about impressing moms and dads."

"True. But I bet I could romance the hardware store—guy's daughter without getting buried in the woods."

Rather than let on he had his own eye on Lauren—not that it meant anything—Ryan let the conversation die and turned up the radio.

Not only was Lauren being at the hardware store a kink in his plan to stay out of her way, but now the whole thing was twisted up. If he kept doing the hardware store runs, there was a good chance he'd keep running into Lauren. But if he sent one of the guys, which made more sense, it would be Matt, since Dill was temporarily unable to drive thanks to a combination of driving too fast and forgetting he hadn't renewed his license. While he didn't see why women found Matt irresistible, he'd seen and heard enough to know they did and he didn't want the man around Lauren.

He was just going to have to make damn sure they planned ahead for the work they were doing and could keep supply runs to a minimum. Considering the way both his brain and body seemed to short-circuit when he was around her, it would only be a matter of time before he said or did something stupid.

Asking a woman he'd been in love with once upon a time out on a date when he was only in town for a month or so would definitely be stupid. Not only would he be starting something he couldn't finish, but she had a teenage son. Things could get messy when kids were involved.

When they got back to the lodge, he left the supplies

for Matt to deal with and went into the house. He had an email from an architect he needed to deal with and the PDF sheet with the specs was too small to read on his phone. He fired up the desktop in the office and waited for it to boot up.

And waited, and waited. When Josh stuck his head in, Ryan growled and gestured at the PC. "How old is this damn thing?"

"I'm pretty sure it's antique in computer years."

"How am I supposed to work with this? And how are you supposed to keep up with a website and a Facebook page when it takes this long just to turn on. I'm afraid if I try to check my email, it'll start smoking and spew computer parts all over the place."

"Mitch has somebody from his company working on the computer crap."

"Finally." Ryan started on the process of signing into his email account. "Were you looking for me or just being nosy?"

"I wanted to tell you something."

"Okay." Maybe he should go fix a snack while the piece of crap took its sweet time opening the attachment.

"Ry."

He realized he was multitasking badly and gave all his attention to his brother. "Sorry. What's up?"

"I just wanted to tell you I appreciate you coming up here. I know you're busy with your business and all. And I'm sorry I couldn't swallow my pride and ask for help before it got so bad."

"I'm sorry I didn't get up here more often. I should have seen what was going on and we all should have realized we'd left you holding the bag." He'd stayed away because of Lauren and wounded pride, and his family had suffered for it. "We'll have the place fixed up in no time and then we'll figure out where to go from there."

When his brother nodded and left, Ryan tried to focus on the spec sheet the computer had finally displayed for him. There was some argument about how far the generator would be placed from the electrical panel and what gauge wire had to be run, and he wanted to know exactly what he was dealing with before calling the electrical inspector.

But he kept picturing Lauren sitting on the stool in her father's hardware store just as she'd been doing for as long as he could remember. When it was his turn to go to town with his dad as a little kid, she'd often be sitting there during the summer, and she'd offer to share the penny candy she'd gotten at the variety store, which had been gone for years now.

Even then he'd been aware of how pretty she was and that her smile made his belly feel kind of funny. As he got older and realized what that funny feeling was, he'd never worked up the courage to ask her to go steady. And then, one day, Dean had.

Ryan was a grown man now, but that smile still made him feel kind of funny. And he suspected if he ran into her too often, he might have to resort to his younger self's way of dealing with it, which involved a lot of time in the shower with plenty of lathery soap.

With a growl, he forced his focus back to the computer screen. Just like Matt, he was there to work, not socialize. But, unlike Matt, he *would* work all the time if it kept his thoughts off Lauren Carpenter.

## CHAPTER THREE

"I CAN'T MAKE it this weekend."

They were the words Lauren dreaded hearing on a Friday afternoon. Nick was going to get home from school expecting Dean to be there to pick him up right after dinner, and instead she was going to have to tell him his dad wasn't coming. It didn't happen a lot, but often enough she'd grown to dread seeing the disappointment on her son's face.

"You and I need to talk," she told her ex-husband, trying not to squeeze her phone until it popped. "He's already had detention this year."

"So we'll talk next weekend. One week isn't going to make a difference."

"It's pretty important, Dean."

She heard him sigh over the phone, and she clenched her jaw. "Look, the kids don't feel good," he said. "Jody said there's something going around at day care and she's already got her hands full. Plus, if Nicky's having trouble in school, getting sick wouldn't be good for him."

Their son hated being called Nicky and she'd forced herself to break the habit when he hit middle school. But trust Dean to turn it around so it looked as if he was doing Nick a favor, even though Lauren knew he'd deliberately called before school let out so he wouldn't have to break the news to Nick himself. The insurance office closed at two on Fridays, so she beat Nick home from school and Dean knew that.

"You and I can meet somewhere and talk," she said.

"I don't know. Like I said, Jody's got her hands full with the kids and I think she'd be pissed if I take off."

And a pissed-off wife trumped a pissed-off ex-wife. "Fine. I hope the kids feel better soon."

She hung up and tossed the phone on the counter rather than giving in to the urge to chuck it across the room. Her ex-husband had that effect on her a lot. He wasn't a bad guy and she knew he tried, but sometimes he really drove her crazy. One of his worst habits was trying to dodge the hard stuff when it came to Nick, leaving it squarely on her shoulders to be the tough one.

Lauren had been having a pretty decent week, too. Nick had done his homework every night. He was in a slightly better mood. And she'd managed two days without seeing Ryan Kowalski. She hadn't gone two days without *thinking* about him, but at least she hadn't run into him again.

Usually she used her free Friday hour to crank up the radio and wash the kitchen floor, but today she didn't give a damn. The linoleum was getting old, anyway, and didn't hold a shine for much longer than it took to dry.

Instead, she turned on the television and, when she got tired of flipping through channels, watched some show about a bunch of housewives who whined their way through spending obscene amounts of money.

She'd just started being able to keep track of which blonde was which when Nick walked through the door. He tossed his backpack down, then froze when he saw her.

"How come you're not washing the floor?"

Gee, at least she wasn't stuck in a rut or anything. "I decided to see how real housewives live instead."

He made a face at the television, then plopped down on the sofa next to her. "Dad's not coming, is he?"

"How did you know?"

"You have that look, like you don't want to tell me something but you have to. That's pretty much the only thing you don't like telling me."

"He said the kids are sick and they don't want you getting sick, too."

"Whatever." He lifted one shoulder.

"You want to do something tomorrow?" What, she didn't know. She had to go grocery shopping before they totally ran out of food and she didn't even want to think about the laundry pile.

"I'll just hang out. See if Cody's around."

Cody had been Nick's best friend since kindergarten, but Lauren had heard from Fran—who owned the Whitford General Store & Service Station with her husband, Butch—that Cody had been getting in some trouble lately, and Nick didn't need any more of that. "Stay out of trouble."

He rolled his eyes. "Like there's any trouble to get into in Whitford. I can't believe you won't let me take driver's ed. If one of us had a car, we could actually go somewhere."

"If you can't handle homework, you can't handle driving." This wasn't the first time they'd had this discussion. "When I see a semester with no detentions, all your assignments done and the best grades you can achieve, we'll talk about it."

"Whatever." He got up and grabbed his backpack. "I have to write a stupid book report about some stupid book, so I'm going to go read."

More than likely, he was going to shove earbuds in his ears, crank some angry rock music on his iPod and stare at his ceiling, but she left him alone. If she tried to make him feel better, she'd have to make excuses for Dean and she wasn't in the mood.

Her phone rang and she saw the library's number in the caller-ID window. Hailey Genest, the Whitford librarian, was not only one of her best friends, but was fun and fairly drama-free, so she welcomed the call. "The dog ate my library books."

"Ha, you're funny," Hailey said. "Though that's actually happened. You should have seen what was left of the book. Anyway, you have to get out of work early on October fifth."

Lauren walked over to the calendar hanging on the fridge. "That's two weeks from today, so it shouldn't be a problem. Why do I need to get out of work early?"

"I made us a salon appointment. You know, for Paige's wedding?"

"Is she definitely getting married on the sixth?"

"I guess Mitch is still waiting to hear from Liz, but the rest of the family can come from New Hampshire, so they're going to do it. Paige said Mitch will get Liz here one way or another."

She grabbed a pen and wrote *wedding* in the Saturday block. "What time is the appointment? Oh… wait. Dean's coming on Friday to pick up Nick. They're going camping for the long weekend, so I had to get out early anyway. What time did you make the appointment for?"

"Two. I'm closing the library at noon and we're heading for the city, baby."

"Dean's picking Nick up at noon. It'll be close."

"We'll make it. And it's my treat. Hair, facials, manicures, pedicures, the works."

It sounded like heaven. She couldn't remember the last time she'd gone to a salon. Usually she ran into the barbershop during a lunch break and had Katie trim her hair. "I'm not letting you pay."

"You can't stop me. It's going to be awesome girl-time *and* we'll look hot as hell for the wedding. Oh, and speaking of hot, what're you wearing?"

"I haven't gotten that far. I looked in my closet, but all I have is a funeral suit and a dress with shoulder pads and sequins I don't remember buying."

"Since you were still a kid in the eighties, I'm going to pretend you went on a drunken shopping spree. We'll find you a dress on the fifth, too. Something sexy and slinky."

Lauren laughed. "I was thinking something warm, since Paige is getting married outside in October."

"Trust me. We'll find the perfect dress. Something you can dance in, too."

She didn't plan on doing any dancing. It was something she wasn't very good at and tended to save for very dark nightclubs that served copious amounts of alcohol. "I have to go wash my floor."

"And I have to batten down the hatches for the homework club. Last week the homework seems to have been to sneak all the sexy romances into the Y.A. room and giggle over them."

"Lucky you. I'd rather mop my floor."

By the time she was satisfied the old linoleum was as clean as she could get it, Nick had come out of his room. "You want a snack, honey?"

"I was thinking, you wanna watch a movie or something?"

She didn't, really. She needed to get started on the laundry and make a shopping list. But it was his way of reaching out, so she nodded. "You get the movie, I'll make the popcorn."

RYAN KNEW HE should be doing the final prep work so he could pull the kitchen windows out and put the new ones in with as little inconvenience to Rosie as possible, but he couldn't be bothered. Instead, he sat on the porch with a beer, enjoying the quiet.

He'd always considered Saturdays just another workday, but he didn't have a lot of ambition today. Matt and Dill had headed back to Massachusetts for the weekend the night before in one of the trucks. Rosie's car was in the shop, so she'd taken Josh's truck to some antique place with Fran Benoit. And because she had Josh's truck, Josh had taken Ryan's truck into town to do some errands.

Ryan couldn't go anywhere without a vehicle and he didn't feel like working, so he'd popped a beer and sat down. An hour later, he woke up, groggy and with a stiff neck from his head flopping over in the chair.

A sound caught his attention and he lifted his head, trying to place it. It was a weird *plink*, like something tapping glass, and probably what had woken him up. It wasn't until he froze, straining in the silence, that he heard the pop of a pellet gun.

Somebody was shooting at the new windows. No doubt the same damn somebody who'd been making a nuisance of himself for weeks.

Ryan's instinct was to go running out back, where the windows were leaning up against the barn waiting to be installed, but he didn't. Instead he crept around the house and peeked until he spotted a teenage boy just in the tree line. Though it would probably cost him a pane of glass, he took his time moving to a spot where the kid couldn't see him and sneaked into the woods. He slowly made his way through the trees and, by the time the vandal saw him it was too late.

The kid made a break for it, but Ryan had momentum and took him down to the ground. The pellet gun went flying and he hauled the boy to his feet by the back of his collar.

"What the hell do you think you're doing?"

The kid squirmed, trying to break free, but Ryan had been in construction a long time and had a strong grip. With his free hand, he slipped his phone out of its holster and dialed the Whitford Police Department.

"Please don't call the cops," the boy pleaded, but Ryan wasn't screwing around. The Northern Star Lodge had enough woes without some punk kid making it worse.

After the dispatcher promised to send an officer, Ryan marched the kid around the house and told him to sit down. "What's your name, kid?"

He got no response, but the sullen disrespect the boy was going for didn't mask the fear on his face. He was probably so afraid he couldn't talk if he wanted to.

"Suit yourself. I bet whoever shows up to cart your sorry vandalizing ass to jail will know who you are."

Ten minutes later, a cruiser pulled up the drive and Drew Miller got out. Mitch's best friend was the police chief now, which boggled Ryan's mind, and they shook hands before Drew turned his attention to the vandal.

"What's up, Nick?" The kid shrugged one shoulder, staring at the police chief's shoes. Drew pulled a sheet of paper from his pocket and unfolded it. "I have a list here of all the incidents Rose and Josh have reported for the last few weeks. You know anything about them?"

The one-shoulder lift again, and Ryan had to give him credit for not lying outright, at least. "You know how much those windows cost? Bet your parents are going to love paying for those."

Nick got pale and finally looked up, locking his gaze on Ryan. "I'm sorry. I'll pay for the windows. And for the other stuff."

"Have a lot of money stuffed under your mattress?" Drew asked.

"No. I can work it off. I can mow and split wood and do whatever you need me to. Please don't make my mom pay. She's trying to save up for new tires before winter and she just had to spend a bunch of it on school stuff for me and she works really hard…."

Ryan forced himself to keep the stern look going when the kid's words tapered off. He was obviously choked up, but there were going to be consequences one way or another. "After all the damage you've done, why would I want you on the property? I have expensive tools and trucks, and the supplies aren't cheap."

"I'm sorry."

"Sorry you got caught. You didn't think anybody was home and, if I hadn't been, you'd have come back and trashed something else when you got bored."

Drew cleared his throat. "Nick, what's your mother's cell number?"

He punched it into his cell phone as the kid mumbled the digits, then stepped away to make the call.

"I'll work it off," the kid said again.

Ryan shook his head. "You sneak around, destroying our property, and now you expect me to believe you have a work ethic? And the integrity to stick it out?"

It was too bad, though. The kid was young, but looked fairly strong. And, if nothing else, he could pick up after he, Dill, Matt and Andy Miller—who was Drew's dad and had been working around the place for a few weeks—were done for the day. Cheaper than paying his guys to pick up tools. But the kid was trouble and he didn't need any more of that.

Drew walked back over, putting his phone away. "Your mom's on her way."

Nick's shoulders slumped and he stared down at his feet. Ryan decided to leave him to his sulk and turned to Drew. "You have that list?"

Drew handed him the paper and a pen. "He's never done anything like this before. He's always been a good kid."

Ryan went down the list, putting estimated dollar amounts to each incident. He wrote in the cost of the windows at the end, but a quick glance had shown him that only two were damaged. The total wasn't huge, just a few dollars over nine hundred, but that wasn't counting the aggravation, either.

He handed the list back to Drew and, with nothing else to do until the kid's mother showed up, decided on small talk. "How are things going?"

"You probably heard Mallory and I split." Ryan nodded. "Other than that, everything's the same old shit. My dad said you run a tight ship over here."

Ryan let him get away with the swing in subject. Divorces sucked. "Dill and Matt are good guys, but if I didn't have my thumb on them, they'd be on those damn phones all day."

"Did you ever find out what happened between Rosie and my old man?"

Rose Davis hadn't spoken to Andy Miller in almost

thirty years and nobody knew why. She'd thrown a fit when Mitch and Josh had hired him to work around the lodge, but something had happened and she'd forgiven him, apparently. For what, none of them knew.

"Nope. I'm not sure if anybody knows but them, and they don't seem to be telling."

Drew went on to say something else, but Ryan's attention turned back to the boy. His name was Nick. He looked to be about sixteen. He was kind of tall, with dark hair and light brown eyes and a nose just like Dean Carpenter's. *Oh, shit.*

"Tell me that's not Lauren's kid," he said, interrupting Drew in midsentence.

"You didn't know that?"

"I haven't seen him since he was a baby." When he'd tried to talk Nick's mother into leaving Nick's father and running away with him.

Great. So much for keeping Lauren out of sight and mostly out of mind. She was pulling up the driveway.

LAUREN PULLED UP behind the Whitford PD cruiser and unclenched her fingers from the steering wheel so she could put the car in park and shut it off. Of all the stupid crap Nick had ever pulled, this was the worst.

Vandalism. Damages. Possible criminal charges. And of all the windows in all the world, he had to break Ryan Kowalski's.

She was so angry she could barely think and she hadn't even heard the entire story yet. Through the windshield, she could see her son sitting on the front porch of the lodge, looking thoroughly ashamed of himself. Not that it was going to save him, because he'd put her in one hell of a bad position, but at least he wasn't copping an attitude. Taking a deep breath, she got out of her car and walked to the two guys.

"Hey, Drew." When he raised an eyebrow, she rolled her eyes. "Chief Miller. Hi, Ryan."

"Hi, Lauren," Ryan said, and she tried not to think about how much she loved the sound of her name on his lips.

She shook off the momentary distraction. "I'm really sorry about this. I have no idea what got into him. Was Cody with him?"

"I didn't see anybody else," Ryan said.

Drew shook his head. "Nope. This was just him."

She pointed at Nick and then at the ground in front of her. He got out of the chair and walked over like a condemned man on his way to the gallows. "What were you thinking?"

"I'm sorry," he mumbled, looking at the ground.

He didn't know it yet, but he hadn't even begun to be sorry. She didn't have the extra money to spend on something like this and neither did Dean.

"How much do I owe you?" she asked Ryan. She wished she could mumble and look at the ground like her son, but she forced herself to look the man in the eye. God, he had gorgeous eyes.

"Nine hundred sixty dollars."

"Jesus, Nick." She glared at her son, not even sure what to say. He'd done almost a thousand dollars' worth of damage to somebody else's property. Screwing up in school was bad enough, but this… She was having trouble wrapping her mind around the fact Drew wasn't there on a social visit. He was there as the chief of police. For her son.

"Mom, I—"

"Don't say a word," she snapped. This was the closest she'd ever come to totally losing her temper with her son. "Don't even open your mouth, because there's nothing you can say that's going to fix this. Over nine hundred dollars, Nicholas."

"He's going to work it off," Ryan said.

Nick's head jerked up. "But you said—"

"I know what I said. But I've had a few minutes to cool off and the chief says you've never been in trouble before."

"I can pay," Lauren said. It would be a sacrifice, but it was only right. There went her snow tires. She'd just have to nurse the ones she had through another winter. Leave herself extra time and pray a lot. She could forget a new dress for Paige's wedding, too. Her shoulder pads and sequins would be quite the conversation starter.

"By the time I'm done making him sweat, he'll never do something this stupid again."

He had a point. Mom writing a check was a punishment too easily forgotten. But the logistics of Nick working off that kind of money made her head hurt. "He can't miss school, and he has to do his homework. By the time I get home from work and drive him here, it would be almost suppertime. And he goes with Dean on the weekends, but I'll just have to tell him it'll be every other weekend until this is done."

It was odd, mentioning Dean to Ryan. It made her think of the day he'd shown up at the crappy apartment she and her husband lived in. She'd had Nick on her hip and he'd been fussy that day because it was hot. Ryan had promised her a nice house with a backyard, and he'd told her he'd love her the way she deserved to be loved. She'd said no because she loved Dean.

That worked out well.

Ryan shook his head. "I don't want to cut into his

time with his dad. We can figure something out. The bus goes by here, so maybe it could drop him off."

Drew nodded and tapped his pen on his notebook. "If he takes the bus here after school, he can do his homework in the kitchen, if it's okay with Rose, and then get right to work. If you don't mind eating just a little later than usual, he could work a couple of hours before you pick him up."

She just wasn't sure. On the one hand, she didn't have almost a thousand dollars to pay for her son's stupidity. On the other, that would be a pretty grueling schedule for Nick. Not that he didn't deserve it, but she didn't want him too tired to pay attention in class.

This was serious, though, and even if she had to be in contact with his teachers every day to make sure he was keeping up, he had to learn this lesson. What he'd done was criminal and she wanted to make sure he didn't forget it for a good, long time. "That would work. I can make it work."

"I think Tuesdays and Wednesdays would be enough," Ryan said, looking at Nick. "Mondays always suck enough, and Thursday you'll need to hang with your mom and get your stuff ready to go to your dad's Friday after school, right?"

Nick nodded. "Yes, sir. But I'll come Mondays, too. It's a lot of money and I'll do the three days a week."

"Fine. I'll see you Monday after school. Make sure you're here."

"I will be."

Lauren would make sure of it, no matter how much it messed with her schedule.

"I'm going to temporarily file this as resolved," Drew said. "But if you don't get off that bus here on Monday afternoon, Nick, I'll be knocking on your door."

"I'll be here."

Drew left then, and Lauren told her son to go sit in the car. Once he'd closed the door, Lauren faced the lodge and blew out a breath. It was such a pretty house—a huge, white New Englander with a deep porch and dark green shutters. It was definitely looking a little ragged around the edges, though, and she was so disgusted her son had been sabotaging their efforts to restore it.

"I know it seems bad," Ryan said. "And it's not good, but it's not like he kicked my dog and set the house on fire, either."

"Do you have a dog?"

"No. Do you?"

As if it mattered. Here they went with the awkward conversation again. "I'm really sorry he did this, Ryan. I don't know where it came from."

"Why isn't he with his dad today?"

She saw where he was heading, but it was the wrong direction. "The kids—Nick's little brother and sister—are sick. Yeah, Nick's disappointed when Dean cancels, but it doesn't happen that often. He wasn't a great husband, but he's a good dad."

He held up his hands, as though surrendering. "Okay. Was just curious."

She couldn't believe she was defending Dean. Maybe it was just a knee-jerk reaction to the one person who'd known years ago that she and Dean were a bad idea. "Is this where you say I told you so?"

The question hung between them and she wished immediately she could take it back. It would have been so much better for them both to pretend that day had never happened. But she'd said it and now he stared into her eyes, his expression unreadable.

"You think I'm happy you're divorced? Because I'm not. I'd rather be wrong every day of the week than for you to be unhappy."

She believed him, but she told herself it didn't matter. "It was a long time ago."

And she knew that during that long time between then and now, he'd gotten married, then divorced. Built a successful business. It's not as though he'd spent his life pining for her.

"I should go," she said quickly, before he could continue the conversation. "Thank you for giving Nick the chance to make things right. Let me give you my cell number in case you have any problems with him. Not that I think you will, but just in case."

He punched the number into his phone as she read it off, and then she did the same with his number. Then she started toward the car because it had to be getting stuffy in there by now, which was as good an excuse as any to get away from Ryan.

"I'll see you Monday night when you pick him up," he called after her, and she lifted her hand to let him know she'd heard him.

Thanks to her son's stupidity, she'd be seeing him Monday night. And Tuesday night. And Wednesday night.

She got her car turned around and sped down the driveway as quickly as she could without kicking up gravel. And a couple of glances in the rearview mirror told her he watched her go until she was out of sight.

## CHAPTER FOUR

"I CAN'T BELIEVE you did this." Lauren forced herself to stop strangling the steering wheel before she drove into a ditch. She should probably wait until they were home to have this discussion, but she couldn't keep it inside. "What were you thinking? And don't you dare shrug your shoulders at me."

"I dunno," Nick mumbled.

"That doesn't cut it. What you did was criminal, Nick. *Criminal*. Chief Miller could have arrested you." She started shaking just thinking about it.

"Sorry."

He could say he was sorry all day long, but that's not what she wanted to know. "Why did you do it?"

"I dunno."

She would have screamed if she thought she could vent her frustration and focus on the road at the same time. "That's not an answer. You've been getting in trouble at school. You've already had detention. And now you're destroying people's property and breaking the law. There has to be a reason."

"I'll do better."

"Damn straight you will. But I still want to know why this happened. Are you doing drugs?"

"No!" He took his eyes off his shoelaces, at least. "I swear."

"If you don't straighten up, I'll buy every home drug test they have at the drugstore, Nicholas. I mean it."

"I'm not, Mom."

"Then what's going on?"

He shrugged, gaze back on his feet. "I dunno. I just screwed up."

"Well," she said as she pulled into her driveway,"now you get to call your dad and tell him you screwed up."

"Can't you tell him?"

"I'm going to talk to him once you're done, but you're going to tell him yourself."

She went through the mail while Nick made the phone call, though she didn't really register the return addresses. Mostly bills, probably, so she tossed them on the counter unopened. Nick sounded on the verge of tears as he told Dean what he'd done, and she could hear her ex-husband's voice, loud and angry, from halfway across the kitchen.

"I'm sorry," Nick said into the phone, and then he held it out to her. "Dad wants to talk to you."

Lucky her. "Hello?"

"What the hell is this about Nick working for Ryan Kowalski?"

"He's going to work off the damages."

"Don't you think you should have asked me first?"

She wasn't in the mood to have a pissing contest with her ex. "No, I don't. Since you cried poverty when I asked for extra child support for school clothes and supplies, I'm guessing you don't have an extra grand in the cookie jar."

"I don't want my kid working for him."

Through the anger, Lauren felt a familiar tiny poke of guilt. Dean had a lot of resentment toward Ryan, but it was for the wrong reason. He didn't know the truth of why his best friend had left town and never looked back. "You don't have any choice."

"I don't like it."

"This isn't about you, Dean. This is about Nick breaking the law and Drew and Ryan giving him a chance to make it right rather than pressing charges, and whether you *like* it or not, he's going to do just that."

"Why did it have to be him?" Dean muttered, and Lauren silently echoed the sentiment.

"I have to go," she told him. "Needless to say, Nick's grounded. I trust you and Jody will follow through with that when he's at your house."

"Yeah."

With nothing left to say, Lauren ended the call and leaned against the counter. Nick was still sitting at the table, picking at his thumbnail. "Do you have anything else to say?"

"I'm sorry."

She shook her head, too frazzled to keep running in circles. "From now until I decide otherwise, your life is school and the Northern Star Lodge. No iPod, no video games, no anything that isn't homework or work."

He nodded, his shoulders sagging a little more.

"You can spend the rest of today cleaning your room." He practically ran for his bedroom. "And don't slam your door."

She pulled a few fun-size candy bars out of her secret stash and sat down in the chair Nick had vacated. This was just the kind of day that had spawned the *what-if* fantasies. As stressful and worrisome as the day was, she was going to have a hell of a time nodding off and imagining Ryan's hands on her had always been just the thing to soothe her to sleep.

It was a little different now that she'd actually seen

Ryan and had a very real, not pretend reaction to the man. And, thanks to her son's stupidity, she was going to be seeing a lot of him.

Popping chocolate into her mouth, Lauren walked to the fridge and slid the shopping list out from under a magnet. After rummaging on the counter for a pen, she wrote, *Chocolate. Lots and lots of chocolate,* on the bottom of the list.

She had a feeling she was going to need it.

"I CAN'T BELIEVE it was Nick Carpenter," Josh said. "His name never even popped into my head as a possibility."

"He's always been a good boy," Rose agreed. "But I can tell you with some authority that teenage boys do really stupid things all the time."

Three of them around the table had the good sense to keep their eyes on their plates. Ryan knew he was a major contributor to her knowledge of teenage stupidity, as were Josh and Mitch, who also developed a keen interest in their meatloaf.

As soon as Paige had called to tell Rosie that Mitch was on his way home from Miami, Rosie had rummaged through the pantry and started throwing together a family dinner. Ryan figured his brother would rather crawl into bed with his fiancée and stay there for a couple days, but you didn't turn down Rosie's meat loaf.

"How's the house hunting going?" he asked before Rose could start trotting out some of their less intelligent, youthful moments.

Paige perked up immediately. "I think I found one! It's a little further out of town than I wanted, so I'll have to drive to work, but it has a big barn and some land and a room that will make a great home office."

"She showed me pictures of the master bathroom, too," Mitch said. "Huge shower."

When Paige blushed to the roots of her hair, Ryan decided not to ask why the shower size ranked so high on Mitch's list of important details.

"Why not just move in here?" It seemed like a good compromise. There was plenty of room, Paige wouldn't be alone while Mitch traveled, and it would take some of the burden off Josh's shoulders.

There were a few seconds of awkward silence, which made Ryan wonder if it was something they'd already talked about.

"We both own businesses," Mitch finally said. "We can help with the lodge, but it can't be a full-time thing. And it's important to Paige—to us—that we have a home that's *ours* to raise our kids in."

"Kids?" Rosie asked.

Paige laughed. "Not yet."

"But soon."

Ryan concentrated on his mashed potatoes while Rosie tried to pin Paige down on how long they were going to wait before starting a family. The woman was desperate for a grandchild. The Kowalskis might not be her kids by birth, as Katie was, but they were close enough for her to claim their grandbabies as hers should they ever get around to giving her any.

"I talked to Aunt Mary," Mitch said, probably to change the subject before Paige got so desperate to avoid interrogation that she dragged him off to make a baby for Rose right that very second. "They can all come Columbus Day weekend."

"The whole weekend?" Rosie asked.

"They're going to come Friday and stay until Monday. They were going to leave Sunday afternoon so the kids would have all of Monday to settle in and get ready to go back to school, but the Patriots are playing the four o'clock game Sunday and they don't want to miss it. So they'll leave early Monday morning."

"So you'll get married Saturday afternoon, then?"

"Yes," Paige said. "I don't want half the family sneaking off to get a score check during the ceremony."

Ryan laughed. "You haven't even met them yet and you've got their number."

"Speaking of which," Mitch said to Paige, "I have a quick trip to make this week, but next weekend, if you can get your shifts at the diner covered, I'd like to take a trip over to New Hampshire so you can meet everybody. Aunt Mary said it wouldn't be right to see you for the first time when you're walking up the aisle."

"Will they *all* be there?"

"She didn't say, but you can almost guarantee it."

"It's like jumping into the deep end of the pool," Josh said. "There's no dipping your toe in. You've gotta cannonball."

"I'll see what I can do," Paige said.

Ryan shoved his empty plate away and leaned back in his seat. "You can either make the drive over with Mitch or, at some point in the next two weeks, the entire family will show up at the diner. Trust me, you don't want that."

"He's right," Mitch agreed.

Paige threw up her hands in surrender. "Fine, I'll make sure I can go."

Ryan sat back and half-listened to the idle banter between the others, sneaking peaks at his phone under the table. An electrical inspection on a key project was supposed to have happened yesterday afternoon and he still hadn't received a status update on it. He keyed in a second text to the foreman on the job and hit Send. He'd give the guy a couple of hours and then he'd call. After all, he'd been away for only five business days, so if things were falling apart down there, he'd be pissed. They should be able to do their jobs without him looking over their shoulders.

"Ryan, are you playing with your phone at the dinner table?" Rosie was giving him the look when he glanced up.

"Nope." He set it on the table, since he was already busted. "I'm working with my phone at the dinner table."

"It can wait until everybody's done eating."

He figured she should cut him a little slack since he was doing them a favor, but it wasn't worth arguing with her. "Yes, ma'am."

"I think we're done anyway." Mitch pushed back from the table and piled his silverware and napkin on his plate to carry it into the kitchen. "I have the preliminary workups for the new website and Facebook page for the lodge, so I thought we could all take a look at those and see what we think. We need to get them up ASAP, because people will be starting to think about reservations soon. It's getting colder and guys'll be pulling the sleds out of storage and tuning them up soon."

"Sounds good," Josh said. "I have some paperwork for the ATV trails, too. They need reading by somebody a little more fluent in legalese."

One of their plans for getting the lodge back on its feet was to connect Whitford to the ATV trail system in the next town over. Not only would businesses like the diner benefit, but the lodge could possibly see more off-season business than the occasional hiker or passer-through. If they got the four-wheelers in the spring, summer and fall and got the sledders coming back in higher numbers in the winter, they could double the income. Whether they kept the lodge or ended up selling it, doubling the income wouldn't hurt.

"Right after you boys are done cleaning the kitchen," Rosie added.

Ryan groaned and shoved his phone in his pocket so he could carry dirty dishes. Sometimes it sucked being home.

LAUREN WAS OUT of words. Because Nick wasn't talking, any conversations they'd had since she'd gotten the phone call from Drew were more like one-sided lectures on her part. And she'd said everything she could think of to say.

She knew he was sorry. And she knew Ryan catching him and calling Drew had scared the crap out of him. But she still couldn't figure out why he'd done it in the first place. Acting out, obviously, but why?

Sick of hearing "I dunno," she'd let him go to his room to sulk, minus his iPod, which was zipped securely in her purse. If he wanted to stare at his ceiling, he could think while he did it, not listen to his music.

She'd thawed chicken breasts for dinner, but she didn't really have time to cook them and she wasn't in the mood for soup. Grabbing her purse, she knocked on Nick's door. "I'm going to the market. I'll be right back."

"Okay." At least he hadn't said "whatever."

The Whitford General Store & Service Station was still open, thankfully. Fran Benoit ran the grocery half of the business, while her husband ran the gas station and garage. They'd cornered the market on food and gas in town, but were smart enough to take advantage of that by putting the screws to the community.

Fran was sitting behind the counter, knitting what looked like a sweater for Butch, when Lauren walked in. Her gray hair was in its customary braid and she was wearing a blue flannel shirt that had seen better days. "You cut it close, honey. Ten more minutes and I'd have been gone."

"I just need to grab a couple of things. I was going to bake chicken breasts for dinner, but I got held up and it's too late."

She grabbed a package of hot dogs, then a box of macaroni-and-cheese because she couldn't remember if she had any in the cupboard. Not the most nutritious of dinners, but it was enough to fulfill her maternal obligations and that was about all her son deserved at the moment.

Grabbing a candy bar on the way, she walked to the register. She'd eat the chocolate on the way home, because she wasn't sharing.

"You look a little stressed," Fran observed.

Because it was Fran, Lauren told her the entire story. "So now Nick has to work over there three days a week after school until Ryan feels he's paid off the damages he caused."

"Kids get crazy ideas in their heads sometimes. He wasn't with Cody, was he?"

"No, he was alone. If he hadn't been, I could have blamed Cody, so maybe it's for the best. This way I can't deny my kid's heading toward a life of crime."

Fran laughed at her exaggeration. "Nick's a good boy and you know it. Maybe he's bored or maybe there's something bothering him, but sweating it out at the Northern Star won't hurt him any. Might even do him some good."

"Plus, Rose will be making him do his homework first so his grades are bound to go up."

"That they will, because she doesn't put up with any crap. And being around Josh and Ryan will be good for Nick, too. Not that Dean's not a decent guy, but the Kowalskis have a work ethic he could learn something from."

Lauren didn't even want to think about Dean. It could be really tiresome, sharing a child with somebody you really didn't like all that much anymore.

"It's probably a good thing Ryan caught him now," Fran said as she rang up the purchases. "Not only because he might have ended up costing so much money that his doing some odd jobs couldn't make up for it, but because Paige seems pretty determined to get married there in a couple of weeks. The guys already have their hands full making sure the old lodge is spiffed up for that."

"I heard he brought a couple of guys that work for him. And he's got Andy there, plus Josh. His leg's doing pretty good, so there's quite a crew. Plus Nick, I guess."

She was still having trouble wrapping her head around the fact her son would be spending that much time with Ryan Kowalski. While nobody knew it but her and Ryan, Nick could just as easily have grown up with Ryan as his stepdad if she'd packed her bags and left town with him.

Fran rambled on about how the Northern Star Lodge had been so pretty when Frank and Sarah Kowalski had run the place, and how heartbreaking it had been to see the toll the crappy economy had on it. And on Josh, who'd tried to shoulder the burden without dragging his siblings into it.

"It was a mistake," Fran said. "But people learn from their mistakes. Josh has, and Nick will, too."

She thanked Fran and carried her bag out to the car. Because she wanted to savor the secret candy bar, she had to drive slowly and even take a little detour to avoid pulling into her driveway before it was gone. Once she'd licked her fingers clean and folded up the wrapper to shove in her pocket, she parked and went inside.

Nick was sitting on the couch, looking as miserable as she'd seen him in a long time. He wasn't crying, but she could see it was taking some effort on his part not to.

"I'm really sorry, Mom. I really am."

She dumped the bag in the kitchen and went to sit next to him. "I know you are."

"I just get mad at, like, stupid stuff. Dad or my teacher or…whatever."

"Me," she supplied for him, patting his knee.

"Sometimes. Anyway, I just get mad and I break stuff."

"How much stuff?" It hadn't even occurred to her until now he might have vandalized more of their neighbors. "Am I going to have other people banging on my door accusing you of breaking *their* stuff?"

He shook his head. "There are lots of trails in the woods behind the lodge and I like to walk there, so I haven't done it anywhere else. I promise."

"We need to find another way to channel that anger. Maybe some hard labor will help."

"He's not going to go easy on me, is he?"

"Ryan?" She laughed. "I wouldn't be surprised if he has you splitting cordwood every day until you can't lift your arms. He'll be fair, though. And you have the punishment coming."

"I know. I just want you to know I'm sorry. Everybody in town's going to know, so I embarrassed you."

"I don't really give a damn what everybody in town thinks. What's important to me is that you don't ever do something like this again, and that you do the right thing now. And you're going to, so we'll get through this."

"Okay." He mumbled something that might have been "I love you."

"I love you, kid. You're still not getting your iPod back, though."

# CHAPTER FIVE

ON MONDAY AFTERNOON, Rose Davis watched the teenage boy chug the lemonade she'd given him and smiled. Their vandal turning out to be Lauren Carpenter's son was an interesting twist in her plan to see all the Kowalski kids and her own Katie happily married before she got too old to enjoy grandchildren, biological or otherwise.

Sean was happily married, of course, but his wife owned a thriving landscaping business, so Rosie wasn't too sure she'd be in a hurry to have kids. Plus, they lived in New Hampshire. Mitch and Paige would be married soon, but they were avoiding answering any questions about starting a family. Once she'd heard Paige was going to rent out her trailer and look for a house, Rose had hoped they'd move into the lodge, but Mitch was adamant that he and Paige wanted their own space.

Now Lauren had been thrown back into Ryan's life. She wasn't sure exactly what had happened right before Ryan had left Whitford to start his job in Mass, but she'd had her suspicions for a while that he'd cared more for Lauren than he let on. He'd gotten over her, of course. Fallen in love, gotten married, fallen out of love. But Rose didn't think it was a coincidence that it was Lauren's son who got busted shooting at the windows. Cupid had a master plan.

"You want some more?" she asked Nick when he'd

drained his glass. She wasn't surprised he was thirsty. It was still early enough in the school year to be hot and the school had no air-conditioning.

"Yes, please."

"Sit down and get your homework done." She refilled the glass and set it in front of him. "The guys are waiting for you. But don't rush. Do it right."

"I did most of it in study hall."

She snorted. "I raised a daughter of my own and five others. You think I haven't heard that before?"

The tips of his ears turned pink, but he started pulling stuff out of his backpack and got to work. Once he was scribbling on a math worksheet, she took the pitcher of lemonade and some paper cups into the backyard.

Ryan saw her first, and she smiled when he scowled and shook his head. She wasn't supposed to care if Dill and Matt dehydrated while putting up the scaffolding? They might draw their paychecks from Kowalski Custom Builders, but they were temporarily living under Rose's roof.

"I told you not to spoil them," he hissed when she got close enough to set the pitcher on a sawhorse.

"It's not a triple-layer chocolate fudge cake. It's lemonade."

"Do you have a triple-layer chocolate fudge cake?"

She laughed and poured four cups of lemonade. "No. I have apple crisp for dessert, though. And yes, I'm sharing it with Dill and Matt."

"And me?"

"Yes, and you. I might even give some to Nick."

That brought his scowl back full force. Not that it bothered her any. "He's going home for supper."

"So I'll wrap some up some for him to take home. And his mom, too."

"By all means, let's punish the little vandal with baked goods."

Time to do a little fishing. "I hear you were hell-bent on getting cash until you realized he's Lauren's son. Then you decided he could work off the debt."

He paused with a cup halfway to his mouth. "Who told you that?"

"Paige. I assume she heard it from Mitch, who heard it from Drew, but you never know in this town." He shook his head and then took a long drink of lemonade, probably so he wouldn't have to talk. "I always thought Lauren would have been better off with you than with Dean back in high school."

When his jaw tightened and his expression got that smoothed-over, fake look, she knew she'd dangled the right bait. She also knew when to give the line some slack. "You tell Andy, Dill and Matt to come drink this lemonade before it attracts bugs."

She walked back into the lodge, shifting the puzzle pieces of Ryan and Lauren around in her head. She didn't have enough fragments to make out the whole picture yet, but she would.

In the meantime, she had some math problems to check.

RYAN HAD JUST set Nick to work painting the shutters he'd taken off the back of the lodge when he heard a vehicle pulling up the drive. For a few seconds, he thought it was Lauren and his whole body tensed at the thought of seeing her again so soon. But it was too early for it to be her, so he forced himself to relax and walked around the front of the house.

It was even worse. Standing in front of a very used minivan was Dean Carpenter. His old friend had aged well—though not as well as Ryan, if he did say so him-self—but his face showed he worried too much, and his gut gave away the beer intake.

Dean didn't smile when he saw Ryan coming, but he didn't really expect him to. They hadn't been friends in a long time.

"Lauren called me. Said my son vandalized your place."

"Small, stupid shit, but it added up."

"I've come to pay. I can give you half the money now and half in a couple of weeks."

Ryan shrugged. "His mother, the police chief and I decided he'd work off the debt. That way he'll be less inclined to do it again."

"I'm his father." There was a hard edge to Dean's voice that made Ryan wonder if he'd have to duck a punch before the conversation was over. "I think it's best I pay you and then he can work off the debt he owes *me*."

"I have the work, though. He's painting shutters right now."

"I don't want to owe you."

That was the bottom line and Ryan didn't see any way around hashing it all out. "Look, I know you don't like me, but—"

"I don't give two shits about you one way or the other, Kowalski."

"You didn't give two shits about her, either. That's why I asked her to go with me. But she said no and that was the end of it."

When Dean got very still, his head slightly cocked to the side, Ryan realized he'd made a very big mistake. Lauren hadn't told him.

"What are you talking about?"

"Forget it." He just wanted to Dean to leave. "I'm not accepting payment. The kid's going to sweat off his debt to me or we can get Drew Miller back out here."

"Don't threaten me, asshole. What do you mean you asked Lauren to go with you? When?"

"Right after I graduated from college. Nick was a baby. I was heading to Mass to start my new job, and I stopped at your house while you were at work and asked her to take him and come with me."

"You tried to steal my wife? And my kid?" Ryan could see the anger hadn't even begun to set in yet. Dean was stunned, and a lot of years of guilt welled up in Ryan's gut. "That's why you never came back. It wasn't because you forgot about me. It's because you couldn't face me."

Actually, it was because he couldn't stand seeing Lauren struggling to raise a baby while her husband partied with the guys and drank half his income. "You treated her like crap."

"I wasn't a good husband to Lauren. I was young and I was stupid." Dean paused, shaking his head. "But she still wanted me more than she wanted you."

"Yeah, she chose you. End of story."

Red crept over Dean's face. "But it's not the end of the story, is it? Because here you are, making my son work for you. Getting Lauren over here."

"Your son is working for me because he was destroying my property and it seemed like a better option than pressing charges."

"Aren't you a fucking hero." Dean started toward the door of his truck, then stopped and turned. "I should kick your ass."

He wouldn't stand there and take a beating for something he'd done a decade and a half ago. "It was a long time ago. And, like you said, she chose you."

"Screw you, Kowalski."

Dean managed to relocate half the gravel in the drive with his tires, spinning and fishtailing his way down to the road. Ryan watched him go, then scrubbed a hand through his hair. That hadn't been fun.

"Was that my dad?"

Shit. Nick had come around the house, probably in time to see Dean's minivan turning the corner. Hopefully not in time to hear any of the conversation. "Yeah. He wanted to pay me for the damages, but I told him you were working it off."

"Ma told him that already."

"I guess he just wanted to see for himself." He couldn't control what Dean might tell Nick later, but he certainly wasn't going to explain what just happened. "How are those shutters going?"

The kid couldn't figure out how to hang the shutters on the wire hangers that Andy had made up as a makeshift drying rack, so Ryan went to help him. Then he checked on Dill and Matt. They almost had the upstairs bathroom window in place, but the lodge was old and, even though he'd paid extra for custom-ordered sizes, it needed a lot of shimming.

Satisfied his crew was working, he went back to his own project, which was preparing to frame in a new back door off the kitchen. The old one was narrow and wooden and the new steel replacement was wider, which meant stripping away some siding and reframing the hole.

It was tedious but easy work, leaving his mind free to wander back to his confrontation with Dean Carpenter and the burning question he couldn't answer. Why hadn't Lauren ever told Dean?

LAUREN DIDN'T SEE Ryan when she stopped at the lodge to pick up Nick, which was just as well. Her nerves were shot, work had sucked and half the town had already heard her kid was a fledgling criminal.

She had to admit she was a little disappointed, though. Under the embarrassment her son had caused her, the thought of seeing Ryan again made her feel jittery, like a schoolgirl who knew she'd see the boy she liked as they passed between classes.

But it was Andy Miller who walked Nick out to her car and leaned against her door. She rolled down the window while her son got in the passenger side. "How'd he do, Andy?"

"Pretty good. Ryan had him painting shutters—so, nothing too physical, but it was nothing the rest of us wanted to do."

"Good. The more tedious the work, the more reluctant he'll be to get in this kind of trouble again." She glanced sideways at Nick, but he was smart enough to keep his eyes on his hands.

He was quiet all the way home, actually, and it worried her. Feeling guilty and being contrite, she expected, but she didn't want him to beat himself up, either. And they didn't dwell on things, as a rule. If there was a crime, there was punishment and they moved on.

"My dad went to the lodge," he said as she pulled into their driveway.

"Today?" Why was Dean at the Northern Star?

"Ryan said he wanted to pay for the damages, but he wouldn't take the money."

Lauren didn't think Dean had that kind of money to

waste, but his son working off a debt to Ryan Kowalski probably dinged his pride. "Did you talk to him?"

"No, he was leaving when I went around the front of the house. He peeled out, too. Gravel went everywhere."

So he'd left mad. "Don't worry about your dad. You're doing the right thing now and that's what's important."

That seemed to pep him up a little, and he told her about his day at school while they ate the stew she'd dumped in the slow cooker that morning. They'd be using that a lot, she thought, until Nick was let off the hook at the lodge.

"Do you have homework?" she asked when he went straight to the television after dinner and turned on the game system.

"I did it at the lodge. Rose checked it for me."

She didn't think he'd lie about that since it was too easy to get caught, but she made him show it to her anyway just so he'd know she was watching. Then she went down to the basement and started another load of laundry before going back out to the car to get the book she was reading from the backseat where she'd tossed it.

The cell phone in her pocket rang as she reached in and she almost hit her head on the roof of the car. Muttering under her breath, she pulled it out and looked at the incoming number. It was Ryan.

She desperately hoped he hadn't changed his mind about Nick, because she really needed new snow tires. Even if she and Dean went halves on the damages, it would be tight. "Hello?"

"Hey, you busy?" Even if his name hadn't come up on the caller ID, she would have recognized his voice. It was the one that made her shiver.

"Nope." She grabbed her book and went to sit on the front step. "What's up?"

"Dean stopped by today."

"Nick told me. Said he sprayed gravel everywhere when he left, too." She stopped herself before apologizing for it. Dean's behavior wasn't her problem.

"He wasn't happy."

"He's probably embarrassed and doesn't want to feel like he owes you."

"You never told him."

It took a few seconds for his words to sink in, and when they did, she caught herself clenching the phone in her fingers. "You told him?"

It shouldn't matter. She and Dean had been divorced for eight years, but she felt guilty for not having told him at the time. She should have let him know. What Ryan had done was wrong, plain and simple, and Dean had a right to know.

But there was some guilt because she'd thought about Ryan—started playing the *what-if* game—while still married to Dean. When things were tough, she'd think about that day and imagine saying yes. She'd picture their home and the big backyard for Nick, and she'd imagine Ryan holding her in bed instead of belching and falling asleep like her husband. It was safe and harmless—just a stupid fantasy—but the fact she hadn't told Dean made it feel worse than it was.

"I assumed he knew, so I misunderstood what his problem was and, yeah, I told him."

"Did Nick hear?" It would explain why he'd been so quiet in the car.

"I'm pretty sure he didn't. I told him Dean was angry I wouldn't take his money, which wasn't totally a lie, though he was probably more angry I tried to steal his wife."

Hearing him say it like that, so flat out, made her cheeks hot, and she was glad he was on the other end of the phone line and couldn't see her. "Why did you?"

"I told you why." His voice had softened and the timbre of it didn't help cool her face any. "He didn't treat you right."

"He was young. We both were and obviously stupid, since we never meant for me to get pregnant. He wanted to try to go to college eventually and make something of himself. Instead he got a baby and a wife and a factory job while you went off to school."

"And he resented me for it and, even worse, he resented *you*. He was a miserable son of a bitch and he took it out on you."

Lauren rubbed the bridge of her nose. "You're not being totally fair. He wasn't a *bad* guy, Ryan."

"He didn't love you."

*And you did?* She didn't say it out loud, because she didn't want to know the answer. "Did he tell you that?"

"He didn't have to."

She'd like to think Ryan was wrong and that, at some point, the man she'd had a child with and married *had* loved her, even if it hadn't lasted forever. "There's no point in talking about this. But I appreciate you letting me know Dean was upset."

"There was a point," he said. "Since he left, something's been bugging me and I have to know why you never told him."

"I don't know." It was the truth, really. "I kept putting it off because I knew he'd be mad, and I wasn't sure if he'd think I'd led you on or something. And you kept not coming back, so I kept not telling him. Eventually, I just didn't see the point."

He was quiet for so long she wondered if the call had dropped. Finally he spoke again. "It must have thrown you for a loop, me showing up like that."

"I didn't know you felt like that. I never guessed."

"Because I was trying like hell to hide it." He cleared his throat. "Actually, I spent a long time trying to deny it, but when I came home from college and you looked so damn unhappy...I had to try."

"It never would have worked out," she said, as much to herself as to him. "I didn't feel the same way about you."

"I know that—I *knew* that—but I thought you'd still be happier."

Lauren didn't know what to say to that. In fact, the entire conversation seemed a little surreal. During all the years she'd harmlessly imagined what life would have been like if she'd said yes to Ryan that day, she'd never once imagined they'd have a telephone conversation about it.

"I have to run," he said when she missed her turn in the conversation. "Josh is waiting for me to go over some numbers."

"Thanks for calling."

"Good night, Lauren."

She liked the way that sounded in her ear, as if his head was next to hers on a pillow. "Good night."

Sitting on the step, the book forgotten in her lap, she wondered if it would be more or less awkward the next time she ran into Ryan. Maybe less awkward because they'd addressed the past and could put it behind them.

But the feelings he was stirring in her now could make things more awkward if she didn't squash them. But wanting Ryan Kowalski wasn't an easy thing to squash.

## CHAPTER SIX

WEDNESDAY WASN'T A fun day at work. Gary was in a bad mood, the customers were cranky, and Lauren was fed up by closing time. She actually sat in her car for a few minutes, head resting on the steering wheel, trying to shake off the negativity that had sucked all the energy out of her.

It was still too early to drive over to the Kowalskis and pick up Nick, but she didn't see any point in going home just to go out again, so she drove to the library.

Hailey was behind the circulation desk, checking in a stack of picture books with her handheld scanner, and the place seemed empty. "Hey, Lauren. Rough day?"

"Does it show that bad?"

"Probably only to somebody who knows you well. Promise."

Lauren dragged a stool from the computer area to the desk so she could sit down. "So, I guess you've heard."

"That your son messed with the Kowalskis and has been sentenced to hard labor? Yeah, I heard."

"I swear, he gets more like Dean every day."

"Lucky you." Hailey carried the books she'd checked in to a rolling cart. On Tuesdays and Thursdays a high school student reshelved them, unless Hailey got bored and did it. Then the lucky kid got to dust. "You know, Nick's not only sentenced to hard labor. You know Rose will be feeding him and giving him that amazing lemonade she makes. Or milk. Depends on what she feeds him."

"Maybe I should break a few of their windows."

"Are you going out there to pick him up? I have a couple of books she reserved, so maybe you could drop them off? Save her a trip."

"Sure. I'd look around, but I still haven't finished the last batch I checked out. And now we're eating a little later and, even though it's not by much, it's throwing my schedule off."

A couple of kids wandered in, wanting to use the computers. Then a few moms showed up with pre-schoolers tagging along. So much for killing time chatting with the librarian.

"I'll get out of your way. I'll probably run a couple more errands and then go pick up Nick." She took the books Hailey checked out for Rose and left.

Even once she'd run out of things to do, Lauren was a little early when she drove up to the lodge and parked between Josh's and Ryan's trucks. Grabbing the books off the passenger seat, she walked up the front porch steps. She could hear power tools being run behind the house and she couldn't help but hope her son wasn't operating one of them.

At least she trusted Ryan to show him how to use the things correctly. But still, they weren't something Nick had a lot of experience with.

When Rose opened the door, she held up the books. "Delivery from the library."

"Lauren! It's nice to see you again. Come on in." She took the books, making an excited sound over the shiny, new hardcover.

"I stopped at the library and Hailey knew I had to come pick up Nick, so she asked me to bring them."

"I appreciate it. Come on into the kitchen. I'm making up a big batch of spaghetti and I don't want the sauce to burn."

The kitchen smelled amazing and Lauren wasn't surprised her stomach growled—quietly, just enough to let her know she was starving and the cube steaks and instant mashed potatoes waiting at home weren't going to taste quite as good tonight.

"Nick's really working hard," Rose was saying as she stirred the sauce. "And he's a quick learner, according to Ryan."

"I'm glad to hear it." Lauren pulled out a chair and sat down, since she wasn't sure what else to do. Almost instantly a napkin appeared in front of her with a fresh brownie on top. She liked this place. "Considering what he did, you've all been very gracious to him. I appreciate that."

"My boys all made their share of stupid mistakes and had to make right on them. They're not going to hold the same against your boy. You two want to stay for supper? I made plenty."

Yes, she absolutely wanted to stay for supper. But she needed to keep in mind, even if Rosie didn't, that Nick's being here was supposed to be a punishment. "Thank you, but I've got meat thawed and I need to cook it."

Lauren heard footsteps crossing the wood floors and looked up to see Ryan stride into the room, phone to his ear.

"She signed off on marble countertops in the master bath and granite in all the other bathrooms. If she wants marble in all of them, she's going to pay for it, plain and simple." He stopped when he saw her and smiled before continuing on to the fridge. "I don't care. You already gave her under-cabinet lighting in her kitchen because you're a sucker. If you don't get her to accept the granite or sign off on the marble as an extra, I'm going to fire you."

Lauren watched as he pulled a bowl of what looked like chocolate pudding out of the fridge. Then she put her hand over her mouth to stifle a laugh when Rose took it away, slapped his hand and put it back in the fridge. She replaced it with a brownie, which Ryan scowled at.

"She has until noon tomorrow to make the decision and then the granite's going in. Tell her that. I'm not going to pay the penalty if this job runs over because she can't make up her mind. Call me tomorrow and let me know how it went."

He snapped the phone closed and shoved it in his pocket. "Women."

"Give me that brownie back," Rose snapped.

"I'm kidding. The problem isn't the homeowner's wife. It's Phil. He's too nice to be in charge."

"You won't really fire him, will you?" Lauren asked.

"No, and he knows it. He has trouble being firm with homeowners, but the younger guys will work themselves into the ground for him. So how you doing today?"

"Better, now that I've had a brownie. You should eat yours. They do wonders for the mood."

He smiled, his blue eyes crinkling in the corners. "My mood's already improving."

She found herself smiling back. So was hers. "How's Nick doing?"

"Good. Andy had him working on the stone wall that runs around the back of the property. Straightening loose stones and yanking any weeds out." They heard footsteps running up the back steps. "Speak of the little devil."

Nick rushed in and grabbed his backpack out of the corner. He was filthy, sweaty and his hair was standing up in about twelve different directions, but he was also smiling. "Hi, Mom. I saw your car out front. Andy said I'm done for the day."

Lauren crumpled up her napkin and tossed it in the garbage, trying to ignore the delicious sauce simmering on the stove. She needed to use the slow cooker more often on workdays. The only time she really had to cook big meals was the weekends, but she was the only one home to eat them. Or maybe she could cook up big batches of sauce to freeze and then reheat during the week. She suspected, though, her efforts wouldn't taste as good as Rose's smelled.

"Thanks for the brownie," she told Rose. Then she turned to Ryan, who'd apparently devoured his in the time it had taken her to walk to the trash can. "Good luck with your countertops."

He smiled again, making that slow heat curl through her insides. "Thanks. I'll see you around."

"Probably."

She drove home listening to Nick's story about the snake they found curled up in the stone wall, but part of her was thinking about Ryan. The most sinful thing in that kitchen should have been the freshly baked double-fudge brownie, but the gooey chocolate had nothing on that man's smile. Or his eyes.

"Are you listening to me, Mom?"

"Yeah. Rock wall. Snake."

"That was like two minutes ago. I said I need more money in my lunch account."

Oops. Time to get her mind off Ryan and back on reality where it belonged.

ON SATURDAY, RYAN scored a parking spot directly in front of Whitford Hardware and gave the door an extra little jerk because he liked the way the old bell sounded when it rang. Always had.

The place looked pretty empty, but he heard paint cans being moved around on the other side of a shelf. "Hey, Dozer, I need a half-dozen tubes of caulking and a couple of guns. Some idiot can't read a supply list and took off for the weekend without leaving me what I need. Maybe if I texted it to him, he'd pay more attention."

The person who stepped out from behind the shelf wasn't Dozer, though. It was Lauren. She had on jeans and a long-sleeved T-shirt, both of which were liberally covered in dust.

"Dad's not in today, so I'm covering for him."

Which was fine with him. He'd never turn down a chance to see Lauren. "Is he okay? He's not sick or anything?"

"He's fine. My mom's been trying to get him to slow down, so she talked him into going to an RV show today. It's a good excuse to get some dusting done. He still gets the eye-level shelves, but you could write a book in the dust on the bottom shelves."

"Not that it's my business or anything, but why isn't Nick doing it?"

"He works here during the summers. And he helps out part-time during school vacations sometimes, but he's with his dad on the weekends and has school, which my dad thinks is more important. Mostly Nick helps shelve the deliveries and replace screens and glass panes and mix paint. Neither of them ever think to dust, and my mother's refused to work in the store for years. She wants him to sell it and take her to Niagara Falls."

He realized the time Nick was spending at the lodge probably took away from the time he spent at the store, but he knew Dozer had been all for it. He'd told him so last time Ryan had stopped in, after he'd apologized profusely for his grandson's behavior. "He could probably go to New York without selling the business."

She smiled, shaking her head. "From Niagara Falls, she wants to visit the Black Hills. And she's always wanted to see a giant redwood tree or whatever they're called."

"That's a long time to hang a We'll Be Right Back sign on the door."

"Yeah. Let me get you that caulking and the guns. I was just about to hang the We'll Be Right Back sign on the door myself so I can go get some lunch. After cleaning all morning, the yogurt I brought in for lunch isn't going to cut it."

"I was going to stop at the diner for a burger when I left here. Why don't you let me buy you one?" The words rolled casually off his tongue, but his stomach knotted up. Did he mean it as a date? Would she take it that way? But, really, they were going to the same place, so it was a friendly and gentlemanly offer to make.

"Okay. Sure." She found an empty box and loaded it with the caulking guns and tubes, but he insisted on carrying it to the register.

He put it on his card instead of the lodge's account because he was always on the lookout for ways to save the family money. Mitch had it in his head they

shouldn't put personal funds into the place because it
needed to sink or swim on its own, without them throwing good money after bad. Ryan felt that they should
do what they had to do to get the lodge back in shape
and then worry about turning a profit. But he wasn't
the oldest.

"I'm going to hang the sign and lock up after you
leave," she told him. "But I want to try to wash up a
little, so I'll be a few minutes."

"I'll get us a table."

He barely noticed the bell ringing on his way out.
After dumping the box in the bed of his truck, he drove
down the street to the diner's lot and then sat in the
truck for a few minutes, getting his bearings.

So he was going to have lunch with Lauren. They
were friends. They were both hungry. It was no big
deal. And really there was nowhere else to eat but the
diner, which, unfortunately, his sister-in-law owned.
Rose would know he was there with Lauren before their
food was even cooked, and God only knew what she'd
make of it.

Since there was nothing he could do about that, he
got out of his truck and went inside, where Paige greeted
him with a kiss on the cheek. "You want to sit at the
counter?"

"Um, actually I'm going to take a table. Lauren's
joining me."

He had to give her credit. She almost managed to
hide the curiosity he knew the simple statement had
triggered. "Okay. Setup for two, coming right up."

There weren't really any private tables at the diner,
but he chose one in the back and listened to Paige make
small talk about the wedding while she laid out the place
mats and silverware.

"I was going to hire a caterer, but Rosie told me Fran's talked to practically everybody on the guest list and turned it into a potluck dinner. Does that sound tacky? I mean, it's a wedding reception, even if it is in the backyard."

"Nobody will think it's tacky. That's the way it's usually done around here, and most people would think you were crazy if you paid strangers to cook you food your neighbors will gladly bring."

"And Steph already has her iPod loaded up with play-lists so she can play DJ. She's been emailing me lists and, I swear, that girl has every song ever recorded on that thing."

Ryan grinned. His cousin's daughter loved her music and her iPod. He didn't get to see her a lot, but he never saw her without it. "More money saved."

"And Gavin's mom is going to be our photographer." Gavin was her second-shift cook and he loved to ex-periment on the locals.

"Spend all that money you saved on alcohol and yours will forever be considered the wedding of the century in Whitford."

She laughed and slapped his shoulder with the menu. "You know Fran is ordering enough champagne to turn the entire U.S. Navy into drunken sailors."

As fascinating as he found wedding planning, or pretended to at least, Ryan kept looking out the win-dow, waiting for Lauren to come into sight. He tried not to be obvious, but he must have failed, because Paige chuckled.

"First-date jitters?"

"It's not a date." He said it firmly, so she couldn't misunderstand. "I stopped by the hardware store and

she was on her way to lunch and I was, too, so I offered
to buy her a burger."

"Whatever you say." She winked at him before she
walked away.

"It's not a date," he muttered again, even though nobody would hear him.


IT'S NOT A DATE, Lauren told herself as she walked down
the main street toward the diner. Dates were planned
far enough in advance for a woman to shave her legs
and pick out something nice to wear. They weren't so
impromptu that she had to show up in jeans with her
hair in a ponytail.

What this was was two friends bumping into each
other at lunchtime and deciding to have lunch. And,
since all the Kowalski guys were a touch old-fashioned,
he'd offered to pay. Simple. And not a date.

He'd found a table in the back, away from the counter, which was filling up with lunch regulars, and he
smiled when she slid into the booth across from him.
"You missed a little bit of dust, right on the side of
your nose."

She wiped at it and he nodded to let her know it was
gone. "Dad uses the cheapest paper towels he can buy.
I washed my face, but that brown paper just smeared
everything around."

"I'm in construction. I like women who aren't afraid
to get their hands dirty."

He didn't say it in any kind of flirtatious way, but
she felt herself blush a little. "I grew up in a hardware
store. I don't think I even had fingernails worth breaking until I left home."

"I remember."

"True." Sometimes she had a hard time connecting this adult, sexy man with the kid she'd grown up with.

Paige stopped by to take their orders, and they both asked for coffee and burgers. She wrote it down, then pointed her pen at Ryan. "I meant to tell you, I was up at the lodge yesterday and I can't believe how much work you've done on the outside. It's going to look great for the wedding, so thank you."

"Dill and Matt have worked pretty hard on it, so I'll pass your thanks along to them. They'll head out Thursday night, since the family's coming Friday morning, and they'll put all the sawhorses and scaffolding and stuff in the barn with the tools before they go."

"I can't wait."

"I hope you realize you owe us a movie night," Lauren said.

"I had to cross movie night off my calendar to write in my wedding," Paige confessed. "I was hoping nobody would notice."

The first Saturday of every month was movie night in Whitford. A bunch of the women took turns hosting it and the host got to pick the movie. There were also snacks and no shortage of drinks.

"When you get your new house, you're going to have to throw an epic movie night to make up for it," Lauren teased. Paige's trailer was so tiny, she'd never been able to host the other women.

"Guess I'd better buy a television then."

"Mitch hasn't bought one yet?" Ryan asked. "I'm surprised."

"He hasn't been home a lot. And, trust me, he's TV shopping. I think he's waiting for me to pick a house so he can measure the living room wall."

The bell rang, signaling food in the pass-through

window, so Paige had to run. She was back a minute later with their coffees, but couldn't chat anymore.

"So tell me about your life since you moved away," Lauren said as they fixed their coffees. "I hear little bits and pieces, but not a lot."

"You know the part where I landed a job with a Boston builder when I graduated from college." He'd told her that the day he'd asked her to divorce Dean and leave with him. "I worked my way up with him, got married, kept working, got divorced, started my own business, worked a lot more, built a house in Brookline…more work. And I'm here. Working."

She laughed, shaking her head. "I suspect that's the abridged version."

"That's pretty much the only version. There's not a lot more to it than that."

"Was your divorce a bad one? I mean, all divorces suck, but did you fight?"

He shrugged. "Not really. We drifted apart and both came to the conclusion about the same time that we didn't really want to be married anymore. Last I heard she'd married a guy from Rhode Island. I think. Or maybe it was Jersey."

"I guess, with no kids, it's easier to move on. At least there's no custody battle and child support and visitation schedule to fight over."

He stirred the spoon in his coffee cup, staring at the swirling liquid. "On the flip side, though, I have no kids."

There was something in his voice that made her sad. Her divorce had sucked. Since the marriage's death blow was her finding Dean in bed with Jody, it had been ugly. And there was no putting him behind her, or being so over it that she wasn't even sure where he lived. There were smiles past clenched teeth and arguments over who had to pay for what and holidays spent alone because it was dad's turn.

But she had Nick. He made everything—from being married to Dean to going to work every day to smiling at the current Mrs. Carpenter—worth it.

"Okay," she said. "Leave it to me to sit here across from a great guy, drinking good coffee on a beautiful day and bring up divorce."

He grinned at her over the rim of his coffee cup. "You think I'm a great guy?"

"I don't think that's a secret. You Kowalskis are all great guys."

The grin faded. "But I'm greater than the other ones, right?"

"Are you serious right now?" She laughed at him.

"Of course not." Then he held up his hand, his thumb and forefinger about a quarter-inch apart. "Okay, maybe a little serious."

"Fine. I think you might be a little greater than your brothers."

He winked at her. "That's what I like to hear."

They made small talk while they ate. They talked about Nick and the snake he'd found in the rock wall and how they'd found out Dill was a little phobic about snakes when Nick tried to show it to him. Luckily, he hadn't actually fallen off the ladder. Ryan told her about Rosie's shopping list for the wedding weekend, which was pushing three pages long, and that was with double columns.

He talked some about the family coming from New Hampshire, and she was captivated by the warmth in his voice when he talked about his cousins and their kids. And his aunt Mary and uncle Leo. He was a man

who obviously loved his family deeply, and she thought
back to that odd note in his voice when he'd pointed out
he didn't have any kids. He was really good with Nick,
according to her son, and he'd probably make a great
dad. Some woman out there was definitely missing out
on a good man.

That was a depressing thought, so she shoved it aside
and focused on the story he was telling her. Something
about a cell phone quacking like a duck. Dill's, she
gathered.

"You're the boss and you don't seem to have any
problem being a hard-ass. Make him change it."

"I'm only a hard-ass when it's called for. Okay, which
is almost all the time. But I don't make him change it,
because it's distinctive and I hate it so it catches my
attention. Helps me keep track of how much time he's
spending playing with his phone and not working."

"I'm surprised you put up with it at all. Aren't there
a dozen other guys who'd take his job and not quack
all day?"

"Dill might be driving me nuts right now, but he's
got a knack for building, strong leadership skills and he
holds himself and the other guys on a job with him to a
standard of quality as high as mine. Once he outgrows
this annoying-puppy stage, he's going to be one of my
best builders. He'll be running jobs in a few years if he
doesn't screw it up in the meantime."

She liked listening to him talk about his business. It
was a world he was obviously comfortable in, and the
relaxed confidence he exuded was pretty damn sexy.

Way too soon, their plates were empty and it was
time for her to head back to the store. It had already
been closed almost an hour, which was going to give
her father fits if anybody complained to him.

"Thank you for lunch," she said when they were standing out on the sidewalk.

"I enjoyed the company. We'll have to do it again sometime."

She nodded, her heart doing a little happy dance in her chest as he walked to his truck. She'd like that. A lot.

## CHAPTER SEVEN

THERE WERE NO power tools running. Ryan closed the door of his truck and listened more closely. No work sounds at all.

Monday morning he'd had to make the drive back to Brookline to put out a few fires. An accounts receivable fire. An HR fire, because one of the dumbass new guys got fresh with his secretary's assistant and only Ryan had the authority to fire anybody. And the electrical outfit they'd subbed a job to because Ryan's regular guys were booked had started pulling wires before they'd pulled a permit and the inspector was good and pissed.

Now it was Wednesday and he'd gotten up at the butt crack of dawn to get back to Whitford so he could bust his ass alongside the guys to make sure the lodge looked as good as possible for his brother's wedding.

But the guys apparently weren't busting their asses. Somewhere, for some reason, they were sitting on them.

And he'd bet a week's payroll Rose would know where they were. He went into the lodge and, after listening for a few seconds, heard some faint noises coming from the guest-room wing. He went down the hall and turned into the room the scuffling noises were coming from.

Rose wasn't in the guest room. Dill and Matt were, though. Matt was standing in front of a set of bunk beds, frowning, with his arms folded across his chest. Dill was up on the top bunk, wrestling with a fitted sheet.

"What the hell are you two clowns doing?"

They both jumped a mile, and the one corner of the sheet Dill had managed to hook over the mattress popped off. "Shit!"

"Rose put us to work," Matt said, as if that explained everything.

"You work for *me*."

"Not today, boss."

It was tempting to walk over and cuff him upside the head, but it wasn't really their fault. When Rosie decided something was going to happen the way she wanted it, it generally happened that way. She'd probably steamrolled right over them.

"This isn't possible." Dill sounded as if he'd jump off the side of the bunk bed if only the drop was high enough to put him out of his misery. "You can't reach the back of the damn mattress from the ground, but you can't pull the mattress up to tuck the sheet in if you're on top of it."

"You can't make a bed, but I let you build houses for me?"

"Oh, you think you can do it better?"

Ryan couldn't even tell them how many times he'd made up that particular set of bunk beds. And the other set in the room. And the others in the lodge, along with the double beds and the queen beds. The chore list when you grew up in a lodging establishment was long and royally sucked.

"Get down," he said. "I have to show you how to do everything. How you even managed to knock up your wife without help is beyond me."

Dill snorted as he climbed down the ladder. Ryan

waited until he was out of the way, then climbed most of the way up the ladder. Reaching across the bunk, he curled the mattress toward him and held it with one hand while he used the other to hook the top, back corner of the sheet over it. Then he switched hands and did the bottom back corner. He yanked on the center of the edge to tuck it all down the side, then slowly rolled the mattress down. Getting the front two corners on and tucking it down the side was a piece of cake.

"No shit," Dill said.

"Give me the flat sheet."

He made quick work of that, too, then moved on to the other three bunk mattresses in the room while the guys handled the less taxing job of smoothing quilts over the sheets. He'd hated this job as a kid, much preferring to work with his dad doing outside stuff, but Rose had kept a chart and the kids had rotated jobs to be fair. She'd paired them off, younger with older. She'd claimed it was so they could watch over and teach the little ones, but he suspected it was because the younger kids would tattle if the older kids slacked off or took shortcuts. Mitch got Josh and Ryan got Sean, who had really sucked at making beds. Liz and Katie were supposed to do chores together, but Liz preferred the baking and cleaning and fussing over throw pillows, while Katie wanted to change the oil in the lawn mower and tag along after Ryan's dad.

"You guys got it now?" He wasn't spending his day making beds. Unless Rose told him to, of course, but he was really hoping it wouldn't come to that.

"Yeah," they both said in unison.

"Where's Andy?"

"He escaped," Matt said. "Saw her looking for us

with a big old list and he ran for his truck. She called after him but he pretended not to hear her and got away."

"He'll come back. Everybody does eventually."

Ryan left them to their housekeeping and went in search of Rose. He found her in the backyard, stringing twine between stakes she'd driven into the ground.

She straightened when she saw him, pushing her hair back away from her face. "You're home. I didn't hear you pull in."

"What are you doing?"

"Trying to figure out where I want the tent."

He shook his head. "Why don't you have Dill and Matt doing this, since you decided to shanghai my crew?"

"Well, for one thing, no matter how many stakes they drive in and how much string they run, they still won't know where I want the tent." She blew out a breath and stretched her back. "And for another, I really, really hate making up those bunk beds."

He laughed, but seeing her press her hands to her back and arch it like that gave him a pang of worry. Whether they kept the place or Rose stayed on with new owners, it wasn't going to be long before she needed help, even if it was just a part-time high school girl to help with making beds and laundry and vacuuming. Rose would fight it, though, because she was stubborn and taking care of the lodge was her business and nobody else's.

"Where's Josh?"

"He went to pick up the canopy I rented. He'll be back in a couple of hours."

"You could have waited for Nick to help you with this," he pointed out.

"I can handle setting a few stakes and running some string, young man."

And that was the end of *that* line of conversation. "Nick show up yesterday and the day before?"

"Of course he did. Did everything asked of him, just like always."

"And Lauren picked him up?"

"No. She abandoned him here so we can raise him as one of our own while she runs off with the circus."

"*You* are a crazy woman." He turned and walked away. "I'm going to find actual work to do."

"You're going to drag the throw rugs out so I can beat them," she called after him. "And next time you want to know how Lauren Carpenter's doing, just ask."

He slammed the kitchen door so hard it was a good thing he'd replaced it with steel, because the old one probably would have cracked.

Rose watched through the kitchen window as Ryan, Josh, Dill and Matt put up the canopy she'd rented. It was a big one and she was sure if she stepped out the back door, she'd get quite an off-color vocabulary lesson.

She didn't want to deal with it after the family arrived tomorrow, even though there would be plenty of guys, so she'd talked Ryan into having the guys help him and Josh before they headed back to Massachusetts for the long weekend.

Andy walked into the kitchen, not looking much happier than the guys outside did. "I'm done."

Because he was tall, she'd asked him to go through the lodge and dust the ceiling-fan blades before she vacuumed a final time. There were a lot of ceiling fans.

"Thank you. I have to haul around a step stool and climb up and down for every one of them."

"I'll go see if I can give them a hand."

She watched him walk across the yard, amazed at the difference not even two months could make. Way back when Katie was a little girl, Rose's husband, Earle, had gone on a sledding trip with Andy, who was his best friend. There was drinking and Andy talked two women into joining them in their motel room. Earle had broken his wedding vows. Blaming Andy had helped her forgive her husband enough to rebuild their marriage into the long and happy one it was until he passed away.

After more years than she cared to remember now of her not speaking to Andy, Mitch and Josh had hired him to do some odd jobs around the lodge. She didn't care if he'd been a friend of their dad's and was Drew Miller's father. She was mad as hell. But having the situation shoved into her lap had caused her to give some thought to it and she'd finally forgiven him. Sometimes it was still strange, the way he was so at home at the lodge, but she was slowly getting more comfortable having him around.

Leaving the men to the canopy, she made a slow, careful tour of the house, making sure everything was ready for tomorrow. They might be family, but Rose took a great deal of pride in the place and she wanted it to look its best for the wedding.

Suddenly feeling a little weepy, she sat down on the staircase and ran her hand over a tread worn smooth by generations of Kowalski feet.

She knew it was selfish, but she hoped the kids didn't sell the Northern Star. She wouldn't tell them that. They all had their own lives to lead and maybe they didn't want to be saddled with it anymore. And Josh deserved the chance to figure out what he wanted to do with his life, even if it meant she'd lose this place.

Logically, it made sense to sell it. Mitch and Paige wanted a house of their own. Ryan owned a beautiful house and a successful business in Brookline. Even if whatever was going on between him and Lauren bloomed into something, he wasn't coming back to Whitford to play innkeeper. Sean was settled with Emma in New Hampshire, and Liz was in New Mexico. And Josh…she'd just about given up on Josh seeing that what he really wanted was right in front of him, because he was so blinded by what he thought he wanted. Katie was doing her own thing and wouldn't care if Rose retired and moved into a little apartment over Main Street.

She was tired. And it didn't seem that she was going to get to hear the thunder of little feet overhead again, so maybe it was time to start letting go of the Northern Star.

*After* the wedding.

By THURSDAY NIGHT Lauren had to admit, although only to herself, that she was disappointed she hadn't seen Ryan since they'd had lunch on Saturday.

It had been a bit of a letdown when she'd pulled into the driveway on Monday to pick up Nick and Ryan's truck hadn't been there. Nick had told her that Ryan had to go back to Mass for work stuff until probably Wednesday morning. Then on Wednesday, he must have been busy doing something, because she didn't see him then, either. It didn't look like she'd see him again until Paige's wedding.

"Is there something wrong with that wine?" Katie asked, jerking her out of her thoughts.

"No, why?"

"Because you're scowling at it."

"Oh. Just lost in thought, I guess." And because she knew the question was coming, she went ahead and made up a fake answer. "Nick's going on a camping trip with his dad this weekend and I'm trying to remember if I packed his wool socks."

Katie waved her hand. "Wool socks are for tomorrow. Tonight is for fun."

On such short notice, and with Mitch taking Paige off to New Hampshire to meet his family on the only free weekend, they weren't able to throw a proper bachelorette party for her. But they'd all gathered at Hailey's for an impromptu Thursday-night potluck dinner, with wine.

It would have been nice to wait until Mitch's female relatives could be there, but their Friday arrival and the Saturday wedding didn't leave enough time. They'd just have to party all over again at the reception.

Paige was currently sitting in Hailey's rocking chair, which had been thoroughly toilet-papered in lieu of white streamers. Whitford didn't have a party store and Hailey had forgotten to stop at one when she'd gone into the city to buy gifts.

"Oh, my God, Fran," Paige said, while Hailey almost doubled over laughing beside her.

Lauren could see why when Paige held up the present. Fran had knit her a short, spaghetti-strapped nightie...out of a nice, sturdy wool. It was the most bizarre thing she'd ever seen.

"Hey, you didn't leave me enough time to knit the matching peignoir," Fran said. "But that'll keep the important bits warm while still looking sexy. Maine-style."

Lauren had lived in Maine her entire life and she'd

never seen a wool negligee, but the gift was definitely the hit of the party, even if Paige did decline modeling it for everybody.

"I'll save it to wear for Mitch," she said, folding it carefully and adding it to the pile of more traditional sexy underwear and nighties she'd received.

When the gifts had been opened, the desserts were broken out and more wine was poured. Lauren opted out, since she was driving, but she doubled up on the chocolate cream pie to make up for it.

"Okay," Hailey said to Paige when they were standing at the counter, eating. "Spill. Where are you going for your honeymoon?"

"I don't know."

"What do you mean, you don't know?"

Lauren had to agree with Hailey. "How can you not know where you're going on your wedding night?"

Paige shrugged. "He doesn't want me to know. He's afraid I'll tell somebody and his brothers and cousins will be able to find us. We're only going for a few nights because of the diner and the fact he has a lot of travel coming up, so it'll be someplace close."

"I can't believe he won't tell anybody where he's going to be," Katie said. She'd skipped the Red Sox ball cap for the occasion, though the ponytail was in place.

"If he told anybody, it would probably be Rose. Or maybe Ryan. He's the least likely to tell everybody else, I think. He told me all I needed was my toothbrush and maybe a robe to put on when room service came around."

Hailey snorted. "If he's just going to keep you in a hotel room the whole time for nonstop newlywed sex, you may as well save money and stay right at the lodge."

"Mitch and I didn't really talk about it, but I suspect

having Rose *and* his aunt Mary under the same roof would be…inhibitive, let's say."

"What about me?"

They all turned, and Katie pointed at her mother. "You're getting sneaky in your old age."

"We were talking about the fact they're going to a hotel for their honeymoon because Mitch can't get it up with you and Mary both at the lodge," Hailey said. Lauren guessed she'd probably downed a glass or two more of the wine than the other women had.

Paige blushed bright red. "That's not what I said at all! I said it would be inhibitive. Not prohibitive."

"No wonder Mitch loves you," Katie said. "You know all the big words."

"Shut up. This is my bachelorette party. You can't make fun of me at my own party."

Katie just grinned and moved in for a second helping of chocolate pudding. Lauren glanced at the clock and winced. She still had a lot to do before Nick could leave with Dean tomorrow. And she couldn't run late because Hailey had made the hair appointment for them.

"You wouldn't believe how amazing Ryan has been," Paige said, and Lauren decided she could stay a few more minutes. "He and the guys who work for him have the outside all spruced up. They even repainted the chairs on the porch so they'd look good in the pictures. He's such a sweetheart."

Lauren thought so, too. In fact, for such a sweetheart and all-around great guy to have gone behind his friend's back the way he did, he must have cared about her a lot more than she'd ever suspected. Granted, that was a really long time ago, so he hadn't been as mature then as he was now, but he'd always been a good guy.

The *what-if* game that had always been just a stupid, harmless fantasy came with a hint of regret now. If she'd known then what she knew now—if she'd been able to see the guy Ryan Kowalski would become—she might have said yes.

"You're looking serious again, Lauren," Katie accused.

"What?" Lauren forced herself to shake it off. "Yeah, I really have to go. Nick's supposed to be getting his stuff together for his camping trip, which I just know means tearing apart the house and garage."

She hugged Paige, who squealed in her ear. "Can you believe the next time you see me, I'll be heading up the aisle to become Mrs. Mitchell Kowalski? How amazing is that? Mrs. Kowalski sounds so awesome. I might put that on my name tag at work instead of Paige."

Lauren squeezed her friend, soaking in her happiness. "You're a very lucky woman."

## CHAPTER EIGHT

ON FRIDAY, THE extended Kowalski family arrived like a parade, their vehicles pulling up the driveway one right after another. Paige jumped back from the window when Uncle Leo, who was first in line, honked his horn, and Ryan laughed at her.

"Why are you so nervous? You've already met them."

"For one day."

"Mitch loves you, they'll love you. It's that simple."

She nodded, but her eyes sparkled with unshed tears. "I wish my mother was here."

Hearing her say that raised Ryan's blood pressure all over again. Donna Sullivan had a new boyfriend, it seemed, and they'd already made plans they couldn't cancel on such short notice. Ryan had been in the room when Mitch had called Donna and offered not only to buy two first-class plane tickets, but to foot the bill for any cancellation fees for the plans, which couldn't possibly be as important as her daughter's wedding. But her boyfriend hadn't wanted to come, so she hadn't either.

"You'll be a Kowalski now," he told Paige. "And we always show up."

"I'm going to love being a part of your family." She took a deep breath and blinked away the wetness in her eyes. "Okay, let's go out and say hi."

Rosie, Josh and Mitch were already on the porch

when he and Paige stepped out, so they all went down the steps to the driveway together.

Uncle Leo and Aunt Mary were first in line for hugs, but when his aunt got a little weepy, Ryan passed her off to Rosie and moved to Terry and Evan's car. His cousin and her husband looked relaxed and happy, which made him smile. They'd had a rough patch a while back and the family hadn't been sure the marriage would survive. Now it seemed stronger than ever. Their fourteen-year-old daughter, Stephanie, squealed and threw her arms around his neck and it blew his mind how tall she'd gotten. He needed to get over to New Hampshire more often.

His cousin Kevin arrived in a minivan, which made Ryan chuckle, with his brother Joe riding shotgun. When Beth got two-year-old Lily out of her car seat, she was off like a rocket, mom at her heels. Keri handed Brianna—who'd had her first birthday late in the summer—to Joe, but she squirmed, wanting to get down and go with her cousin.

Then the doors to Mike and Lisa's minivan opened and their kids spilled out, grumbling and throwing elbows. He shook his cousin's hand, trying to remember how old Rosie had said their boys were. The youngest, Bobby, was eight, so working backward he figured out Brian was ten, Danny was thirteen and Joey was sixteen. Damn, they grew up fast.

Pulling up the rear was a pickup that said Landscaping by Emma down the side, and his brother Sean—aka the middle child—was standing in front of it, stretching his back.

His wife, Emma, had her hands on her hips. "If you'd let me drive part of the way, your back wouldn't be so stiff."

Sean just shook his head, then grinned when he saw Ryan approaching. Ryan shook his hand, pulling him in for a shoulder slapping, then kissed his sister-in-law's cheek. "Glad you guys made it."

"Wouldn't have missed it. You haven't lived until you've been in a McDonald's with seven kids who will do anything to not get back in a vehicle."

"Better you than me." Ryan took Emma's bag from her. "Although I get the privilege of making the six-hour round-trip to pick up Liz at the airport. Josh pulled the whole healing-broken-leg card."

"The bastard." Sean didn't seem to be in any hurry to wade into the throng of loud Kowalskis blocking the porch. "How's the work going?"

They chatted a few minutes about the renovations on the lodge, and Ryan wasn't surprised when Emma wandered off to join the rest of the family. He stood and watched them while he talked to his brother, and he *was* surprised when he saw Emma press a hand to her lower belly before shoving both hands in her pockets. He looked at Sean, one eyebrow raised.

Sean grinned and nodded. "Yeah. But she doesn't want to tell anybody yet."

"Between Rose and Aunt Mary, there's no way it's going stay a secret."

"If they suspect, they suspect. But she doesn't want to tell anybody until Thanksgiving. It's still early, plus you know all the women are going to flip out. Especially Rosie, since it's the first baby for our side of the family, but Emma doesn't want to take any of the focus off Paige."

"Holy shit, you're going to be a daddy." The grin and the glow that lit up his brother's face warmed Ryan's heart. It had taken Sean a long time to settle and across the country so we couldn't be in his business anymore. He took you away, so yeah...we're not huge fans. Doesn't mean I'm not sorry you ended up here, kid."

She took a deep breath and let it out slowly. "I'll be okay."

"Are you coming home?"

She shook her head. "I miss you guys, but my life's in New Mexico. I'll be making some changes, though, and one of them is coming home at least twice a year from now on."

He reached across the center console and squeezed her hand. "That sounds like a good plan, but once Rosie knows Darren's out of the picture, it's only a matter of time before all your shit's in a U-Haul headed east."

"And that's why you're going to keep your mouth shut. I'm going to wait until it's time to walk out the door and then tell her quick before we drive away. She's less effective over the phone."

"Keep telling yourself that."

"Whatever. So tell me how the family's all doing? Any good gossip?"

Since he couldn't tell her Emma's news, he told her about Kevin's new business venture. And he told her about Nick and the vandalism and how Rosie was treating him like the grandchild she so desperately wanted. "Isn't he Lauren Carpenter's son?" She said it casually enough, but she was full of crap. She knew full who Nick was.

"Yeah."

"So you must see a lot of her then. And she's friends with Paige, isn't she? I bet she'll be at the wedding tomorrow."

"Yeah."

he could see, without a doubt, his younger brother was ridiculously happy. "Congratulations, man."

"Thanks. I don't know if we'll be able to keep the secret until Thanksgiving or not, but I'd appreciate it if you didn't say anything until after the wedding."

"Not my good news to share." He pulled out his phone to check the time. "Shit. I've gotta hit the road soon. Mitch checked about an hour ago and Liz's flight is on time, so I should be, too."

It was another forty minutes before he managed to free himself from the tangle of family and his truck from the tangle of vehicles and hit the road. Kevin, along with a partner, was in the process of opening a second branch of Jasper's Bar & Grille on the snowmobile trails in northern New Hampshire, and wanted some advice on hiring a contractor. Aunt Mary wanted to know how Josh was really doing, and Uncle Leo wanted to know every detail of the work they'd done on the lodge.

But he finally extricated himself and the almost three-hour drive was actually a nice break. He wasn't going to get a lot of quiet time this weekend.

He hung around the baggage claim area for what felt like forever before passengers began streaming toward the carousel. Liz spotted him immediately and he grinned. She looked great, with her long, dark hair loose and frazzled around her face. While they were all losing their summer color already, her tan set off the blue eyes crinkling as she smiled.

She came at him on the run and he caught her as she threw herself into his arms. It had only been a few months since she'd flown home for Sean and Emma's wedding, but he'd noticed then that she seemed to have a hard time leaving when it was time to go home.

"It's good to see you," he said around a mouthful of her hair.

"I can't believe Mitch is getting married." She moved toward the carousel as bags started dumping off the belt, and he had to walk fast to keep up. "What do you think of Paige?"

"She's awesome. She's kind of quiet and she's a bit of a homebody. Doesn't take any crap from Mitch."

"I always thought we'd end up with a sister-in-law who was a Vegas stripper or a Miami Beach bunny. What does Rosie think of her?"

When she grabbed hold of a massive, battered suitcase, he reached past her and took it away. The thing weighed a ton and he thanked his lucky stars the wheels were still in fairly good shape. "Rosie loves her."

"Then she must be awesome."

They walked out to his truck while she filled him in on the sick kid and the cranky woman and the snoring guy on her flight, and he hoped her chattering covered the sound of his grunt when he had to lift her suitcase into the bed.

"Growing weak in your old age?" Apparently, it hadn't. "It's under the fifty-pound limit. Just barely, but still."

"Shut up and get in the truck."

She was quiet while he navigated his way out of the airport to the open road. Actually, she was more quiet than usual, just staring out the passenger window. Usually she at least sang along with the radio.

"How's Darren?" Not that he cared, but he figured it would be rude not to ask.

"I moved out last weekend."

Ryan almost drove off the road. "What? What happened? Are you okay? How come I didn't know this?"

"You didn't know because I haven't told any And you can't, either. I don't want people wor about me instead of enjoying Mitch's wedding."

When had he become the keeper of the whole ily's damn secrets? "You didn't even tell Rosie?"

"I'll tell her before I leave, but not until after M and Paige leave for their honeymoon."

"So what happened? And are you okay?" Th been trying to get her to dump the guy for year that didn't mean it was any easier for her.

"Nothing happened really. It was just anothe day like every other long day and, after anoth about money—or the lack thereof—and why he set an alarm to remind him when I'd be home s he could at least throw leftovers in the micr thought to myself, 'I'm thirty-two years old. I to do this every single day for another forty, f years.' And I couldn't do it. I couldn't do i more day."

"That's no way to live."

"It wasn't bad."

"But it wasn't good."

She sighed, tapping her fingers on he want more. When I think about havin years left to do what I'm doing, I want enough, not that it's too long."

"I'm sorry, though. You guys were

She laughed. "Don't lie. You—al ways hated Darren."

"We just wanted him to man up responsible. Get a day job so al on you. Instead, he talked you i

"Good. Somebody to dance with who doesn't swim in the same DNA pool."

"I'm not much for dancing," he said.

"Not much to it. Hold her close and sway to the music, big brother."

She was trying to kill him. There was no way in hell he was going to hold Lauren close and sway to the music, especially in front of his family.

He might think about it a lot, though. Later, when he was alone.

LAUREN EYEBALLED THE small mound of camping and ATV gear in the driveway. "You're sure you have everything? It's going to be cold at night."

Nick gave her an exasperated look. "Yes, since you made me check everything off the list as I packed it and then you practically unpacked and repacked everything making sure."

Dean and Jody were standing by Jody's minivan and Lauren could hear Nick's little brother and sister—five-year-old Alex and three-year-old Adrienne—squabbling in the backseat. Time to get the show on the road.

"Let's get it loaded up then," she said.

When they started picking up bags, Dean stepped forward to help and, within a few minutes, they were ready to take off for the long weekend. While she'd gotten used to not having her son around Saturdays and Sundays a long time ago, she still didn't like it and always felt a pang in her chest when she hugged him goodbye.

"Have fun and be safe," she said, trying not to squeeze him too hard.

"I will." And she knew he would. Dean wasn't always on the ball, but he didn't mess around with the four-wheelers. Nick had as much safety gear as a moto-cross racer. "Have fun at the wedding."

"Thanks, honey." At least there was one day she wouldn't rattle around the house alone. "I'll see you Monday afternoon."

Lauren waved until the minivan was out of sight and then rushed into the house to grab her purse and car keys. She was meeting Hailey at the library so they could go to the salon together and she was already running a few minutes behind.

When she got to the library, she saw Hailey locking the front door and got out of her car to read the sign taped to it. " 'Closed early for personal reasons. Re-opening Tuesday morning as usual.' How many people do you think are going to complain?"

"A few, but I don't care. There's been a sign up at the circulation desk for a week and I've told everybody I could think of, so I did what I could."

"Well, let's go because we're running late."

"I don't even know why we're spending the time and money," Hailey said once she was buckled up. "I think the only single, non-Kowalski guys that are going to be there will be Drew Miller and his dad. Drew's not divorced yet, plus Mallory's my friend so he's permanently out, and his dad's too old."

"This was *your* idea."

"I know. It sounded like fun at the time. Today it's just reminding me I have nobody to look hot *for*."

"Why are you discounting the Kowalskis? Josh is single. And hot."

"I'm discounting him because someday he's going to wake the hell up and realize he's in love with Katie Davis and I'd rather not be his girlfriend or, God forbid, wife, when that happens." She turned sideways a little so she could stare at Lauren. "I notice you didn't mention Ryan. Any particular reason you don't think I should hook up with him?"

There wasn't a damn thing she could do about the blush, but she tried to sound as nonchalant as possible. "He lives in Mass. You live here. Would never work out."

"Perfect for a short, smoking hot sexfest, though, don't you think?"

She should say yes. Yes, Ryan would be perfect for a short, smoking hot sexfest and Lauren would know since she'd been giving that very subject a great deal of thought lately. But in no way, under any circumstances, did she think Ryan was perfect for *Hailey's* sexfest.

"I'm just pushing your buttons," Hailey said, and then she laughed. "You should see your face right now."

"I don't have any claim on him."

"Maybe not, but you want to and that's enough to make him off-limits to me. Which brings me back to why we're spending time and money at the salon with no hope of getting laid. Well, you might. But I won't."

"I won't be getting laid. And we're going to the salon because Paige is getting married and it's a party in October in Whitford. That alone is worth an eyebrow waxing."

Hailey turned back to the windshield and crossed her arms. "My vibrator doesn't care about my eyebrows."

"Your vibrator also can't take out the trash."

"Doesn't leave dirty clothes on the floor."

"Can't haul the Christmas decorations down from the attic."

"You and I have different priorities."

Lauren couldn't argue with that. Vibrators and Christmas decorations aside, she and Hailey had very different priorities when it came to men. Lauren, more than anything, wanted company. She wanted somebody to share her life with, especially since Nick would be going off to college in a couple of years. Hopefully.

Hailey was looking for a man to start a life with. Lauren knew, under the flippant talk of smoking hot sexfests, what her friend really wanted was a husband and kids, and she wasn't getting any younger. So, while they both might be looking for a man—though Lauren wasn't putting a great deal of effort into the hunt—they needed men at very different stages of their lives and looking for very different things.

"I've been thinking about moving," Hailey said.

"Moving? You love your house. And your job. What are you talking about?"

"If Mr. Right was in Whitford, don't you think I'd have found him by now?

She had a point, but giving up her job and her home and leaving a place she loved to go track him down was crazy and Lauren said so. "How would you pick a place to move to? Say some kind of magic spell, close your eyes and see where your finger lands on a map?"

"If I move to a city, like Portland, there's a much bigger pool of guys to choose from. One of them's bound to be right."

"Yeah, except for the fact you hate being in the city and he obviously wouldn't."

"I'd live in the city for the right guy."

"You're being crazy."

"I know. I said I've been thinking about it, not that I'm putting my house on the market tomorrow."

Lauren didn't want Hailey to move. Not only was it not a good plan to find her happily-ever-after, but Lauren needed her in her life. Whenever she started getting stuck in the rut of routine, Hailey would pull her out.

They argued about how wacky Hailey's plan was until they arrived at the salon and Lauren had to subject herself to the painful process of looking good for Paige's wedding. The haircuts and facials weren't bad, but they both whined their way through having their eyebrows done. And, when it came time for manicures and pedicures, Hailey went for hot-red nails. Lauren wasn't a bright kind of girl and she didn't have a dress yet, so she went with a French manicure look.

The next stop was the mall for a dress. Or rather, they would be looking for a dress after Hailey stocked up at Victoria's Secret. Lauren never went in the place. She couldn't afford to spend that kind of money on underwear nobody but her would see. She wasn't sure she'd spend that kind of money even if somebody *was* going to see it.

But while she waited for Hailey outside the dressing room, a bra caught her eye and she found herself touching the delicate ivory lace. It was gorgeous. It was also expensive. She needed snow tires. There were the constant deposits made into Nick's school lunch-money account because he ate like a horse. With winter coming, the heating bill would go up. With his hours cut because of the economy and two little kids, Dean was maxed out on the child support he could keep up with. She could come up with a million reasons why it was stupid to buy the bra-and-panty set.

She could try it on, though. It wouldn't hurt and maybe it would pinch or cut into her skin and she'd hate it.

A few minutes later, though, she was looking in the mirror and trying to find a dollar she could cut from the budget for every dollar the set cost. She could buy the store brand yogurt instead of the more expensive brand she liked. Same with the toilet paper. She'd do better at bringing lunch from home to cut down on running out of the office for something to eat.

She couldn't really make it add up in her head, but she wanted the lingerie. Maybe more than she'd wanted anything in a long time. It was soft and feminine and sexy and made her breasts look amazing.

"Oh, there you are," Hailey said when she emerged from the dressing room. "I thought you left—oh, those are so pretty! Tell me you're buying them."

"I'm buying them." It was stupid and maybe a little irresponsible, but she couldn't remember the last time she'd splurged for herself.

She was forced to try on an endless stream of dresses in an endless stream of stores before Hailey finally declared they'd found the right one.

Lauren looked at her reflection in the mirror. The dress had long sleeves and was shimmery and clingy, but with a loose drape to the neck and back. And it was a pale silvery-blue, while she'd been thinking of going with autumnal shades like a hunter-green or russet or navy. "Are you sure?"

"It's gorgeous and, when you're wearing the bra you just bought under it, it'll be killer. I swear. Every guy there will drop their jaw when you walk in the room."

That wasn't a big selling point for Lauren, who preferred *not* to be the center of that kind of attention, but she had to admit she wouldn't mind seeing Ryan's reaction to the dress.

And if she did dance with him, not that she planned

to, his hands would glide over the dress, and she wondered if she'd be able to feel the heat of his skin through the fabric. "I'll take it."

## CHAPTER NINE

RYAN WATCHED HIS sister retying Mitch's tie for what seemed like the hundredth time and, though he chuckled at the very unweddinglike word that crossed Liz's lips, he was having a hard time swallowing past the lump in his throat. His big brother was getting married today.

All five of them were in Mitch's room. Liz was fussing over Mitch while Ryan leaned against the door and watched. Josh was stretched out on the bed and Sean was sitting in the wingback chair in the corner.

Paige hadn't wanted anything too fancy, so they were all wearing simple button-up shirts with dress pants, while Mitch had on one of his business suits. His brother probably could have tied his own tie in about two seconds flat, but it seemed to mean something to Liz to do it for him, so they were all waiting for her to figure it out.

It took her another three tries before she patted the knot and took a step back. "There."

Even from his vantage point, Ryan could see it was a little loose and crooked, but Mitch kissed her cheek and left it alone. "Thanks, Liz."

"Getting cold feet yet?" Josh asked. "We can tell her you shimmied down the rain gutter and took off into the woods."

"We haven't changed the brackets on the gutters yet,"

Ryan pointed out. "If he tries to shimmy down that pipe, he'll spend his honeymoon in traction."

Sean laughed. "With all those pulleys to elevate body parts, maybe he can keep it up more than two minutes."

"I'm not shimmying anywhere," Mitch said. "I don't shimmy. And my feet aren't cold and I don't need pulleys to keep anything up, thank you very much. Stop deflecting your dysfunction onto other people."

"Hey, Emma doesn't complain."

Liz gave him a sweet smile. "Not to you, anyway."

They all laughed, except Sean, whose expression just made them laugh harder. "She's kidding! Jesus, Liz, tell them you're kidding."

They heard the sound of feet running down the hall and then a fist pounded on the door. Ryan stepped aside and pulled it open.

Bobby, Mike and Lisa's youngest son, had already messed up his hair, and his shirt was half-untucked. "Grammy said the bride—that's Paige—is ready so you all need to come down now."

"I'm glad you specified. I'd hate for Mitch to marry the wrong woman." The kid just blinked at Ryan. "Tell her we're on our way."

Bobby took off at a trot, which seemed to be the slowest speed setting he had, and Ryan closed the door again. "You ready?"

Mitch nodded, and Ryan couldn't see even a hint of doubt or hesitation on his brother's face. He was happier than he'd ever seen him before.

"Oh, for chrissake, Liz," he heard Josh mutter and he turned to see Liz struggling to open a travel pack of tissues she must have dug out of her purse.

Sean took it from her and a few seconds later handed

her an unfolded tissue. "If you're crying already, you'll be dehydrated before it's over."

"Did you see how much wine Fran ordered? *Nobody's* dehydrating today."

"You didn't cry at my wedding." Sean almost sounded insulted.

"How do you know? You never took your eyes off Emma. And I didn't think Mitch would ever get married."

Ryan suspected the tears had more to do with the end of her relationship leaving Liz emotionally raw, but he kept his mouth shut. With the lodge damn near overflowing with love and laughter, he could understand why she didn't tell anybody she'd left Darren yet.

"Jilly Crenshaw is taking pictures, right?" Josh asked.

Mitch nodded. "Yeah. She's always had a thing for photography, I guess. She's pretty good at it and, since her son really loves cooking for Paige at the diner, she offered to do it as our wedding present."

"Make sure she gets a picture of us, okay?" Josh said. "Just us."

"On the porch would be nice," Liz added quietly. "Like the picture Mom took."

Ryan knew even Josh, who was only five when their mom died, remembered that day. Their mother had dressed them all up and, even with the promise of going into town for ice cream and threats from Rosie, it had taken forever to get all of them smiling at the same time.

"I'll make sure it happens," Mitch said. "Let's go before we run out of tissues."

Ryan led the way to the great room, where they were having the ceremony before moving outside for the reception. And, because he was in front, when he caught sight of Lauren and stopped dead in his tracks, the groom plowed into his back.

She looked incredible. Her hair was soft and loose around her face, and she had on a dress that was a silvery pale blue and had a soft, draped look while still clinging to her curves. She looked damn good in her everyday clothes, but in that dress…holy shit.

"Why'd you stop?" Mitch asked. "You can't have cold feet. It's my wedding."

Ryan started walking again and all heads turned toward them. Including Lauren's. Through the corner of his eye, he saw her walk to her seat, with Hailey Genest beside her.

Then Mitch elbowed him and he had to pay attention. Once the groom was deposited in front of the fireplace, Ryan and Sean went back to the staircase for Aunt Mary and Rose, whom they escorted to the row of seats in the front. Once that was done, he took his own seat between Uncle Leo—who, being a smart man, had a whole package of tissues at the ready—and Sean.

Everybody hushed when Steph's iPod began playing the wedding march and Paige appeared.

Her dress was simple and elegant. It was white satin, with a square neckline and a slightly flared skirt that ended about mid-shin. Her hair was up and she was wearing his mother's pearl earrings. She looked beautiful.

Mitch and Paige had chosen not to have attendants and instead stood, just the two of them, in front of the notary who was officiating. Ryan could hardly hear their vows over the sniffling around him, but he could see the love and joy on their faces and he found himself hoping that someday a woman would look at him that way.

Cindy, his ex-wife, hadn't. At the time they'd both thought they felt the real thing, but it had only taken them a few years to amicably and mutually come to the realization it wasn't. Now though, looking at the real thing, he could see the difference.

They all erupted in cheers when Mitch kissed his bride, and they rose to their feet when the newlyweds walked back down the makeshift aisle and turned toward the kitchen. They were followed by the notary and by Rose and Aunt Mary, who'd be signing the paperwork as their two witnesses.

"Everybody head outside," his cousin Terry yelled over the noise.

Ryan was only too happy to oblige. It was a beautiful day and, though the guest list was small, it had gotten hot inside very quickly.

Most of the guests were ignoring the monster canopy they'd put up, choosing instead to enjoy the autumn sun. There was food under the tent, though. Tables and tables of food, thanks to the women of Whitford. They loved a potluck dinner and had been more than willing to save Mitch and Paige the cost of a caterer.

Fran and Katie were pouring champagne into the glasses lined up on the table, but Ryan made a beeline for the cooler tucked under the end and grabbed a beer. He was only having one, since he'd volunteered to drive anybody home later who'd had too much to drink. Whitford didn't have a taxi service, so that meant he'd probably also spend a good part of tomorrow reuniting those people with their vehicles.

But watching Mitch dance with his wife in the yard they'd played in as kids, and surrounded by pretty much everybody they cared about it, it was worth it. He'd worry about shuttling guests and cars later. For now, he had a wedding to enjoy.

LAUREN WAS HAVING the time of her life. Some of it was probably the seemingly bottomless glass of champagne in her hand, but mostly it was being free of responsibility, being surrounded by friends, and the fact that every time she looked at Ryan Kowalski, he was looking at her.

And, again thanks to the champagne, she was looking at him more than she usually did. She couldn't help herself. There were a lot of good-looking guys in the yard. God knew the Kowalski men had been blessed in that department. Drew Miller was no slouch, either, and there were some others who'd probably pass for hot with less competition. But it was Ryan her gaze kept landing on.

"Ask him to dance and be done with it."

Lauren elbowed Hailey, who almost dropped her bowl of pasta salad. "Shut up."

"So what if somebody hears me? Anybody who's looked at you more than three times has seen you watching him."

"I'm not asking him to dance. I don't dance."

"Liar. You've danced with almost every man here. Speaking of which, who knew Butch Benoit could dance like that?"

"His mother was a ballroom dance instructor."

"How do you know?"

Lauren shrugged. "No idea. Must have heard it somewhere. Did you try the ambrosia salad? It's amazing."

"Stop trying to distract me with food. You're not changing the subject."

"Fine. I'm pretty sure I heard Butch's mom was a dance teacher from—"

"You are going to dance with Ryan before this party ends. I don't care if I have to stand on a chair and announce to everybody that he has to dance with you."

"If you do that, I'll go to the library on Tuesday and check out every Nicholas Sparks book you have and not bring them back so you'll have to tell everybody you don't have any of his books. Forever."

"You wouldn't."

Lauren smiled over the rim of her champagne glass. "Oh, I would."

"Fine. But you'll be sorry you spent all that money if you don't at least dance with him."

"I bought the underwear and the dress for *me*, you know."

"Uh-huh."

"Enjoying the party?" Rose was standing right behind them and they both jumped.

Lauren hoped she wasn't blushing as hotly as it felt like she was. The woman was practically a mother to Ryan and if she'd overheard their conversation, Lauren would just melt into a puddle of humiliation on the grass.

"We're having a great time," Hailey said, which was good since Lauren's voice didn't seem to work at that moment.

"Good. They'll be cutting the cake soon." Rose smiled. "And then Paige will be tossing her bouquet. I hope one of you girls catches it."

Lauren thought it would be hard to catch the flowers with her hands clasped behind her back, but she didn't say so. She wanted no part of the bridal bouquet. And neither did Katie, who had come up behind her mother, judging by her expression.

After Rose reached between them to grab a few crackers and then wandered off, Lauren slapped Hailey in the arm. "Thanks a lot."

"She wasn't there long enough to hear anything good."

"Neither was I," Katie said, stepping closer. "What did I miss?"

"Lauren's being a chickenshit and won't ask Ryan to dance."

Katie looked her up and down, then shook her head. "Total waste of that dress if you don't."

Lauren returned the look. Katie looked nice, if unremarkable, in a skirt-and-jacket set that was a little too big. If Lauren had to guess, she'd say it was something pulled out of Rose's closet. "I haven't seen you dancing with Josh."

Katie scoffed, but the color in her cheeks gave her away. "Please. I can barely walk in these shoes, never mind dance."

"You're wearing flats," Hailey pointed out.

"And they're slippery in the grass. I tried to get to the French onion dip before little Brian could double-dip his carrot stick and almost ended up on my ass."

"You're both chickenshit," Hailey declared. "Now come on, I want a good view of the cake cutting."

Hailey pulled her forward and she shouldn't have been surprised when they ended up only a few feet from Ryan, who was talking to Sean and Kevin. She wasn't trying to eavesdrop, but she was so close that she really couldn't help it.

"I haven't seen Liz for a while," Sean was saying. "She's going to miss the cake."

"I haven't seen Drew, either." That was Ryan. "Joey and Danny were looking for him because they made a sign to cover the back window of Paige's car, but Lisa wants them to make sure Mitch won't get a ticket because it blocks the whole back window."

"Drew and Liz are both missing, huh?" Kevin asked, and the suggestion was obvious in his voice.

"Don't even think about it," Ryan said. "Drew's Mitch's best friend. He knows if he messed with his little sister, Mitch would break him in half. Drew might have gotten called away for an emergency or something."

Ryan turned around, probably to look for Liz, and Lauren froze when his gaze fell on her instead. She felt like an idiot, standing there staring at him with the glass of champagne halfway to her mouth, but the look in his eyes seemed to hold her and not let go.

The man was not impervious to the dress, that much was obvious. With the way he was looking at her, she was surprised the fabric didn't spontaneously combust, and she shivered all the way to the tips of her shoes.

He crossed the space between them in a couple of steps. "You look beautiful tonight. Are you having a good time?"

"Thank you. And I'm having a great time. Your family knows how to throw a party."

"I hear the champagne's really good." He nodded at the glass in her hand.

"It's not only really good, but there's a lot of it. And somebody keeps refilling my glass when I'm not looking."

His grin made all the nerve endings in her body sizzle. "Don't do anything you don't want showing up on Steph's Facebook account."

"I won't." She hoped.

"I should go find Liz. They want to cut the cake and she'll have a cow if she misses it."

She took a quick sip of liquid courage and, before he got too far away, called after him, "Save a dance for me."

He looked back over his shoulder and the grin had been replaced by a look she couldn't quite decipher. "I will."

"See?" Hailey said when he was out of earshot. "That wasn't so hard."

Lauren drained her glass and looked around for the glass-refilling fairy. One more glass wouldn't hurt.

HE WAS AN idiot. That was the only word for what he was and, the worst part of it was that he couldn't even blame alcohol. He was totally sober.

Ryan stormed into the lodge, cursing himself for a fool as he yelled his sister's name. He couldn't dance with Lauren. He should have told her he was too busy doing something wedding related or come up with some other lame excuse.

Just watching her in that dress all night had turned him into a walking erection. He'd spent more time hiding behind tables and chairs than anything else, and appearances were the least of his problems. He was afraid his balls were going to explode if he didn't get to escape soon. Holding her in his arms in front of his entire family was nothing but a recipe for disaster.

He was halfway up the staircase when Liz appeared at the top. She was a little flushed and he wondered if she'd had too much to drink.

"Everybody's looking for you," he said. "They're

going to cut the cake in a few minutes and you don't want to be missing from the pictures."

"I'm coming." She didn't stagger on the stairs, so he figured she must not be too drunk.

"You doing okay?" he asked when she'd reached him. He didn't imagine there was much worse after ending a long-term relationship than suffering through a joyful wedding.

"I'm fine."

"You tell Rosie yet?"

"No. I told you, I'm going to tell her right before I leave."

"Yeah, but she has a way of knowing when secrets are being kept, and that's a pretty big one."

She rolled her eyes and smoothed her hands over her dress. "I'll tell her soon. But for now, I'm going to go have cake and try not to catch the bride's bouquet."

He was turning to go back outside when he heard a thump from upstairs and frowned. Running through his immediate family members in his mind, he realized everybody who had a room upstairs was out in the yard. The extended family was staying in the guest rooms.

"Who's up there?"

"Probably one of the kids," Liz said, but the flush across her cheeks grew more pronounced.

Oh, crap, he thought. Drew freakin' Miller was upstairs. And the chief of police had put the color in his sister's cheeks, not the champagne.

He did *not* want any part of that. God only knew how Mitch would take it. Not that it was necessarily his business, but there was kind of an unspoken code. Drew was Mitch's best friend and Liz was his little sister. And Ryan was going to pretend he couldn't add two plus two.

"I hope if the kids are running around, they don't break anything," he said, and kept on walking.

Somehow he ended up on the opposite side of the cake table from Lauren, which put her squarely in his line of vision.

When she laughed at something Hailey said, her eyes sparkling with amusement, Ryan's breath caught in his throat. He wanted to be the one making her laugh. His body ached to be close to her, but at the same time he thought that might be a very bad idea.

He couldn't take much more torture and that's exactly what seeing Lauren and not touching her was. And he didn't think dancing with her would be nearly enough. In fact, he was pretty sure that would only make it worse. And he'd been doing a good job of hiding his feelings from his family, he thought, but if he led her out onto the makeshift dance floor, everything he felt would be on display. Not only to the family—and his brothers would be merciless—but to Lauren.

"Ten bucks says she shoves cake up his nose," he heard Kevin say, and he realized the cake had been cut.

"Done," Josh said. "She won't do it."

Mitch had a small slice between his fingers and Ryan watched as he held it to Paige's mouth so she could take a dainty bite off the end. The crowd groaned and the bride and groom both laughed. And, when Paige did the same for Mitch, he heard his cousin groan.

"Ten bucks," Josh said in a gloating tone as the crowd applauded the happy, frosting-free couple.

When Ryan caught Lauren watching him over the rim of her glass, he forced himself to give her a polite smile and turn away. Maybe he could help Fran serve the cake or something. Anything to keep himself distracted.

He'd told her he'd save her a dance, though. Because of that short-circuiting effect she had on his brain, he hadn't been able to think on his feet fast enough to come up with a good excuse not to.

Just thinking about holding her made his body ache, and he knew his only hope was that she was so tipsy she'd neither notice nor care if he didn't dance with her. Or, if he couldn't avoid it, at best he wouldn't make a fool of himself. But he was about out of self-control when it came to Lauren.

# CHAPTER TEN

THE CAKE HAD been cut and the bouquet had been tossed—which Liz caught, much to her apparent horror if the look on her face was any indication. She'd tried to sit it out, but Rosie had been quick to point out that she wasn't married and was therefore technically eligible to take part in the tradition.

Lauren was relieved she'd escaped the curse of the bouquet and now she was about to give up on dancing with Ryan and head home. She was starting to get the feeling he was avoiding her for some reason, and she could take a hint.

He should have just told her he was busy or tired or come up with some other excuse if he didn't want to dance with her. It would have been less awkward then dodging her, and she would already be on her way home.

She wasn't quite sure how she was going to get there, though. They'd come in Hailey's car, but Hailey had enjoyed the champagne almost as much as she had. Neither of them would be driving.

"They're getting ready to leave," Hailey said, dragging Lauren toward the front yard. It wasn't easy to keep up with her in the grass, wearing heels, but she managed not to fall down.

Mitch and Paige were on the front porch of the lodge, posing for a few last pictures, and Lauren had to stifle a laugh when she saw Paige's car. She'd never seen that many ribbons and cans tied to a vehicle before, and there was a huge sign in the back window that said Make Way for the Weddingmobile of Doom! Just married!

"How legal is that car right now?" she asked Drew, whom she'd ended up next to, and who looked more relaxed than he'd been since Mallory left him.

"Not very. The backseat being full of balloons is definitely a problem."

She got a little sniffly when Mitch hugged Rose and his aunt before leading his new bride through a veritable gauntlet of Kowalskis to the car. He honked the horn all the way down the driveway until they were out of sight. Then the guests all drifted around to the backyard again.

Lauren set her empty glass on the table and waved Fran off when she held up yet another bottle. "I've had enough."

When she saw Ryan walking toward her, her breath seemed to catch in her chest. Maybe she shouldn't dance with him. She didn't think she was drunk, but she definitely wasn't sober and the last thing she wanted to do was make a fool out of herself in front of these people.

"I'm told you rode over with Hailey," he said.

Was he going to offer to bring her home? Or maybe tell her she should stay at the lodge? With him? "Yeah."

"She won't be driving anywhere tonight, so I'll be driving you both home. Just let me know when you're ready to go."

"Oh." That was a bit of a letdown. "Okay."

"Wait," Hailey said, mysteriously appearing next to her. "You guys haven't danced yet."

She'd never wanted to stuff a sock in Hailey's mouth more than she did at that moment. "It doesn't matter."

"She's right. I said I'd save you a dance." He smiled and held out his hand, but Lauren noticed the smile didn't quite light up his eyes.

His fingers closed around hers, warm and strong, and he led her to where a few people were still dancing. The song was slow and romantic, and she sighed when he rested the hand not holding hers on her hip.

Then, they simply danced. There was no sliding of his hands across the fabric of her dress. No pulling her close. No resting her head against his chest to hear if his heart was beating as fast as hers.

Instead, he held himself so straight he was almost rigid, carefully leaving space between their bodies. His mouth was set in a straight line and he seemed content to blankly stare over the top of her head.

Okay, so she'd misread his earlier signals. Just one more thing to blame on the champagne. Rather than suffer in excruciating silence, she tried for polite small talk. "Where are Mitch and Paige going for their honeymoon?"

"They wouldn't tell us." His voice was as tense as his body.

"She wouldn't tell us, either." She paused, but he didn't say anything else. "Probably smart. Nobody likes pranks on their wedding night."

"Nope."

She gave up. The song seemed to go on forever, which would have been a good thing if Ryan wasn't holding her as if she was Typhoid Mary.

When it finally ended, he dropped his hands and took a step back. "Just let me know when you and Hailey are ready to go."

She was done. "Anytime you are."

"Let me round up a couple more people and then we'll go."

She nodded and walked back to Hailey, who was frowning, a little of the glow gone from the evening.

"That was painful to watch," Hailey said.

"We danced. That's what you wanted and now we're going home."

"Yeah, about that. Fran took my car key away like hours ago."

"Because Drew and Ryan are driving people home. And, lucky me, Ryan will be our chauffeur this evening."

"I'm going to flash the world climbing into that truck." Hailey looked down at her short red dress as though trying to figure out what to do about it.

It turned out she didn't need to worry about it because, obviously foreseeing that particular risk, Ryan was using Rose's car to play taxi service. Lauren scooted into the middle of the backseat and Hailey slid in beside her. Carl, who cooked for Paige at the diner, got in the front seat after helping his wife in on Lauren's other side.

During the drive to Carl's house, Lauren swore Ryan's eyes must have met hers in the rearview mirror a million times, and it was starting to piss her off. The guy couldn't *not* look at her, but when he had the opportunity to touch her, he turned into a walking, barely talking plank of wood.

She narrowed her eyes at his reflection and saw him lift an eyebrow at her. Then she folded her arms and stared at the back of Carl's head.

Once the cook and his wife were safely deposited at home, Lauren slid to the seat by the door, which made it easier to avoid looking in the mirror. She hoped she was next on his delivery schedule, but he turned toward Hailey's house and she sighed. Logically, she knew it made sense since Hailey's house was on the way to Lauren's, but didn't really want to be in the car alone with Ryan.

When he pulled up in front of Hailey's, he put the car in park and walked around to open her door.

"Call me tomorrow," she hissed before climbing out of the backseat.

No, thanks. She didn't particularly care to relive tonight. "'Night, Hailey."

Ryan leaned down to speak to her. "You want to move to the front seat?"

"I'm fine right here, thanks."

He closed the door and, after Hailey was safely inside her house, he got back in the car and put it in gear. For a minute he looked as if he was going to say something, but then he hit the gas and drove in silence.

NORMALLY WHEN HE drove a woman home, especially if she'd been drinking, he'd get out of his vehicle and walk her to the door, as he had with Hailey. But Ryan was afraid if he got that close to Lauren again tonight, he wouldn't be able to keep his hands off of her, so he kept them on the steering wheel while she got out of the backseat.

After she closed the door, she walked around the front of the car, which made the headlights spotlight how freaking amazing her body looked in that dress. When she walked to the passenger door, he rolled down the window and she leaned in. If he was a gentleman, he wouldn't look at the lace bra-edging the position gave him tantalizing glimpses of.

"Thank you for the ride. And for the dance."

He wasn't sure what to say to that. "I enjoyed it."

"Really?" She tilted her head, scowling. "You didn't seem very happy about it. Before the wedding, I kept thinking about what it would be like to dance with you, and it was a lot different in my imagination."

Don't ask, he told himself. She wasn't sober. What he should do was shrug, wait for her to go in the house and then drive away. "How did we dance in your imagination?"

"Really slow." Her voice was soft and a little husky. "And really close. Our bodies were touching and then you put your hand on my back and held me even tighter so my breasts were pressed against your chest."

Every rational and responsible thought in Ryan's head scrambled as her words formed an image in his mind. "And that's how you wanted me to dance with you?"

"Yes, but I guess *you* didn't want to dance with *me* like that."

He didn't even turn off the ignition or close the door behind him. Before his brain started firing on all cylinders, he walked around the back of the car. "I'm not very good with words, so I'll just show you how I wanted to dance with you."

She made a breathless sound that wasn't quite an *oh* when he pulled her into his arms. Holding her like that, with her body against his, was even better than he'd dreamed it could be.

"I didn't look happy, because it was killing me to have my hands on you and not be able to touch you the way I wanted to because my whole freaking family was watching. And not only would my aunt and Rose be scandalized, but if you shot me down, I'd never hear the end of it."

She hadn't thought about it like that. "How did you want to touch me?"

"Like this." He cupped her ass with one hand, pulling her against him, while sliding his other hand up her rib cage. "And I didn't hold you close because my dick was so hard it ached and I didn't want you to feel it."

"I can feel it now." He held his breath as her mouth moved toward his, almost close enough to kiss. "But you know what I *really* want to feel?"

She was going to feel his balls explode if she didn't stop grinding her hips against his. "What do you want to feel?"

"I want to feel like you think I'm the sexiest woman in the world.

"Honey, I do think that."

"Show me."

Ryan dug deep and came up with a tattered shred of self-control. "You've been drinking and there's a good chance you'll hate me in the morning."

"I'm not sober, but I'm not drunk, either." He must have looked unconvinced, because she laughed. "Want me to do a sobriety test? Bend over and touch my toes?"

"Honey, you bending over in that dress is the last thing I need. Say the alphabet backward or something."

"Z. *X?* Can even sober people do that?"

"I don't care." He gave in to the temptation and cupped her breast, feeling her nipple harden under his thumb as he stroked it through the silky dress. "All I care about is you not regretting this in the morning."

She kissed him, standing up on her tiptoes and wrapping her arms around his neck. Their breath mingled as she teased him, flicking her tongue over his bottom lip and chuckling when his entire body shuddered.

With a growl, he plunged a hand into her hair and held her head as he took control of the kiss. Her mouth was hot and sweet and he took his time tasting her. He could feel the urgent hunger in her body and the bite of her fingernails in his scalp, but he didn't care. He'd waited a long damn time to kiss this woman and he kept on kissing her until she moaned against his mouth in surrender.

"I want you," he whispered.

"Then turn off the car and come inside."

He wasn't sure he could walk that far. Not that it mattered. He'd crawl on his hands and knees to get to her if he had to.

She walked toward the house, being a smart-ass with her arms held out straight and placing each foot directly in front of the other. When she got to the steps, she turned and laughed.

With her eyes sparkling and her skin flushed from his kiss, she was the most beautiful woman he'd ever seen.

Then she stopped laughing, her gaze locked with his. "The way you're looking at me right now makes me feel sexy. But if you're going to stand there all night, I'm going to start without you."

That got him moving. He shut off the car and used the walk between it and the front door to move a condom from his wallet to his front pocket. He only had one, so he had to make it count.

When he walked through her door, he found her in the living room. She'd slipped off the dress and stood there in nothing but two scraps of ivory lace.

She was, no question, the sexiest woman in the whole

world and, by the time he was done with her, she was going to know without a doubt that he thought so.

THE INSECURITIES THAT had started creeping in as she stripped off the dress—she'd gained a little weight and there were a few stretch marks and, ohmigod, she wasn't twenty anymore—evaporated the second Ryan stepped into the room and stopped moving.

The overpriced bra-and-panty set were worth every single penny as his gaze swept over her almost naked body. She knew every flaw was on display, but there was no cooling off in his look when he turned those sizzling blue eyes back to her face.

His naughty grin twisted her up inside. "I'd hate to disappoint you, like I did with the dancing, so maybe you should tell me if you've been thinking about this, too."

"I've thought about this a lot."

He started slowly toward her, unbuttoning his shirt as he walked. "When did you start thinking about it?"

"A long time ago. Years," she confessed, feeling the heat of the blush across her exposed chest. "If I was stressed or wired or, for whatever reason, just couldn't get my mind to shut off so I could go to sleep, I'd…you know…fantasize. About you. Us."

"Thinking about having sex with me puts you to sleep?"

She would have laughed if he hadn't looked honestly perplexed, and maybe a little wounded. "No, thinking about having sex with you distracted me from all the crap in my life, because it was intense and amazing and so perfect I could fall asleep to very, *very* happy thoughts."

"So what you're saying is you've built us up for so

long in your head, I can't possibly live up to your expectations."

This time she did laugh. "You'll just have to try a little harder."

He yanked the shirt out of his waistband to undo the last couple of buttons, and she itched to slide her hands across the expanse of his chest.

Instead, he gently nudged her backward across the room until her back was against the wall, and she sucked in a sharp breath when he raised her arms above her head and pinned her wrists there with one hand.

"You are so...freaking...beautiful," he said, punctuating his words with playful nips at her neck.

Then he hooked the index finger of his free hand in one lacy cup of her bra and yanked it down, exposing her nipple. She moaned when his mouth closed over it, the gentle sucking seeming to pull at her very core, and she arched her back. He used his teeth to pull back the lace and expose her other breast, and then grazed them over the sensitive flesh.

"I was like a walking erection at that wedding. Every time I'd start to cool off, I'd see you again in that dress and get hard all over again."

He licked and sucked, all the while holding her hands over her head so she couldn't touch him.

"If I'd known you were wearing this underneath," he said, his breath warming the nipple moistened by his mouth, "I would have had to sneak up to my room and jerk off so I wouldn't explode."

She pulled against the hand holding her wrists, wanting to touch him, but he held her tighter and increased the pressure on her nipple until she whimpered. "I want to touch you."

"I'm not done touching you yet." He slid his hand

thumb until she was panting. "Come for me
d then you can touch me as much as you want
n inside of you."

want to—" He was bossy and again she wanted
but he nudged her legs further open and, be-
ould get any more words out, his tongue took
is thumb and the words choked off.

gers curled in the sheets. She tried to say his
t it came out a whimper as he twisted his fin-
ching her with his knuckles. All the while he
d sucked at the sensitive flesh until her hands
nto fists and all she could do was ride it out.
he went limp, breathless once again, he knelt
er legs, a smug grin on his face. "Told you I'd
come again."

off." She grabbed the condom wrapper off
and and threw it at him.

u I was better at showing," he said, catching
bounced off his chest and tearing it open to
dom on. "Of course, if you'd rather stop and
ke or something…"

ked her ankle behind his ass and pulled so he
onto his hands. With them braced on either
head, he kissed her long and hard.

ake," he asked when he came up for air,
o an elbow so he could run his other hand

e to choose between you and cake, I'll

her again and she sighed against his mouth
d between their bodies and guided him-
As his tongue teased hers, he moved his
each slow, steady stroke, he pushed fur-

down her stomach, his fingertips sliding under the lace
edging of her panties.

She wanted to argue with him, but his mouth covered hers, stealing her breath along with the words.
Pinned between the length of his body and the wall,
all she could do was surrender to feeling. Feeling his
hot breath on her mouth. Feeling the brush of his chest
across her nipples. Feeling his fingers—so strong and
work-hardened and different from her own touch—sliding under lace.

Her hips bucked against his hand when he hit the
sweet spot and she whimpered, but he held her fast.

"If I'd known you were this hot from thinking about
me fucking you," he said in a low, hoarse voice that was
barely more than a whisper, "I'd have skipped the damn
cake cutting and taken you in the barn."

"A woman should never have to choose between sex
and cake."

He drew back his head so he could see her eyes as
he slipped one finger inside her. "Which would you
choose?"

She hesitated, savoring the friction while he waited
for her answer. "It was pretty good cake."

"Really?" The hand holding her wrists tightened and
he worked another finger inside her. She sucked in a
breath, grinding against his hand. "Did it make you
this wet? Did that cake taste so good it made you come,
Lauren, because I'm going to."

And he did, stroking her and kissing her until her
hips bucked against his hand and she strained against
his hold. He held her, relentless in his touch, until she
sagged—flushed and breathless—against the wall.

"So fucking pretty." He nipped at her jaw, then released her wrists.

She couldn't touch him enough. His shirt was already unbuttoned and she shoved it down off his shoulders so she could run her hands over his chest and his arms while he slipped his hands out and tossed it away. His back muscles rippled under her fingertips and she smiled as she licked his throat, making him growl.

Lauren wanted more. She wanted Ryan naked and in her bed. Stepping out from between him and the wall, she unclasped her bra and let it fall to the floor. His gaze was hot and hungry as he kicked off his shoes and reached down to pull off his socks, and she started down the hall as she pulled down the waist of her panties. Halfway to her door, she paused and kicked them off.

Looking over her shoulder, she saw Ryan was right behind her, and he stopped to lose the pants and boxer briefs at the same time. The man put her imagination to shame, and it was a good thing her bed was only a few more feet away or she might have taken him down right there in the hallway.

She hadn't made her bed that morning, but he didn't seem to care. After tossing a condom packet onto her nightstand, he shoved the lump of covers back and lowered her onto the mattress.

Lauren relished the weight of his body as he settled on top of her and a little off to the side, so his knee rested between her thighs. He smiled, seemingly content to stare down at her face for a minute.

She smiled back. "Has anybody ever told you that you have the most beautiful eyes?"

Then she felt stupid because women probably told him that all the time, and that wasn't something she wanted to think about at the moment.

"If they're beautiful, it's only because you're seeing yourself reflected in them."

There were a few seconds laughed. It was so corny, she

He scowled. "You're not th my eyes, but I'm pretty damn who's ever laughed at me in

"Oh, come on. That was She tried to take her amusem "You don't have to try so ha naked."

"I noticed. I like that ab thumb over her nipple wh pressed between her legs. telling you I'm better at sh

When he lowered his he nipple he'd been gently ru body arched, increasing th and she clutched his shoul with his foot, parting her l her body and his knee. It to pull her thighs together

"I'm not finished touch

This time he wasn't ho touched him back. She tr back, then felt his abs ti under the arm pinning h fingers around the hard

He sucked in a brea curses she took as a co inside her, she stroked low growl from his thr

"You should stop d

She threw his own ished touching you yet

He plunged his fing

with hi
again ar
while I'
"No,
to argue
fore she
over for
Her fi
name, bu
gers, stre
licked an
clenched
When
between
make you
"Show
the nights
"Told y
it before i
roll the co
go have ca
She hoo
fell forwar
side of her
"So no
leaning on
up her thig
"If I ha
choose you
He kisse
as he reach
self into he
hips so wit

ther into her. Digging her fingernails into his back, she urged him deeper.

"You feel so good," he said against her ear. "I don't know if I'm going to last long enough to live up to those expectations."

She smiled and turned her face to nip his earlobe. "You're way better than the imaginary you was."

He reached down and tucked his hand behind her knee, pulling her leg up. The change in angle allowed him to thrust deeper and she moaned when he filled her completely. "Now, when you close your eyes at night, you can think of the real me."

His pace quickened and she rocked her hips, meeting him stroke for stroke. He let go of her knee and took her hand. He pressed it flat, palm to palm, on the bed beside her head and then curled his fingers around hers, interlocking their hands. Harder and deeper he took her until her entire world became the exquisite sensation of Ryan inside her.

The orgasm rocked her and she squeezed his hand, aware of his breath coming in ragged, hot bursts against her skin and the uneven thrusts as he found his own release. He collapsed on top of her and she wrapped her arms and legs around him to hold him close as the aftershocks rippled through his body.

After several minutes, he shifted and she sighed as he pulled out and away from her. When he didn't stumble or swear getting to the bathroom and back, she realized half the lights in the house were still on. And she didn't care.

He climbed back into bed and stretched out beside her with a groan. "That was way better than cake."

"That was even better than a triple-layer fudge cake." She pulled the covers up, trying to straighten them.

He hauled her against his chest and flicked the blankets over them both with a snap. "Honey, that was better than nachos and a beer at the ballpark watching the Sox spanking the Yankees in the ninth."

His arms tightened around her and she melted against his chest, closing her eyes. And, as she drifted off to sleep, she was certain of one thing. Her fantasies would never be the same again.

# *CHAPTER ELEVEN*

"Ma!"

Lauren groaned, keeping her eyes squeezed shut against the light. She wanted to yell at him again to stop bellowing, but her head hurt too much to yell. Instead she nestled further under her covers. As she nestled, an arm curled around her, hauling her back against a warm, hard and very naked body.

Ryan Kowalski was in her bed. And Nick was home a day early. "Oh crap. Oh crap, oh crap, oh crap."

"Ma?"

And her bedroom door was open. Oh, and there were clothes strewn down the hallway. "Oh crap."

"I'm not hiding in the closet," the warm lump next to her mumbled.

"I'm coming," she yelled, hoping to halt his search for her, but it was too late.

Her son saw her, clutching the covers to her chin, saw Ryan and then turned and walked back toward the living room. She started to call after him, but what was she going to do? Have a conversation with him while she hid behind the blanket?

She managed to snag her bathrobe off the foot post and pull it on so she could at least close the door. Then, rather than face her son and possibly her ex-husband that way, she pulled on a pair of underwear and her jeans under the robe and then, keeping her back to the bed, pulled on a bra and a sweatshirt.

"I thought he wasn't coming home until tomorrow."

She turned to find Ryan sitting up, looking utterly delicious with his hair tousled and the blankets around his waist. "He wasn't supposed to. Something must be wrong."

After taking a few awkward seconds to gather their clothes from the hallway, which she tossed into the bedroom before closing the door, Lauren went out into the living room to find Dean and Nick sitting stone-faced, one on each end of the couch.

"Nick didn't feel good, so I brought him home," Dean said in a grim voice. "Surprise."

Her embarrassment at being caught in bed with a man was instantly squashed by concern. "What's the matter? Is it your stomach? Headache? Fever?"

He lifted one shoulder in a half-ass shrug. "Just don't feel good."

She reached out to feel his forehead, but he flinched away from her. Great. They'd already had to have the *sometimes even single mothers get to have a life now and then* talk once. Looked like they were going to have it again.

Her bedroom door opening and then the bathroom door closing sounded unnaturally loud. She'd been hoping maybe Ryan would go back to sleep, or at least stay in bed until Dean was gone.

And, speaking of her ex-husband, she didn't miss the look he gave her, though she refrained from either returning the look or flipping him the bird, since their son was in the room. But he'd been married to Jody for almost six years, had two kids with her and was disgustingly happy. What was it to him if his ex-wife had a man in her bed?

It was something to him, judging by the waves of attitude rolling off him. Maybe it wasn't just the man that was the problem. Maybe it was the fact it was Ryan. But, again, not his business. Dean needed to go home to his wife and other kids.

"Thanks for bringing him home," she said, trying to make it an obvious dismissal. "I'll let you know if it turns into anything serious."

He either didn't take the hint or chose to ignore it.

"I'm going to my room." Without looking at either of them, Nick went to his room and slammed his door. Not a good sign, since that was one rule he almost never broke.

"You think this sets a good example for our son?" Dean asked.

She couldn't believe he'd said it. The anger was instant, burning the back of her throat like acid indigestion. And there was no way she was going to stand there and take it.

"Since the first time I met Jody, she was coming down that very same hallway, pulling her clothes on while you tried to tell me it wasn't what I thought, while our son stood there and watched—you can kiss my ass." She pointed to the door. "You can also get the hell out of my house."

He was instantly contrite, as was his way. "Lauren, look—"

"Get out of my house. Now."

"I'll call you when you've calmed down and we can talk about this," he said on his way to the door.

"You and I are not talking about this. Ever. It's none of your business."

He paused for a second at the threshold and gave her a wry smile. "I guess he got what he wanted. Kowalskis always do."

He was gone before she could come up with a response, not that one was really necessary. But she was still standing there, staring at the closed door, when Ryan walked up beside her.

"I should probably go."

She nodded. "Sorry about this. I guess this is a little messier than you're used to."

He cupped the back of her neck in his hand and she closed her eyes. "Are you going to be okay?"

"Yeah. Nick will calm down and I don't really give a damn what Dean has to say."

"I hate leaving while you're upset. Especially since it's my fault."

She tilted her head to look up into his face. "It's not your fault. It's just…my life."

He kissed her, still cradling her neck. "Call me when things calm down, okay?"

"I'll try." The look on her son's face flashed across her mind. "I have to make sure Nick's okay, you know?"

"I'll wait." He kissed her again, then he left and it was time to deal with her son.

Nick was lying on his bed, staring up at the ceiling when she knocked and walked in. He looked a lot more angry than sick, and she braced herself before sitting on the edge of the bed. No doubt this was going to be awkward and painful for both of them.

"How are you feeling?" When he didn't respond right away, she forced herself to be patient. "Your dad said you were sick."

"Yeah, sick of being there."

Lauren sighed. "So you ruined your dad's vacation

and cut it half a day short because you were bored? He said you were all having a great time."

"No, he and Jody were having a great time. I only got to go riding one time and we had the kids so it was all like ten miles an hour. Dad said he'd take me out again, but he didn't. They just left me with the kids so they could go riding alone. Last night they were so late I was worried about them and I had to feed the kids and put them to bed and Adrienne wouldn't stop crying. Then, this morning, after she made breakfast, he said they were going for a ride again, and I said I felt sick. It just sorta popped out of my mouth."

"Do they ask you to watch Alex and Adrienne a lot?

"Just like all the time. And they don't really ask. They just tell me they're going out and leave."

"I can talk to your dad about it, if you want." As soon as she could talk to her ex without destroying the years of goodwill she'd established for Nick's sake, despite having every reason to hate his stepmother. "But I think you should be the one to do it."

"Whatever."

"You're sixteen. You should be able to have a discussion with your dad without me being in between."

"Maybe." He shrugged. "I'll try."

"So you're not really sick, so on to the next thing." She picked at the hem of her sweatshirt, wishing she knew what to say.

"We've had this talk before, Mom. You're an adult, he's an adult, blah blah blah. Whatever."

"Someday—"

"Yeah, someday I'll understand. I remember that part of the speech."

"Watch your tone," she snapped.

"Sorry," he mumbled. "So, is this what you do on the weekends?"

His tone was okay, but she didn't care for the question. "That's none of your business. But, no, I very rarely…have a man over."

Nick kept staring at the ceiling, but he was bobbing his foot, tapping his toes against the air. "So he's, like, special, then?

That was a loaded question if she'd ever heard one, and she had no idea how to answer it. She didn't want her son thinking she was having indiscriminate, champagne-fueled sex, but she also didn't want him thinking there was something special between her and Ryan. *She* didn't even know what was between her and Ryan and she'd lost the opportunity to get a feel for it this morning when their time together came to such an abrupt end.

"We're not running off to Vegas, if that's what you mean," she said, trying for lighthearted. He didn't look amused. "Honestly, I don't know if he's special yet."

"Let me know when you figure it out," he said, and then he rolled onto his stomach and turned his face away from her.

She took that as her cue he'd had all the talk about mom's sex life he could stand, and she left him to brood in peace. If she'd known spending a night with Ryan would lead to so much drama, she might have passed.

Then she stretched, feeling that delicious soreness in neglected muscles, and smiled. Spending the night with Ryan had been worth the drama and she'd do it again. But after being rudely awakened by her son and ex-husband, she wasn't sure Ryan felt the same.

Eventually she'd work up the courage to call him and find out.

Ryan sat in Rose's car at the end of what looked like a veritable parking lot. Even subtracting the cars and trucks that belonged to family staying at the lodge, he'd be lucky if he got everybody's vehicles back to their rightful owners before the game started.

Assuming he ever got out of the car.

There was no way in hell he could get through that house without being seen. There would be Kowalskis in the front room and Kowalskis in the hallway and Kowalskis in the dining room. And Rosie and Aunt Mary would be in the kitchen, so sneaking in the back door was out.

The knock on his window made him jump and Josh grinned as Ryan hit the button to lower it. "Your absence has already been noted."

"I'll tell them I got up early and went out for...something."

"In the same clothes you wore last night?"

Good point. He looked at the flannel shirt his brother was wearing over a T-shirt. Flannel wasn't usually his style, but he was desperate. "Give me your shirt."

"Hell no."

"I'll give you fifty bucks for it."

"Give me your truck."

"Kiss my ass."

Josh shrugged. "Then put on your dancing shoes because you're about to face the music."

"Some brother you are."

"Because you *are* my brother, I'll give you the heads-up on the betting pool."

Ryan drummed his fingers on the steering wheel. "What betting pool?"

"Whether you went home with Hailey or Lauren."

"Hailey? They think I spent the night with Hailey Genest?"

"You have to admit, she's smokin' hot and she doesn't have a kid."

"She's got nothing on Lauren."

"That's money in my pocket. I knew it was Lauren. So did Liz and Rosie."

"Rosie bet on who I spent the night with?"

"Hell, Rosie and Aunt Mary have a side bet going." Josh slapped the side of the car. "We won't be having Aunt Mary's lasagna for supper now, by the way. It'll be Rosie's shepherd's pie."

"I'm not going in there."

"Chickenshit."

Worst morning-after ever. Ryan dropped his forehead onto the steering wheel, resisting the urge to do it again and again. All he'd wanted to do was wake up with Lauren in his arms. Maybe take a long, lazy shower together. Have some breakfast. Instead, he got a moody teenager, a pissed ex-husband, a baby brother who thought he was funny and his entire family waiting to watch his walk of shame. Plus, Aunt Mary made a killer lasagna and they wouldn't be getting any.

Screw it. He couldn't sit in the car all day. With Josh laughing at him, he walked in through the front door and looked around. Most of the family looked back and it was only a minute before Rose and Aunt Mary popped in from the kitchen.

"I hear we're having shepherd's pie for dinner," he said, and then he walked up the stairs to take a shower, ignoring the outburst of whispers below. At least he knew that while his family would give him crap about this at every possible opportunity, it wouldn't go any further than that. What happened in the family, stayed in the family. Usually.

Once he was safely behind the locked bathroom door, he turned the shower on as hot as he could stand it and prayed the rest of the family had left enough in the ancient tank to rinse off the soap lather.

Letting the hot water pound his muscles, Ryan leaned his head against the shower wall and closed his eyes. Despite the decidedly shitty morning-after, he wouldn't change anything about his night with Lauren. It had blown every fantasy he'd ever had right out of the water.

Well, he'd change their first dance because it bugged him he'd let her think he didn't want her. If he could, he'd go back and dance with her the way he'd wanted to, and screw what anybody else thought.

All he could do now was hope she called him. Not that he wouldn't reach out if too much time went by, but he really wanted her to call him, because her morning-after had been messier than his and he needed to give her time to straighten it out.

By the time he went back downstairs, the family had gotten over their fascination with his sex life. Either that, or the presence of the kids kept them from butting into his business some more. Whichever it was, at least they were done talking about it for the moment.

"Who's going to help me get those cars back to where they belong before the game starts?" he asked after he'd downed a couple cups of coffee.

"Everybody seemed to show up while you were in the shower," Rose told him. "Most folks have two vehicles, so they drove over and picked them up. A few called and they're going to come by later. I think the only person who doesn't have a ride over is Hailey Genest, so I told her you'd drop it off in a little bit."

"I'll follow you over," Josh said.

He was still annoyed with his youngest brother, but it made sense. If they got separated, his cousins didn't know the way to Hailey's house. Sean *might* remember, but he was keeping the kids occupied with a thumb-wrestling tournament, so Terry and Lisa wouldn't thank Ryan for breaking that up.

Rose must have called Hailey when they left, because she was sitting on her porch when he drove into her driveway. She met him halfway while Josh let Ryan's truck idle at the curb, and he dropped her key into her hand.

"Thanks," she said. "A little embarrassing to need a ride home."

"Better than Drew getting called out because you wrapped yourself—and Lauren—around a tree."

"She got home okay, too?"

"No, I dumped her out on the curb a few miles up the road."

She laughed. "Dumb question. What I was really asking was what happened after you dropped me off."

"I brought her home."

"And then…you went home?"

"Yeah." Eventually. In the morning.

Hailey looked disappointed, but he wasn't going to kiss and tell. He wouldn't have been surprised if Lauren had already called her friend and filled her in, but since she hadn't, Ryan kept his mouth shut.

She narrowed her eyes. "Are you lying to me?"

"Absolutely not." Technically he wasn't.

Sighing, Hailey shook her head. "Your loss. She looked hot as hell in that dress."

She looked even hotter in the Victoria's Secret number *under* the dress, but he wasn't telling that, either.

"You have a good day, Hailey."

"Thanks for bringing my car home."

When Ryan reached his truck, Josh refused to get out of the driver's seat and instead cracked the window enough so he could talk, but not enough so Ryan could reach in and choke him.

"You've gotten soft if you need heated leather seats, dude."

"Get out of my seat."

"Or what? You gonna drag me out? You can try, but I'm younger and I wasn't up all night trying to keep a lady happy."

"I'm sorry you have to work so hard at it. I, on the other hand, can keep my lady happy and still kick your ass up and down this street."

He shrugged. "The fact remains, your truck is locked, your keys are in the ignition, I'm in the driver's seat and you're on the sidewalk."

Muttering every curse he could think of, and combining them into interesting new combinations, Ryan walked around to the passenger side and, when he heard the lock release, climbed in.

"I'd reach over and punch you in the face, but I don't feel like taking shit from Rosie for bruising her precious baby boy."

Josh grinned, cranked the radio and left half the tires on the asphalt as he took off. Rather than encourage him, Ryan gritted his teeth and rode home in silence as his brother tried what seemed like every satellite radio channel. Twice.

ROSE TRIED TO keep a stiff upper lip, but she only got halfway through hugging the kids before she was leaking tears. They were a rowdy bunch, this family that had made her one of their own, but she couldn't have loved them more. The big lodge was going to feel too quiet for a while.

She almost came undone when it came time to hug Sean. He'd been gone so long during his time in the army, she'd hardly gotten to see him more than she saw Liz, and then he'd gone and fallen in love with a woman already settled in New Hampshire. He was happy, though, and that was all that mattered.

After looking around for a second, he pulled Emma close and put an arm around each of them. "We're not telling anybody else yet—okay, I told Ryan because he kind of guessed—but I have to tell you because you're… our Rosie. Emma's pregnant."

She almost came undone, weeping all over the poor girl and then Sean. But she tried to do it discreetly because she didn't want them to have to explain to Mary why saying goodbye was especially hard this time around.

"I've been waiting to knit a blanket for a grandbaby for years," she said once she'd composed herself. Then she realized what she said and hoped Emma didn't mind the housekeeper claiming her baby as family.

But Sean's wife smiled and squeezed her hand. "We have plenty of room for Nana Rose to come stay for a while when he or she is born."

Nana Rose. She liked that a lot. So much, in fact, it was a few seconds before she could find her voice. "I'll be there."

She forced herself to let Sean and Emma go, then moved on down the line. When she came to Mary, she squeezed extra hard. A long time ago, the woman had been nobody to Rose but her employer's sister-in-law. Then Sarah Kowalski had died and they'd bonded while helping Frank raise his children, Rose day to day and Mary the best she could from a state away and while raising four kids of her own.

"It was a beautiful wedding," Mary said. "And thank you for making us feel so at home. I know we can be a little overwhelming."

"I loved having you. Honest."

They left the way they'd come, all in a line. With the windows down, there were hands sticking out waving from all the vehicles, and Rose laughed as they pulled out of sight.

"I need a beer," Josh said.

"I'll join you," Ryan added. "Love 'em, but I'm going to sit on the porch and listen to the damn crickets for a while."

"I don't hear any crickets."

"Even better."

Rose shook her head at the guys and followed Liz and Katie into the house. She only had a short time left before Ryan took Liz back to Portland to catch her plane, and it might not be long enough to ferret out what was wrong with the girl.

They went into the kitchen because that's where the leftover chocolate cake and coffee were and took supersize helpings of both to the table. The girls talked about the wedding, but Rose had a hard time focusing on the chatter.

Liz had been drinking and disappeared from the reception for a short time. Drew Miller hadn't been drinking, but he'd also disappeared for the same amount of time at about the same time. And, as far as Rose could tell—and she'd been paying attention—the two of them hadn't circled within twenty feet of each other or made eye contact for the remainder of the night. She didn't like where her thoughts had gone during the reception, but she was starting to suspect she wasn't wrong.

Liz got halfway through her cake before she set her fork down. "Stop staring at me like I've done something wrong and you're trying to will me to confess."

"Ouch," Katie said. "Hate that look. Always works."

"I'm not staring at you."

"Yes, you are. And I left Darren last weekend. I moved out."

The relief practically knocked Rose out of her chair. Not only the relief that Liz had finally cut loose a man who was no good for her, but that if something happened between Liz and the police chief, she hadn't cheated. Rose could forgive a lot of flaws in a person, but having been on the short end of that rope, she had no tolerance for cheating. And, no, Drew technically wasn't divorced yet, but his marriage was definitely over.

Another consideration was the fact Drew Miller was Mitch's best friend and that relationship *wasn't* broken. It was best for everybody if Liz and Drew's whereabouts during the reception went undiscovered.

"Are you coming home?" she asked, because that was the first question that popped into her head.

"No. And you're not going to change my mind. I like New Mexico and I have plans there."

Rose sighed, but it was a start. "Are you okay?"

"Yeah. It was a long time coming, I guess."

"Oh, damn, I have to run." Katie got up from her seat and dumped her dirty dishes in the sink. "Mr. Wilcox likes his hair cut at noon on Mondays and he doesn't recognize Columbus Day as a real holiday. He's ninety-two now and it's a lot easier to go in and cut his hair than try to convince him I should get the day off with everybody else."

After kissing her mother's cheek, she rushed out, leaving Liz and Rose alone with the rest of the cake. After a moment's consideration, she cut them each another slice. Sometimes a woman couldn't have too much cake.

"I wasn't going to tell you until I was going out the door," Liz said. "I didn't want you to make a fuss and harass me about coming back to Whitford."

"I don't harass you kids. I persistently guide you in the right direction."

"You thought I cheated on Darren," she said, her voice heavy with accusation.

Rose reached across the table and laid her hand on Liz's, looking her in the eye. "I was trying my best not to believe it because it wouldn't be like you."

"It was stupid, but it wasn't cheating. I just wanted you to know that." She pushed the cake around on her plate. "Just a stupid rebound thing for me and a stupid rebound thing for him, and that's the end of it. I made him promise not to tell Mitch."

"That's probably for the best, but it might eat at him, you know. Even without telling him, it might hurt their friendship."

"So he'll tell him. Not only am I an adult, but I'm an adult who lives all the way across the country. They can do whatever they want."

She could say the words, and maybe even believe them, but Rose could see the unhappiness in her eyes. And in the way she went back to inhaling the chocolate cake. Liz cared a lot about what Mitch thought, and she also wouldn't want to be responsible for breaking up his friendship with Drew.

"Hopefully it didn't mean any more to him than it did to me," Liz said in a quiet voice. "Then he won't care enough to have guilt and nothing ever needs to be said again."

Rose could only hope. Lord knew, with the kids finally starting to find happiness and love, that wasn't the kind of family drama she wanted popping up. "Ryan's going to come looking for you soon. Are you all packed?"

Liz laughed. "I haven't started yet."

"Maybe that's a sign you don't really want to go back to New Mexico."

"Or it's a sign I've been sitting in the kitchen eating cake with you instead of packing."

Rose laughed and pointed toward the stairs. "Let's go. I'll help you because if you miss your flight, you're calling Mitch to tell him you need a new ticket and interrupting his honeymoon, not me."

## CHAPTER TWELVE

DILL AND MATT showed up about midmorning on Tuesday, slightly sluggish after the long weekend and complaining about traffic. And Ryan greeted them with happy news.

"While the family was all together, we looked over the house and we looked over some numbers and we decided to go ahead and put a new roof on. The house *and* the barn *and* the shed." They groaned in unison. "If you guys don't want to do it, that's fine. I pay my roofers a little more than my rookie carpenters, so I won't have any trouble finding other volunteers."

"Roofing in October, boss?" Dill didn't look convinced.

"Originally, we thought the roof would be okay, but it's got some punky spots and if we get a heavy snow load and it collapses, we're screwed." Since he was there and able to do it, they'd voted to go ahead and get it over with. "We'll start with the house and move fast. Stripping it totally, right down to new sheathing, but Josh and I will be up there, too, so hopefully with four of us it won't be bad."

Matt looked past him at the lodge. "Man, that's a lot of roof."

Dill slapped him on the shoulder. "And that equals a lot of money."

"Good point."

Ryan knew they'd both stick it out. "Start taking measurements then. I want to be damn sure we have everything on hand before we strip a single shingle. Long-range forecast looks decent, but I don't want to be wasting time making supply runs while the roof's open."

While the guys got busy on that, Ryan grabbed his clipboard and went through the smaller things left to be done. A lot of it could be done during downtime or when it rained. There were a few inside things he wanted to address, like the basement stairs. They were old and narrow. It wouldn't take long to replace them, and new ones would not only be safer, but would be more attractive to a potential buyer if they put it on the market.

He looked at his phone's clock for the umpteenth time, but the day was refusing to do anything but crawl by. He'd given Lauren some space over the weekend to deal with her son and Dean, but he was anxious to talk to her. Not so anxious he'd be obnoxious and call her at work, though.

He threw himself into work to take his mind off her, hoping the hours would fly by. He made a few phone calls, looking for the best deal on a construction Dumpster. The guys had been making dump runs with the pickup as needed, but there was no way that would work for stripping the roofs.

Once the guys started seriously taking measurements, he joined them on the roof. At this time of year, he didn't want to chance any screwups, so they checked and rechecked every measurement. Once they'd sketched out the house, they moved to the barn.

He must have lost track of the time after all, because Rosie appeared at the base of the ladder and hollered to him. "I heard the bus go by and it didn't stop. Did you know Nick wasn't coming today?"

His stomach sank. *Shit*. "No, I didn't."

"Lauren would have called us if she'd known he wasn't going to be here. Something's wrong."

What was wrong was the kid had walked in on him in bed with Lauren and now he didn't want to face him. Ryan climbed down the ladder and pulled out his phone. "I'll call her now. Let her know he didn't get off the bus."

Rose was giving him the look and he knew she had more she wanted to say. He didn't want to hear it, to be honest, but a lifetime of experience told him to let her say her piece and get it over with.

"That boy was doing really well," she said. "Not only was working with you guys good for him, but he was doing better in school."

"Jesus, Rosie. Maybe he didn't feel good or something."

"So it's just a coincidence that Saturday night you didn't come home and today he didn't show up?"

"Fine. And Sunday morning Lauren and I woke up to Nick standing in her bedroom door and Dean in the living room. Happy?"

"Oh, no." She put her hand over her heart. "What a mess."

"Yeah, so that's probably why he didn't get off the bus."

"I still think Lauren would have called if she'd known he wasn't coming."

He held up the phone. "Which is why I'm going to call her."

When she just stood there watching him, he turned around and walked to his truck. Once locked inside, he pulled up Lauren's number and hit Call. It rang twice and he would have smiled when he heard her say hello if not for the circumstances.

"Hey, it's Ryan."

"Hi." She paused for a couple of seconds. "I was going to call you. I just…wasn't sure what to say. And I'm at work, actually."

"I know. I was going to call you later tonight if you didn't call me first. But I'm calling now because Nick didn't get off the bus."

He could practically feel the exhaustion in her sigh over the phone. "He seemed okay this morning. I would have called if I didn't think he was going to show up."

"Which is why I called you."

"It's pretty slow today. I'll sneak out early and go talk to him."

He didn't want the call to end. "Is everything okay? I mean, I know this is a problem, but…in general."

"Everything's okay. I'm sorry there was such a scene. I was looking forward to making you breakfast, you know."

"Is Nick going to his dad's this weekend?" He knew he shouldn't push, especially in the middle of a situation with Nick, but he couldn't help it.

"Yes, but I have to see if he's okay. It's…complicated."

It wasn't a no, so he'd take it. "We'll play it by ear."

"I really need to go. I want to make sure he went home and isn't getting in more trouble somewhere."

"Call me and let me know how it goes. And if he'll be here tomorrow."

"I will. Bye, Ryan."

He closed his phone and sat there drumming his fingers on the steering wheel. What a mess.

as sixteen now. He needed to learn how to deal with
ther men as a man.

"Apology accepted. So what are you going to do?"

"I'll work if you let me. Starting tomorrow, if that's
okay."

"As long as you understand my relationship with
your mom and my relationship with you are connected,
but still separate."

The word *relationship* echoed around in Lauren's
mind. She knew what he meant—or she was pretty sure
she did—but the word still stuck.

Nick stuck out his hand and Ryan shook it. "I'll be
here tomorrow."

"Good. Now go in and apologize to Rose for worrying her. And tell her I said you could have some of those
oatmeal raisin cookies she baked this morning."

Nick was through the front door in an instant. Lauren laughed, stepping closer to Ryan. "You handled that
perfectly. Thank you. Although, he probably doesn't
deserve any cookies."

"I was on the receiving end of that kind of talking-
to more often than I can even count." He grabbed her
hand and pulled her close. "I missed you."

She didn't get a chance to respond before he kis
er. He slid his hands over her shoulders and
des of her neck so he was cradling her head
ted like oatmeal raisin cookies and she
lips.

"Hey, boss?" The shout from
ge made him end the kiss
Let me take you to dinner o
Ryan!" The voice—she thought
ng closer.

But for once in his life, this was one mess he wasn't
in any hurry to extricate himself from.

LAUREN HAD JUST pulled out of the insurance company's
parking lot when her phone rang again. Thinking it
had to be Nick, she answered it without looking at the
screen. "Hello?"

"You haven't called me." It was Hailey, and Lauren rolled her eyes. "I know you're at work, but I heard
Rose Davis's car was parked outside your house all Saturday night and I'm pretty curious why I didn't know
about that."

"I'm not at work. I'm on my way home because Nick
didn't get off the bus at the Northern Star today."

"Possibly connected to Rose's car spending the night
at your house?"

"I'd say probably." She really didn't want to go into
it, but she might as well get it over with. "Dean brought
Nick home early. Sunday morning, actually. We were
still in bed."

"Oh, shit. Was it bad?"

"Dean was a jerk about it and I had to throw him
out. Nick's been quiet, but I thought he was doing okay.
He's having some issues with his dad and Jody, too, so
maybe it was just too much."

"What a freakin' headache. But was Ryan worth it?"

Lauren smiled, even though Hailey couldn't see her.
She couldn't help it. "He was worth it."

"Oh, customers. Call me later."

When she got home, Lauren was relieved to see
Nick's backpack dumped inside the door, as usual.
Though she'd been pretty sure he had come home instead of going to Ryan's, not knowing exactly where
he was wasn't a good feeling.

"Nick?"

He came out of the kitchen, opening a can of soda. "What are you doing home early?"

"I'm home early because I got a phone call you didn't get off the bus at the lodge."

"I was going to call you. I just wanted a drink first."

"What about calling *them?* They were expecting you and it's not like it was a social visit. You have an obligation to be there."

He set his jaw in an imitation of Dean's stubborn look. "I didn't feel like it today."

"You keep telling me you're responsible enough to take driver's ed and drive my car, but then you pull something like this?"

"Something like what? I don't want to see him. It's *weird.*"

She had no doubt it was a little weird. But it didn't change the fact he'd made a deal with Ryan and now he wasn't living up to it. "You see Jody every weekend. That's not weird."

"Dad married her. It's different."

He certainly hadn't been married to her in the beginning, but Lauren let that whole thread drop. "Fine. Put your shoes back on and get in the car."

"Where are we going?"

"We're going to the lodge so you can apologize for not showing up and tell them you'll be there tomorrow."

"Can't you just pay what's left?"

"No, I can't." She prayed for patience because she was about out. "This is your mess, you gave your word and you're going to honor it."

"Whatever." He shoved his feet into his sneakers and stormed out to the car.

Nick ignored her for the entire drive, which was fine

with her. Her stomach was twisted up and her starting to ache. By the time they parked behin truck, she was ready for the entire male specie appear off the planet.

Until Ryan walked out onto the porch and s her. She didn't want him to disappear anytim Then he turned his attention to Nick and his exp was a little less warm.

She had to give her son a little nudge to get h on the porch, but then he straightened up and l Ryan in the eye. "I'm sorry I didn't call and tell wasn't coming."

"You worried Rose and probably your mother,

"But not you, right?" He said it with a little bit of a sneer, but Lauren stayed back. If Ryan didn't like his tone, he'd let him know.

"Not really. I know why you didn't show up."

Nick squirmed under Ryan's calm stare. "It's just. . weird. I thought my mom would pay what's left, but s said I had to keep working it off."

"Good for her. You're not seven, Nick, and it's weird. What it is, is none of your business. Y your business is this—I like your mother. I resp mother. I like you. And, up until this afterno spected you."

"You did?"

"You screwed up, which happens, but you very day you said you would to work it off u're here ready to throw your mother ial bus because seeing me might be a m sorry."

ren hoped Ryan could see that w ssion as he'd get from her son o watch silently and not n

She stood on her tiptoes to give him a quick kiss. "I'd like that."

Nick exited the house at the same time Dill turned the corner. Though her son's expression closed off a little when he saw her standing so close to Ryan, he just said, "See you tomorrow," and walked to the car.

"Sorry to interrupt," Dill said, "but we want you to take a look at the flashing on the big chimney."

"I'll see you tomorrow when I pick up Nick," Lauren said, moving toward the stairs.

"If I'm not around, I'll give you a call. Five o'clock Saturday?"

She nodded and lifted her hand in a wave before going to the car. Once they were on the main road, Nick took a folded-up napkin out of his pocket and unwrapped an oatmeal raisin cookie.

"I stole a cookie for you."

It was an apology and a peace offering and an I-love-you all wrapped up in one small cookie theft. She grinned and took a bite.

THE NEXT DAY, when Nick got off the bus at the lodge, he still seemed a little off, so Rose broke out the secret weapon. Fresh-from-the-oven apple pie with French-vanilla ice cream melting into the nooks and crannies. She set it in front of him, then poured him a glass of milk.

"Your after-school snacks are awesome, Mrs. D. Thanks."

She took the cup of hot tea she'd just brewed and sat down across the table from him. "So how are things going, Nick?"

"Good. I got a B on my ELA quiz."

"ELA?"

"English Language Arts."

"Oh." She scowled, making him laugh. "Back in the olden days, we called it English class. I'm very proud of you for getting a B. And how are things going at home?"

His face closed off immediately and he gave her the one-shoulder shrug. "Fine. Whatever."

"*Whatever* usually means a person doesn't want to talk about something that needs talking about."

He moved some pie around on his plate, watching the ice cream melt into streams running through apple chunk boulders. "It's not like it matters."

"If something's bothering you, it matters. And unless I think you're into something dangerous or bad for you, what you say to me stays with me. You can ask my daughter or almost anybody in this town. I'm not a rat." He still hesitated and she guessed at what was holding him back. "Even if the person you're having a problem with is family to me."

When the tips of his ears got pink, she knew she'd nailed it. It didn't take a math genius—assuming it was still called math nowadays—to see that, even though he'd shown up, he was still having some kind of problem with Ryan.

"Whatever," Nick said after shoveling down a few mouthfuls of pie. "He'll probably marry my mom and they'll have new kids and they'll only remember I exist when they need a babysitter."

Whoa. There was a whole lot of telling information in that one sentence, and Rose took a long sip of her tea to give herself time to parse it out. "Do you babysit your brother and sister a lot?"

"On the weekends, Dad and Jody go out all the time and I watch Alex and Adrienne. I mean, they're kind of cool for little kids and I love them and everything, but

Dad takes Jody shopping and they go to the movies and whatever they want. I'm just, like, the free babysitter."

"Have you told your dad you feel that way?" He shook his head, digging into his pie again. "Or your mom?"

"Whatever. It's no big deal."

"Young man, if you say *whatever* again in the course of a conversation with me, that'll be the last baked good of mine you ever eat, do you understand?" He looked stunned, and she waited until he nodded before continuing. "It *is* a big deal. You need to tell your dad you'd like to do something with him on the weekends once in a while. Or at least something as a family.

"As the oldest, you're going to babysit sometimes. That's how it works in real life. But you're his son, not a sitter, and he needs to know you feel like they're taking advantage of you instead of looking forward to spending time with you on the weekends."

"I don't know how to say it."

"Just say it straight out. 'Dad, I don't mind babysitting Alex and Adrienne so you and Jody can do things, but sometimes I'd like to do stuff as a family because I only get to see you on weekends,' and go from there." He nodded, washing the last of his pie down with half the glass of milk. "And about your mom and Ryan…"

"Wha—" He stopped. "I mean, I don't really want to talk about my mom."

"And that's your business. But I'll say one thing. You're sixteen so you know a little about attraction between a man and a woman." He blushed, of course, but she kept on. "And sometimes it's just an attraction. Maybe Ryan and your mom have more than attraction and something will come of it, or maybe they don't and he'll go home and that'll be the end of it.

I honestly don't know. But I do know two things. Ryan's a good man and your mother loves you very, very much. No man or having more children or *anything* will change that."

He didn't say anything, but he did give her a little smile, which she took as a small victory. While Liz and Katie had had no trouble pouring out their troubles to her growing up, she'd had her hands full with Mitch, Ryan, Sean and Josh. She knew getting them to just listen was something to feel good about.

"Okay," she said, standing up to take his plate. "Go get to work now before the boss comes looking for you."

Nick passed Andy on his way out the door and Rose shook her head once he'd closed it behind the boy. "You smelled that pie, didn't you?"

"Is there any left?"

"Just like a man. I give an inch and you take a mile." She took out a clean plate and served another slice. "Took me thirty years to forgive you and now here you are, hanging around my kitchen and begging for pie."

"Your pie's worth the wait." He took the plate from her and had the audacity to wink at her.

And, good Lord, she blushed. Turning her back abruptly, she made herself busy at the sink so he wouldn't see. "Eat that quick and get back to work before Ryan accuses me of corrupting his help again."

"Why don't you sit down and have a piece of pie with me?"

"I just had one with Nick," she lied.

"There was only one slice gone and one dirty plate. If you shared his, you must not have gotten much. Sixteen-year-old boys eat like wolves."

"I'm fine." His chuckle made her cheeks flame again

and she threw the dish towel on the counter. "I'm going to vacuum. Rinse your plate when you're done."

She'd liked Andy Miller a lot more when he wasn't allowed in her house.

# CHAPTER THIRTEEN

WHEN RYAN HEARD the bus stop at the end of the drive the following afternoon, he realized he wasn't sure what to do with Nick. He couldn't really have him on the roof, but that's what they were focusing on for the time being.

He thought about it while the kid was inside doing his homework and probably scarfing down apple pie with Rose. The guys could spare Ryan for a couple of hours. Hell, they'd probably be happy as pigs in shit not to have him looking over their shoulders for a while.

"Hey, Josh, those four-wheelers have gas in them?"

His brother frowned, then shrugged. "Yeah. And there's a gas can in the garage that's still got some in it if they need more."

"You mind if Nick and I take them out? He can't be up here, so I was thinking we'd go work on the trail."

"Sounds good."

Ryan climbed down from the roof and went into the barn to get the keys. He fired two of the machines to let them warm up for a few minutes while he grabbed the chain saw off the shelf and secured it in its rack on the front of the bigger ATV. Then he grabbed a couple pairs of work gloves and branch cutters and threw them in the cargo box.

By the time Nick came out of the house, Ryan had scrounged up a few helmets for him to try on. "You go four-wheeling with your dad, right?"

Nick looked confused, but he nodded. "Yeah. Not a lot anymore, but sometimes."

"I thought we'd go cut some trail today, if you're up to it."

"Yeah. Cool!"

Once Nick had a helmet on, Ryan led the way into the woods. At first they were on established trails he'd ridden since he was a kid, but out toward the back corner, a new trail cut off.

Part of the plan to connect Whitford to the ATV trails was an access trail that cut across the lodge's property, and that of several other landowners. The hope was, of course, that direct access by ATV to both the food and gas in town and the trail system would build up year-round business for the Northern Star. But it was up to them to cut the trail.

The new path was still pretty rough, so Ryan kept a close eye on Nick, but the kid was a good rider. He kept a steady pace and it wasn't long before they reached the spot where the fresh trail dead-ended into the woods.

Ryan killed the engine and grabbed the gloves and cutters out of the box. "See how it's marked?"

Josh had been out several times with members of the ATV club and a guy from the state and they'd used orange flags and spray paint to mark where the trail needed to be.

Nick nodded. "Everything between the orange markers has to go, right?"

"You got it."

They worked side by side, cutting away brush and moving rocks. Occasionally Ryan had to fire up the chain saw and take down smaller trees. A patch of puckerbrush almost got the better of them, but they managed to clear it with only minor scratches.

There was one large pine they skipped over. "My brothers and I will come out and deal with this one later."

"What about the stumps?"

"We'll deal with them later, too. Some weekends the guys from the ATV club come over and give a hand, so it's not too bad." Ryan pulled off his glove and wiped his arm across his forehead. "You know, you can come over and go riding sometime. With me, of course, or one of my brothers. You can't be running around alone out here."

"Sure. Thanks." He didn't seem too excited about the offer. "That'd probably make my mom happy."

"I'm not sure why, since I didn't invite her."

Nick shifted his weight from one foot to the other. "You know, 'cause we'd be bonding or whatever. Because I'm her son and you're her...you know, whatever, so that would make her happy."

Ryan had to laugh. "I guess since I am her *you know, whatever*, it might make her happy if I bonded with you, but that's not why I made the offer. When I was your age, I wanted to live on my four-wheeler and it doesn't sound like you get a lot of seat time right now."

"Not too much. But Alex and Adrienne are getting older now, so we might ride more."

"It's hard with little kids." While he had his glove off, Ryan pulled out his phone and looked at the time. "Oh, shit."

"What?"

"Don't tell your mother I said shit."

"Pretty sure I've heard that word before."

"Yeah, but as her *you know, whatever*, I have to be on my best behavior with you. As it is, it's later than I thought and she's probably at the lodge waiting to kill me right now."

They packed up the tools and hit the trail, with Nick leading this time. He'd have to look back when they reached intersections so Ryan could point in the right direction, but he was comfortable on the machine. Not reckless, but confident, and Ryan had to admit Dean had taught the kid well.

He wasn't surprised to see Lauren's car parked in the drive when they came out of the woods. Hopefully, Rose was keeping her distracted so she wasn't fuming over the fact it was already getting dark.

They parked the four-wheelers and put the chain saw and keys back in the barn. When they went through the back door into the kitchen, everybody turned to look. The four guys—Dill, Matt, Josh and Andy—were crowded around the sink, washing up. Rosie was at the stove and Lauren had been on her way to the dining room with a stack of plates.

She looked at Nick, then at Ryan with one eyebrow raised. "What did you do to my son?"

He looked at the kid, trying to figure out what she meant. He was a little sweaty and flushed from the fast ride home. His clothes were definitely filthy. Even dirtier than his skin, although the dried blood from the puckerbrush scratches probably made his arms look worse than the clothes overall. He'd even managed to get a pretty good scratch on his cheek.

As far as Ryan could see, there was nothing wrong with him. "What do you mean?"

Lauren laughed and gave him a look that seemed to promise good things in the near future, then continued on to the dining room, shaking her head.

Nick elbowed him, distracting him from the delicious view of Lauren walking away. "Do I look as bad as you do?"

"Probably about the same." He looked down at himself. "But your mom doesn't buy my clothes, so you're in more trouble than I am."

"Since you can't tell time, I invited Lauren and Nick to stay for lasagna," Rosie said.

Andy laughed. "Actually she *told* Lauren she and Nick were staying for lasagna."

"You, on the other hand, are welcome to go on home and open up a can of something for your dinner," Rose told him.

Ryan couldn't see Rose's face because she was at the counter, transferring dinner rolls from a baking pan to a plate, but he could see Andy's. The man definitely liked pushing the housekeeper's buttons, and Ryan thought that was pretty ballsy for a man who'd spent several decades on the woman's shit list.

Lauren took the plate of rolls from Rose and, by the time Ryan and Nick managed to get clean enough to eat, everybody was sitting around the dining room table. Josh sat at the head, as he had since their dad had passed despite Mitch being the oldest, so Ryan sat at the foot of the table. Nick pulled out the chair on the other side of Lauren, so they were both on his left. It felt right to him, having them there at his family's dinner table.

Maybe it felt a little too right. It was so easy to picture them doing this every night, like a family. But this wasn't *his* table. His was down in Mass, and Lauren had her own table.

"Get much cleared out there?" Josh asked him when they'd all filled their plates.

"A bit. About a quarter-mile from the brook now." They'd have to build a bridge over the brook to preserve it, but they were hoping if they supplied the lumber, the ATV club would give them a hand with the construction.

"Excellent. I think we might be able to break through to the main trail before the snow flies. Won't be in good enough shape to groom it for sleds yet, but it'll be settled for spring."

Ryan nodded, then pointed his fork at Nick. "You already know the kid's a good worker, but he's a hell of a rider, too. If you need a hand, you should give him a shout and see if he's free to come over."

Nick beamed, but Lauren didn't look quite as pleased with the praise. "Umm…I don't find my son being deemed a hell of a rider by a Kowalski very comforting for some reason. You weren't going fast, were you, Nick?"

"Of course not." The kid obviously wanted to deflect his mother's attention, because he pointed at Ryan. "He was cursing in front of me, though."

Ryan's jaw dropped and, when Lauren turned to look at him, Nick mimicked pointing and snickering at him behind her head.

"You little rat." He picked up his dinner roll and cocked his arm.

Rose slammed her hand down on the table. "Ryan Kowalski! If you throw that roll, you'll be cleaning the entire kitchen, *alone*, every night for the rest of the time you're here."

"You do realize I can get in my truck and go home anytime, right?" She just kept giving him the look, waiting him out. He set the roll back on the edge of his plate. "Sorry."

Everybody but Rose, including the miscreant who'd

thrown him under the bus and the two guys he paid to respect his authority, laughed at him.

"It's all right, kid," he said to Nick. "Rose can't save you forever."

Then he winked at Lauren and went back to his lasagna.

By the time they were done eating and Lauren had helped with the cleanup over Rose's objections, it was getting late and Ryan knew she had to get home. He'd rather have sat on the porch with her for a while, but he walked her and Nick to her car instead.

"I'll call you tomorrow night," he said, and then he leaned in through the open window to kiss her goodbye. "Have a good time with your dad this weekend, Nick."

"Yeah, thanks."

He watched until the taillights faded into the darkness, then went back inside to take a long, hot shower. Physical labor might be good for the soul, but keeping up with a sixteen-year-old wasn't good for the body.

ON FRIDAY MORNING, Ryan realized they didn't have enough flashing on hand, an oversight for which he thoroughly reamed Dill and Matt.

Of course, mentioning he was going to run into town real quick and grab some at the hardware store caused Rosie to remember she was out of half-and-half and she didn't have enough eggs for baking, and ten minutes later he had an entire list. And Josh decided he just *had* to get a haircut.

"It's tickling my ears," he said when Ryan rolled his eyes.

"Twenty minutes," he grumbled as they climbed into his truck. "It was going to take me twenty minutes, tops, and now half the day's going to be gone."

"How do you not have an ulcer? You should relax."

If Ryan was an asshole, he'd point out Kowalski Custom Builders ran further into the black every year, while the Northern Star was barely treading water, and ask if maybe his brother thought there was a correlation to the whole "relax" thing. It would be a shitty thing to say, though, so he kept his mouth shut.

Besides, once Mitch had really dug into the books and laid it all out for them, Ryan didn't see how Josh had kept the place going on his own for so long. It certainly hadn't been by relaxing.

They swung by the barbershop first. Ryan's original intention was to drop Josh off and go to the market alone, but he hadn't seen a lot of Katie and the day was already half shot to hell anyway.

With the Red Sox knocked out of the post-season, Katie had transitioned to football. The Patriots logo on her ball cap matched the sweatshirt, and Ryan smiled when he saw her. She wasn't a woman who wasted a lot of time shopping. A trip through a sporting goods store, a few pairs of jeans and she was good.

"Hey, kid," Ryan said, giving her a quick hug. "How's business?"

She waved her hand around the empty barbershop. "Gee, I'm not sure I can fit you two in."

"I'm all set, actually. But the princess here says his hair's tickling his ears."

"When it starts getting long, it curls over the tops of my ears and drives me nuts."

Katie shoved him toward the chair. "I told you your hair grows fast and if you don't come in every four or five weeks, it's going to tickle your ears."

"I don't see why you can't cut it when you're at the house."

She snapped open a clean cape and draped it around his shoulders. "Because you don't pay me when I cut it at the house."

"I didn't charge you that night you spent at the lodge because you stayed up too late playing cards with Rosie, did I?"

"That's not the same thing."

Josh held up his hands to Ryan, as though looking for support. "How do you figure that?"

"Because I have very sharp scissors a fraction of an inch from the tip of your ear and I said so."

As usual, their arguing quickly turned to sports and Ryan tuned them out. He should have just gone to the market as he'd originally planned. Instead, he pulled out his phone and read through email, flagging some to respond to when he got home. One was urgent enough that he went through the laborious process of typing out a response on the tiny phone keys.

Finally, Katie brushed Josh off and removed the cape. "Fifteen bucks."

"You still owe me twenty because of that blown field goal last Sunday."

Ryan shook his head. Those two would bet on anything.

"That's football. This is my business. I keep them separate and you owe me fifteen bucks."

Josh grumbled while he dug out his wallet, but he kissed her cheek before they left. "See you later, kid."

Since Josh was already heading out the door, Ryan knew he hadn't seen the pink that tinged Katie's cheeks or the way her mouth twisted when he called her kid. The guy was hopeless.

"See ya, Katie."

The hardware store was next just because they'd have

to drive past it to get to the market. Ryan had to park a few spaces down the street. "You want me to leave it running?"

"I'll go in with you."

"It's going to take me two minutes." When Josh opened his door and got out, Ryan cursed and shut the truck off.

He followed his brother into the store, then stepped aside for a couple who were on their way out.

"How goes it?" Josh asked, walking straight to the counter.

"It goes."

Ryan looked around for a minute, but he didn't feel like wading into the back room. "Hey, Dozer, do you have any flashing?"

He crossed his arms and gave Ryan a flat stare. "You can call me Mr. Dozynski, I think."

"What?" Ryan had never heard anybody call him that. Ever. He'd been Dozer since he'd moved to Whitford and bought the hardware store in the seventies. "What did I do?"

"You molest my daughter and then come in here and think I'll sell you flashing?"

"Whoa!" Ryan held up his hands. "Your daughter's thirty-four years old. Nobody molested anybody."

Dozer looked at Josh. "Is that not the word I wanted?"

Josh shook his head. Albert Dozynski had grown up speaking Polish at home and English at school and still had some trouble with the more outside-the-classroom words. "People use it joking around, but it's not cool if you're throwing out serious accusations."

"What word do I want?"

Josh considered for a few seconds. "Soiled."

"You soiled my daughter," Dozer threw at Ryan.

He glared at his brother. "You asshole."

"Hey, he needed a word."

"Look, I didn't soil Lauren, okay? I spent the night with her, yes. And I'm taking her to dinner tomorrow."

"And you don't come and talk to me about it, like a man?"

"Uh…no."

Dozer looked at Josh, who shook his head slightly. "That's more for marrying, not soiling."

Ryan made a mental note to kick Josh's ass later.

But Dozer wasn't finished yet. "You seduce my daughter, and *then* you buy her dinner? And you think that respects her?"

Ryan wasn't sure who had seduced whom, but "seduce" was a better word than "soil" any day of the week. He mentally flailed for a way to answer the question.

"I'd taken her out for a meal before," he blurted. Meeting her at the diner and paying for her burger probably wasn't what her father had in mind. And even though they hadn't technically gone together, he added, "And we went to my brother's wedding."

Dozer narrowed his eyes. "So you're dating my daughter?"

"Yes, sir." He thought so, anyway.

"I suppose you want a discount."

"No, sir. I just want to buy some flashing so I can get back to work."

"My wife will want to meet you."

Ryan was going to start downing a shot of something hard before coming into town. "Mrs. Dozynski has known me my whole life."

Not that anybody saw much of her. She refused to learn to drive and preferred staying home to going out and socializing.

"True. But now you're dating my daughter, no?"

"I'll mention it to Lauren."

"Good. I'll get the flashing. How much do you need?"

Ryan told him and he disappeared into the back room. Josh managed to wait until he was out of sight before he broke into laughter.

"I knew I should have left you in the truck."

"You should have seen your face when he accused you of molesting Lauren."

"I just wanted flashing."

"Fran's good friends with Mrs. Dozynski. I hope we don't have to tell Rose she can't have half-and-half for her coffee because you were soiling Lauren."

"I should have let Sean drown you the day he got you stuck in the toilet trying to give you a swirly."

"We could have gone to the diner, you know," Lauren said, trying not to laugh at Ryan's expression as he read the offerings of the upscale restaurant they'd driven an hour to get to.

"The diner's not a date. It's just…the diner." He flipped the menu over, saw the back was blank, then flipped back to the front. "Oh, steak tips. We're in business."

"So this is our first date?"

"Let's call it our third."

Maybe his definition of a date and hers weren't quite the same. "How do you figure that?"

"I think lunch the day you were working at the hardware store should be our first date. That way Mitch's wedding could be our second date. And then I spent the night." He grinned across the table at her. "I don't want people to think you're easy."

She laughed. "Funny. You're a real funny guy."

"Actually, that's kind of how your dad thinks it went."

She stopped laughing. "My dad? What are you talking about?"

"I went to the hardware store for some flashing and he wouldn't sell me any because I'd soiled you, so I had to convince him we'd been dating before I, you know, soiled you."

"Wait. *Soiled?*"

"Josh was helping him with his words."

"Great. So you convinced him we were dating."

"I really needed the flashing." He winked. "Did you know Nick refers to me as your *you know, whatever*? He called me that the other day when we were working on the trails."

"That sounds about right for Nick." She traced a trail in the condensation on her water glass. "What word would you use?"

"Helpless sex toy," he said without any hesitation.

"You're shameless."

He lifted his water glass, his gaze locked with hers. "When it comes to you, absolutely."

The waiter appeared to take their order, breaking their eye contact, though his presence didn't put a dent in the hot anticipation she'd been practically tingling with all day. The diner might not have fit his definition of a date place, but if they'd gone there, they'd probably be in her bed already.

They talked about a little bit of everything while they ate. The lodge and his family and Nick. Then they moved on to books and music and television shows and movies.

"Here's something I never thought I'd say," she said, "but I can't believe I had sex with a man who can quote every line of *Spaceballs*."

"It was pretty good, though, wasn't it?"

*"Spaceballs?"*

"No, the sex."

She shrugged. "A little short on quotable dialogue, but it was pretty good, yeah."

He narrowed his eyes. "I guess I'll have to try even harder."

If he tried too much harder, it might kill her, but she just smiled at him while he tucked his credit card back in his wallet. It was going to be a very, very long ride home.

They were about halfway home when it hit her that he'd never given her the word he'd use to describe his place in her life. He'd used humor to deflect her and, while "helpless sex toy" wasn't a bad thing, she would have liked a serious answer to the question. If she introduced him to somebody as her boyfriend, would he balk?

But that moment had passed. He was telling her a funny story about the time Matt had called him from a customer's home because he needed an answer from the homeowners before he could continue working. Unfortunately, they were occupied in the bedroom and he didn't want to interrupt them having sex, so Matt wanted the office to call and ask them and then call him back.

It didn't really matter if he had a label, she told herself. She was just going to enjoy his company.

She was laughing so hard at a Dill story, she almost

fell out of the truck when he parked in her driveway and come around to open her door.

"You're lying," she said when she'd caught her breath and unlocked her front door.

"Ask him tomorrow. I swear it happened."

Lauren was a few feet inside when she realized Ryan hadn't followed her in. He was still standing in the open doorway. "What are you doing?"

"Waiting for you to invite me in. Or at least kiss me good-night."

She laughed and walked back to the door. "Really? So if I just kiss you and say good-night, you'll just go home?"

"Well, plan B would be to kiss you good-night until you're so crazy with lust you forget you weren't letting me in. But plan C would be going home."

"What's plan A?"

He braced his hands on the doorframe and leaned forward so that he was almost close enough to kiss her without technically being *in* her house. "Plan A is a race to your bed, stripping on the way, and the first one there naked gets to be the choreographer."

"I don't think so."

He almost managed to hide his disappointment. Almost. "On to plan B."

"We can't leave our clothes scattered all over the house again, and we have to close the bedroom door, just in case."

"Okay."

"But we can still race. Go!" She took off running, then called over her shoulder, "Make sure you close the door!"

She laughed when she heard him curse, but he had

long legs and she lost her little bit of advantage when she fumbled with her bra hooks.

Just as she kicked off her panties, a jumble of clothes landed at her feet, her bedroom door slammed closed and Ryan launched himself—totally naked—past her, hitting her mattress so hard he bounced. "I win!"

"How the hell did you get your clothes off so fast?" She put her hands on her hips and glared at him. "And why didn't you let me win?"

"I'm a Kowalski. We're genetically incapable of taking a dive." He rolled onto his side and propped himself on his elbow. "Standing like that makes your boobs look great, by the way."

She walked over to the bed and lay down next to him. "Fine. Choreograph me."

He lifted her arm by the wrist and let it go, then laughed when she let it flop bonelessly back to the mattress. "Somebody's a sore loser. I never would have guessed that about you."

"I think you cheated."

"Hey, you should be proud. You came in second."

She rolled to her side and then shoved him to his back so she could straddle him. "Didn't anybody ever tell you it's not nice to gloat?"

He reached up and cupped her breasts. "Yeah. Usually the people who come in second."

She pinched his nipple and his body jerked under hers.

"Ow! Be nice."

"Oh, did that hurt? She leaned forward and kissed the same spot, then flicked her tongue over the sensitive nub. "Is that better?"

He moved his hands to her hips. He pulled her forward and then pushed her back so his erection glided between her legs. "A little."

Lauren swiveled her hips and his fingertips gripped her hips tighter. When she leaned forward to brace herself on her hands, Ryan lifted his head and captured her nipple between his teeth.

"Don't you dare," she hissed.

He dared, just enough to make her squirm, but not enough to hurt. She whimpered as he switched to her other breast and did it again.

Then he flopped back onto the pillow. "Shit. Condoms are in my pants, which are in a ball…somewhere. I threw them."

"I tucked one under the pillow earlier. Just in case."

Seconds later, he was wearing it and she lowered herself onto him. Slowly—so slowly she could hear him grind his teeth—she rocked her hips, taking him deeper and deeper.

He rolled her nipples between his thumbs and forefingers as she rode him. With her hair falling around her face, she looked down at him, keeping her gaze locked with his. There was no doubt, when he looked at her like that, that he thought she was the sexiest woman he'd ever seen.

Ryan reached up and tucked her hair behind her ear before stroking a fingertip down the side of her face. "*Yours*. That's the word I'd use."

She wasn't sure what he meant but, then again, most of her brain cells were being thoroughly distracted by the exquisite sensations going on in other parts of her body. "What do you mean?"

"If somebody wants you to pin a label on my place in your life, just tell them I'm yours. It's that simple."

"That simple, huh?" She ran her thumb across his lower lip and he nipped at it. "Mine?"

"Yours." Then, in one swift movement, he rolled them so that she was on her back and he was buried deep between her thighs.

With hard, powerful thrusts he sent her over the edge and then he said her name in a low and raspy voice, his face pressed against her neck, as his orgasm racked his body. He shuddered, collapsing on top of her with a groan.

"Jesus, Lauren, you're going to kill me."

She chuckled and snuggled closer to him. "Have I ever told you I love the way you say my name?"

"I didn't realize there was more than one way to say it."

"Smart-ass." She jabbed him lightly with her elbow. "I meant I like the way it sounds when *you* say it. It's warm and sexy."

"I've always thought you have the most beautiful name I ever heard."

"My dad learned English watching Bogey and Bacall movies. It's probably a good thing I didn't have a brother."

"Yeah, a name like Humphrey Dozynski wasn't going to help in the getting laid department." He nuzzled her hair before rolling over to dispose of the condom. Then he pulled her up against him, one arm thrown over her to hold her close. "Although you know everybody in Whitford would have just called him Little Dozer anyway."

"Dad would have loved that. Now I'm almost sorry I *don't* have a brother."

He chuckled softly, but she could already feel the

muscles in his arms going slack as he started dozing off. She closed her eyes, and without even having to work at relaxing, drifted off to sleep with a smile on her face.

## CHAPTER FOURTEEN

RYAN WAS BEAT. He'd started his day with an hour-long telephone call trying to convince a homeowner she was totally in the wrong while simultaneously soothing her ruffled feathers. Then he'd spent the rest of the day laying shingles. He wasn't in the mood to see Dean Carpenter's truck pulling up the drive.

He dropped his hammer on the roof with a thud and made his way to the ladder.

"You want me to come down?" Josh asked.

"I'm all set." He paused a few rungs down. "But if he starts something and it looks like he's kicking my ass, then yeah, come down."

Nick was picking up the ties they'd been cutting off the bundles of shingles and throwing over the side all day.

"Hey," Ryan said. "Your dad's here."

"I told him I'm almost done."

"So you knew he was coming?"

"Yeah, I called him to come get me. Mom left a message at school that she's sick so she wanted me to come straight home from school since she couldn't come pick me up here, but I called my dad and he said he would."

"Your mom's sick? What's the matter with her?" She was fine when he'd left yesterday afternoon.

"She started getting stuffy last night and she had a

sore throat this morning. Got worse, I guess. Wicked bad cold."

"That sucks." But nothing so bad he had to be mad she hadn't told him. Although she could have called and asked him to drive Nick home. It bugged him she thought he wouldn't do it. "Next time, you don't have to call your dad. I don't mind giving you a ride home."

"Okay."

"You did call your mom, right? To tell her you weren't going straight home?"

"Yeah."

Nick was going to be at least another ten minutes cleaning up and then he had to go inside and get his stuff. In the meantime, Dean was going to be hanging out in his driveway like the giant ex-husband elephant in the room.

Ryan walked over to where Dean was leaning against his truck, staring off into space. "Hey."

"Just here to pick up my son."

"He told me. I wouldn't have minded driving him home, but he didn't ask me. Sorry you had to drive all the way over."

"Not a problem."

Ryan looked at the man whose childhood was so entwined with his own that he could barely think of a memory that didn't include Dean.

"I did a shitty thing to you," he said, without knowing he was going to say it out loud. "I can't honestly say I'm sorry, but I acknowledge it was shitty."

Dean looked at him then, more resignation on his face than anger. "I loved you like a brother."

"But I loved *her*."

"Do you still?"

That was a really tough question, but Ryan guessed

he owed Dean the most honest answer he could give. "That Lauren? No. That faded a long, long time ago. Mostly what kept me away was embarrassment, I guess. I wasn't pining away. This Lauren? I don't know yet. It's really…complicated."

"I hurt her and I lost her. And I love Jody more than I thought I could love a woman, but I still care about Lauren and she's my son's mother. If you end up walking away, do it straight up. Don't screw with her head."

With anybody else, Ryan might have gotten belligerent, because he didn't need a lecture on how to treat a woman. But Dean had the right to say it. "I'm going to try my damndest not to."

"Nick says you're a good guy. He likes you."

"The feeling's mutual. You have a great son."

Dean nodded, then took a deep breath. "You and I are never going to be friends."

"I regret that, but I understand it."

"We don't have to be enemies, though."

It was more than Ryan had hoped for. "No, we don't."

Nick walked out onto the porch at that moment, and both men turned. He had his backpack slung over one shoulder and was munching on a cookie.

Rose followed him out. "Remember. You use that hand sanitizer I gave you. And wash your hands a lot. And don't share a cup or a fork or anything with your mom."

"I won't," he called over his shoulder. "See you tomorrow."

"I'm surprised she didn't dig through my stuff for a painter's mask for you to wear," Ryan told him when he got to the minivan.

"Believe it or not, she mentioned those."

"Oh, I believe it. See you tomorrow, kid." He lifted a hand to Dean, then walked back to the ladder.

Josh was on his way down and they met at the bottom. "Looks like it went okay."

Ryan nodded. "Better than I expected."

"For the record, if there had been a fight, I'd have stepped in, but I'd have let him get one good shot in first."

It took a few seconds for his meaning to sink in. A guy didn't let his brother take a hit from a guy who'd been an ex-husband for eight years. "What the hell do you know about it?"

"Remember when I went through my secret-agent ninja phase?"

"Yeah. You were one seriously messed-up kid, by the way."

"I was under your bed when you were practicing your 'divorce my best friend and run off with me' speech in the mirror."

"Are you shitting me?"

Josh raised his right hand. "I shit you not."

"And you never said anything to anyone? Not even to me?"

"A secret-agent ninja never reveals his secrets," Josh said solemnly and headed for the barn.

"You're a seriously messed-up adult, too," Ryan called after him.

Josh just laughed and kept walking.

LAUREN KNEW IT was Ryan's truck as soon as the headlights splashed across her living room window, and she pulled the blanket up over her head.

"You want me to tell him to go away?"

"No, that would be rude."

"Not if I say please."

She laughed, but that hurt her throat. And it was hot under the blanket, so she pulled it back down. The static did wonders for her hair.

Nick let Ryan in when he knocked, then hefted his backpack. "I have an essay due Friday. I'm going to go work on it in my room."

Even with a fuzzy brain, Lauren appreciated the gesture. He wasn't going away to sulk, but to give them some privacy.

She could see Ryan battling not to look amused by her appearance, but he lost. "You were fine yesterday. What the hell happened?"

"It's always that way. Colds hit me hard and I have sensitive skin, so the red nose and puffy eye thing happens fast."

"I can see that." He held up a plastic tub of something. "Did you eat?"

"I'm not really hungry. Nick had some leftovers. There should be a couple more slices of homemade pizza in the fridge if you want them."

"This is Rose's miracle chicken soup. She told me to make sure you eat it."

She sniffed and reached for her best friend, the tissue box. "I'm not hungry."

"Maybe you missed the part where she told me to make sure you eat it."

"Fine." She pushed back the blanket and swung her legs off the couch.

"Nice outfit."

She was wearing faded flannel sleep pants and a fleece pajama top with Christmas trees on it. And no bra. Whatever. Any man who got past the hair, eyes and red, runny nose wasn't going to be put off by fleece and flannel. Not that she was trying to attract one.

She heard Ryan rummaging around in her kitchen and a few minutes later he brought her a bowl of soup, a spoon and a napkin, which he set on the coffee table in front of her. "Eat."

He went back into the kitchen and a couple minutes later, she heard the microwave ding. She stared at the chicken soup, trying to work up the will to spoon it into her mouth.

Ryan sat down on the couch beside her, setting a plate with reheated pizza slices on the table. "Eat."

She picked up the spoon and ran it through the bowl. There were bite-size chunks of chicken and some veggies and rice in a dark, rich broth. She wished she could smell it. Then she took a bite, flavor exploded in her mouth and her eyes watered a little.

"Oh, yeah. I forgot to tell you it has a little more bite than the average chicken soup."

"What kind of spices does she use?"

"I don't know, but it's delicious. And keep those tissues close, because it won't be long before your sinuses start breaking loose."

"Oh, that's sexy," she muttered.

He eyed the outfit again. "Were you going for that?"

She gave a short laugh and then dug into the soup again. He was right. After the initial shock faded, it really was delicious.

"So how come you didn't call me? I had no idea you were sick, and you know I would have given Nick a ride home."

"I know, but you're trying to get the roof done and I didn't want to be a bother."

"That's pretty lame."

"You can't be mean to me right now. I'm sick."

"Which I found out when your ex-husband showed up in my driveway."

She winced. "I honestly didn't think he'd call Dean. After he called me and told me he did, I was going to call and give you a heads-up, but I think I fell asleep. He seemed okay, though. Dean, I mean. He even apologized for acting like a jerk the day he brought Nick home early."

"We talked a little. Enough."

That was good. It made things a bit less awkward, at least. "I mostly didn't call you because I knew you'd come running over, just because you're that kind of guy, and I didn't want you to see me like this. Not exactly a fun, sexy look."

He had the nerve to chuckle at her. "It's not as fun and sexy a look as the underwear you wore to the wedding, but it takes more than a stuffy nose to run me off. I'm that kind of guy."

She was surprised when she looked down and her bowl was empty. "That was delicious."

"There's more in the tub for tomorrow night if you still feel crappy. Never have seconds, though. Whatever she puts in it will knock the hell out of the cold, but too much will eat up your stomach."

She could already feel her stuffy nose transitioning to a runny nose, and she curled back up on the couch with her blanket and box of tissues.

When she looked at his plate, she laughed. There was nothing left but a little pile of mushrooms. "Not a fan of mushrooms, huh?"

"No, but I'm a big enough fan of pepperoni to pick the mushrooms off."

"Oh, it's almost time for *Survivor,*" she said, noticing the time. "I have to tell Nick. We never miss it."

"I'll get him."

She watched him walk down the hall and knock on Nick's door. "Your mom said it's almost time for *Survivor.*"

"I'm coming!" he yelled back.

"He's coming," Ryan told her as he sat back down on the couch.

When he lifted her feet and set them on his lap so he could lean back, she smiled to herself and dug the remote out from under the blanket so she could put the TV on the right channel.

"Do you watch this?" Nick asked Ryan when he'd dropped into the easy chair.

"When I get a chance. I haven't seen much of this season because I have a lot of paperwork and stuff to do for my office after I'm done working on the lodge. But I've seen a few."

"Did you see the one where…"

Lauren tuned them out and blinked bleary-eyed at the television. There was less pressure in her sinuses and she wasn't comfortable, but she wasn't quite as miserable as she'd been. Especially with Ryan's thumb rubbing the bottom of her foot.

She managed to stay focused on the first challenge, mostly because Ryan and Nick liked two totally opposing players and there was much shouting and trash-talking in her living room. But eventually their voices blended with the voices on the television and she started drifting in and out.

One of the times she drifted in, she found herself in Ryan's arms as he carried her toward her bedroom. She smiled and nestled closer to his chest.

"Be still. I'm trying not to drop you or bash your head on the doorjamb."

He got her to her bed without causing her injury, though, and waited for Nick to turn down the covers. Once he'd gotten her tucked in, he kissed her forehead. "I'll call you tomorrow and check on you."

"Okay."

"'Night, hon," Ryan said.

"Good night, Mom," Nick echoed.

Lauren smiled and drifted back out.

ROSE'S MIRACLE CHICKEN soup must have been exactly that, because by Wednesday she felt better enough to pick Nick up at the lodge herself. She didn't see Ryan when she got out of the car, so she waved to the guys on the roof and to Nick, who was painting the trim on the barn's windows and door, and went inside to say hi to Rose.

"Hi, honey," Rose said when she went into the kitchen. "How are you feeling?"

"This is the fastest I've ever gotten over a cold. Thank you for sending the soup over with Ryan. Have you ever thought about canning and selling the stuff?"

"Nope. Wouldn't be the same. I don't give out the recipe anymore, either, because people always screw it up and then blame my recipe. When you or Nick catch a cold, you call me. I'll get you some soup."

From somewhere in the house, Lauren could hear Ryan. She couldn't make out the words, but his voice was raised and he didn't sound happy.

"I guess it's hitting the fan down south," Rose told her. "The poor boy's been working on this place a month now and I think his business is starting to suffer. He'll probably have to go back to only coming up on weekends like he was doing. And once they finish the roof, Dill and Matt won't be coming up anymore. It's going to feel empty around here."

On the outside, Lauren nodded and made an appropriate "oh, that's too bad" sound, but on the inside, she was reeling.

Logically, she'd known all along Ryan's stay in Whitford was temporary. It was never intended to be anything but that. But it hadn't *felt* that way. Their relationship was becoming comfortable and familiar and he'd made himself a part of her life. He hadn't called her last night to check on her—he'd come over again and he'd brought supper and stayed to watch some television with her and Nick.

Almost like a family.

But Ryan's life was in Massachusetts. He had a house she'd never seen. He had friends she'd never met and a business she knew nothing about. She knew he didn't have a dog, but other than that, his life was a closed book to her.

The Ryan that was here—*her* Ryan—was just a visitor.

A few minutes later, he walked into the kitchen. His mouth was set in a grim line and the tension in his body didn't ease when he saw her, though he did give her a quick kiss. "Hi, hon."

"I hear you're having troubles."

"Yeah. Nothing I can't fix, but I have to head home and deal with it." Her heart twinged at the word "home." "If all goes well, I'll be back by late Friday afternoon or early evening."

"When are you leaving?"

"In a few minutes. I need to throw my stuff in my bag and then I'll head out."

Rose turned to look at him, a half-peeled potato in her hand. "It's a four-and-a-half-hour drive, Ryan. Can't you leave in the morning?"

"Not and make a seven-o'clock meeting."

"I should probably grab Nick and get out of the way," Lauren said, heading toward the door.

Ryan gave her a funny look, then grabbed her hand and pulled her in for another kiss. "You're never in the way. And I'm going to go talk to Nick. I want to tell him I'm leaving, but he's also done with his punishment."

Lauren felt her eyes widen. When Ryan started wrapping things up, he really went all out. "Okay."

"Starting Monday, if he wants to keep working, he'll get paid. I've already talked to Josh and there's plenty of busywork around this place."

So he wasn't cutting Nick loose. She nodded and tried to smile. "I think he'd like that."

"But I've gotta make it quick. Rosie, can you—" He turned to the housekeeper, but she was already pulling deli meat and the mayo out of the fridge. "Thanks. I'll be right back."

He went out the back door, bristling with angry energy, and Lauren sank onto one of the kitchen chairs. "That's a long drive."

"Yeah, it is."

"After Josh broke his leg, Ryan was really driving up here on Friday nights and driving home on Sunday?"

"Not every weekend. And whenever he could, he'd take the Friday or Monday off so they could get more done up here."

That would never work for an extended period of time, though. And how hard would it be on a relationship to only see each other on weekends? It would be especially hard for Ryan and Nick, since Nick spent those days with Dean.

"I can practically hear the wheels turning in your head, girl. Are you borrowing trouble over there?"

Lauren sighed. "Not borrowing it. I already own it, but I guess I chose to ignore it until now."

Rose set down her knife and crossed her arms. "You got married and had a baby young. You went through a divorce and you've been a single mother for eight years. You've been keeping a sixteen-year-old boy on a mostly straight path in a town with nothing to offer. And now you're going to let two hundred and thirty miles kick your ass?"

Wow. She wasn't sure she'd ever heard Rose say "ass" before. "It's not just about the miles. He's already a part of our lives, but I know nothing about his. I don't even know what color his house his."

"It's beige. Inside and out, everything's beige because he builds beautiful houses, but can't decorate worth a damn."

"Do you think he's thought about it?" Lauren hated sounding needy, but nobody knew Ryan the way this woman did. "That we're not a part of *his* life?"

"I don't know. But I bet he will when he's all alone in that big beige house for a couple of days and nights, missing you."

Lauren smiled, imagining him stretched out on a beige couch, staring at the ceiling with nobody to talk to. Of course, there was always a chance he'd be happy to have the peace and quiet and decide he didn't need the complication of a woman with a teenage son who lived hours away.

This time, when Ryan walked through the door, he smiled at her, looking a little bit more relaxed. Nick was at his heels and he grabbed his backpack out of the corner. Guess they were leaving.

Lauren stood up and gave Rosie a smile since she couldn't really thank her for the advice in front of Ryan. "We should probably go. You've got a long drive ahead of you."

He stepped close to her. "I'll miss you."

She certainly hoped so. "Call me when you get a chance. It's going to be insane at work because Gary destroys the office if I'm gone an hour, never mind three sick days, but anytime after work hours."

"I will." He kissed her, maybe a little longer and harder than he should have in the kitchen, but nobody complained. "I'll see you Friday."

She drove home listening to Nick's excitement that he'd be getting paid to work at the lodge now. There weren't many jobs in Whitford and, since the economy had suffered, adults had taken the jobs the teens used to do. Plus, his penance was over and his debt paid, which was a weight off his shoulders.

"That's great, honey," she said. "I'm proud of you. It might have started as a punishment, but you earned yourself the job."

"When I get my first paycheck, I'm going to take us out for ice cream at the diner."

Lauren couldn't help but smile at his enthusiasm. "I can't wait."

"I'm going to get a banana split because you never let me. I bet Ryan will get a sundae with chocolate ice cream and hot fudge because he loves chocolate. What are you going to get?"

A son with a broken heart if Ryan went home and remembered he liked his uncomplicated beige life, she thought. Maybe not broken, but bruised. Hers would be the broken one. "Coffee ice cream with caramel topping and extra whipped cream."

He gave her a sideways look. "Will they charge me for extra whipped cream?"

Laughing, she shook her head. "Paige won't charge us for extra whipped cream. Neither will Ava."

Some of the tightness eased in her chest. She'd be okay. No matter what happened in the future with Ryan, she had Nick and they'd both be okay.

# CHAPTER FIFTEEN

"You can't keep doing this."

Ryan scrubbed his hands over his face. He knew Wendi, his office manager, was right, even without Phil nodding his agreement from the other chair.

"If you're still in charge," she continued, "you need to be here. If you want to be there, then somebody else has to be in charge. And not just somebody you delegate stuff to and communicate through. Somebody has to be *the boss*."

Phil leaned forward. "When we have to keep telling homeowners and real estate brokers and architects and suppliers over and over you're unavailable, even if we can give them a reason, they lose confidence in the company."

As much as he'd tried not to think about this day, it was time to quit with the denial and come back to reality. He'd asked a lot of his people over the past month, especially Wendi, who'd been with him since the end of his first year in business. She'd started out part-time, out of her house, and he'd pretty much eaten peanut butter and jelly sandwiches for months to scrape up the money to pay her. But he sucked at remembering to return phone calls and file paperwork, and he couldn't run his growing business out of his pickup anymore. She was as important to Kowalski Custom Builders as he was, and he could see she was nearing the end of her rope with him. He couldn't lose her.

"We've just about wrapped up the projects they need me for," Ryan said. "Once the roofing's done, I'll be done except for some weekend side work. Another week, so you can start telling people I'll be available starting the twenty-ninth."

They both sagged back in their chairs, relieved smiles lighting up their faces. All he felt was grim resignation and a knot in his gut. This was going to change everything.

"Except on weekends," he said. "No Saturday meetings."

"You got it," Wendi said. "As long as you're here during the week, we can handle anything that comes up on a Saturday."

Once they left, Ryan leaned back in his oversize leather office chair and folded his hands behind his head. There were piles on his desk. He hated piles. And he knew Wendi had kept on top of the urgent things, but she'd leave anything she could for him as punishment.

It had been a long drive home and a short night's sleep, followed by a very long, intense day of meetings and phone calls. All he wanted to do was hit the drive-through of the first fast-food joint he came to and then stretch out on his couch. He'd drift off to the sound of the TV and then, at some point, wake up enough to stagger off to bed.

By the time he pulled into the driveway of his big, empty house in the middle of a gorgeous neighborhood full of families, and grabbed his paper bag of dinner off the passenger seat, he was almost ready to skip the couch nap and head straight to bed. He knew that no matter how tired he was, though, if he went to bed now, he'd be up at four, ready to face a day that hadn't started yet.

He watched a rerun of *Bonanza* while he ate, because that was what was on and he couldn't reach the remote.

Then he stretched out on the couch and pulled out his phone. Lauren answered on the second ring and he smiled at the sound of her voice. "Another couple minutes and you would have missed me. I was going to jump in the shower before our shows start."

"I won't keep you. I just wanted to say hi. I said I'd call."

"You sound tired," she said after a few seconds.

"I'm pretty beat. It was a very long day with a lot of tense people in it."

"Is everything okay?"

"It will be." He didn't want to talk about work. "Tell me about your day."

She told him how excited Nick was about the fact he'd be earning a paycheck and how today he'd brought home an A on his history quiz, which was a first. Ryan could feel the tension easing out of his body as he listened to her voice.

Lauren was what he needed at the end of the day.

"You didn't fall asleep on me, did you?" he heard her ask, and he realized he'd been dozing off to the comfortable lull of her voice.

"Of course not."

"Liar. Go to bed. I'm going to go jump in the shower."

"Good night, Lauren."

After she said good-night and hung up, he pushed himself up off the couch and tossed the paper debris from his supper. Then he went into his room, stripped down and climbed into bed.

He'd always loved his bed. It had a firm mattress and

was big enough for him to stretch out if he wanted. To-night, though, it felt hard and cold. And he didn't want to stretch out. He wanted to spoon his body around Lauren's and hold her while she fell asleep.

Looking around the room, he wondered what she'd think of it. Her house was neat and not too cluttered with knickknacks and crap, but his room bordered on austere. The only bright spots were the family photos on the wall.

It could probably use some color. Neutral tones like beiges and tans were attractive to buyers, but he didn't see selling the place anytime soon. Maybe some throw pillows and new drapes wouldn't hurt, either. And a woman. It needed a woman and a teenage boy to muck things up. Maybe more kids to really make a mess. But, mostly, nothing would warm up the house—and his bed—like Lauren.

It wasn't too late yet, so he took his phone off the bedside charger before he could squash the impulse. He scrolled through his contacts until he found Mitch's number and hit Call. It rang three times before his brother answered. "Hello?"

"Can I borrow your bike for the weekend?" Once he'd popped the question to Paige, Mitch had had the motorcycle shipped to Whitford, where it lived in the Northern Star's barn until they moved into a house with a garage.

"The whole weekend? Aren't you supposed to be working? You're always working."

"Just looking to blow off a little steam." And as far as Ryan was concerned, that was all he needed to know.

"Sure. I won't be home until close to noon Satur-day, so you'll have to get the key and my helmet from

Paige. And I'm sure she wouldn't mind lending out her helmet, too, if you need it."

As fishing expeditions went, it wasn't subtle. "Thanks."

"Going anywhere special?"

He might as well skip being discreet. The Kowalski family didn't know the meaning of the word. "I want to bring Lauren here. I'm in Brookline, by the way."

"Paige told me you had to go home. So, you're going to drive back to Whitford tomorrow, then ride down on the bike with Lauren and then drive back on Sunday? In October, when it's not really all that balmy, of course."

"I want her to see my house, and weekends are the only time it can happen, so yeah."

His brother was quiet long enough that Ryan guessed he probably wouldn't like whatever came out of his mouth next. "I thought you guys were just fooling around. I didn't realize it was that serious."

"You say that like it's a bad thing."

"No." Again with the hesitation. "Just a lot of hurdles, that's all."

"I got a ribbon in track and field. I can handle it."

Mitch laughed. "Dumbass, that was a *participation* ribbon. You sucked at track and field."

"Screw you." He hung up. Mitch called right back and Ryan answered it. "What?"

"The throttle sticks a little shifting from first to second and you might have to goose it a little. Try not to dump Lauren off the back." Then he hung up.

It was too late now to call Lauren back and see if she even wanted to go on the ride he'd just suffered taking his brother's crap for. She was probably already in the shower, and then she'd be watching TV with Nick. It would give him a good excuse to call her tomorrow afternoon since, judging by the looks of his schedule, he wouldn't be pulling into Whitford until pretty late.

Yawning and forcing himself to close his eyes, he wondered how long he'd be able to keep up with driving back and forth from Brookline to Whitford on the weekends. Eventually, balancing his business with seeing Lauren was going to wear him down and one or both would suffer. But he couldn't see giving up either of them, so he'd make it work. Somehow.

WHEN HER PHONE RANG, Rose wasn't surprised to see Liz's number pop up on the caller ID. At the end of the last message Rose had left on Liz's voice mail, Rose had threatened to send one of her brothers to New Mexico in person if Liz didn't call her back.

"Don't you dare send any of the boys here," Liz said once they'd said hello.

"Then don't ignore my calls."

"I've been busy."

"Then send a text that says 'busy, will call later' instead of breaking up with a long-term boyfriend and then dropping off the face of the planet. I watch *Criminal Minds* and *20/20*. I worry."

"Okay, I'm sorry. What's going on in Whitford? The condensed-digest version."

Rose sighed. "Pretty much the same as was going on when you left."

"What's going on with Ryan and Lauren?"

She put the phone on speaker and picked up her knitting. She loved newfangled technology. "Nobody's really sure. If they lived in the same state and she didn't have a teenage son to consider, they'd probably be pretty serious. But it's about time for him to go back to Brookline and nobody knows what's going to happen. He's not saying."

"He probably doesn't know. And being a Kowalski, he's probably too stubborn and thickheaded to ask."

"Speaking of stubborn, thickheaded Kowalskis, when are you moving home?"

Liz laughed and it made Rose smile. Her girl sounded less tired than she had in years, as though a weight had been lifted off her shoulders. A weight named Darren. "I'm not, Rosie. But I'm going to try to come home for Christmas."

It was more than she'd had of Liz in the past and it would be enough. "I'm going to ask Sean and Emma if they'll come, too. It's been too many years since we've all been together for Christmas. Did you have a good time at the wedding?"

Rose knit half a row of stitches before Liz answered. "Yeah, I had a good time."

There was an odd note to her voice, as if she really didn't want to talk about the wedding, but before Rose could poke at her for a reason, Liz claimed she had to get to work and they said their goodbyes. She sat in her rocker, mindlessly knitting rows, until she heard the kitchen door open and close. A few seconds later, Andy wandered into the living room.

"There you are," he said. "Not used to seeing you sit still."

"Liz called, so I sat down to knit while I talked to her and just kept on sitting."

"How's she doing?"

"Good." She would have said more, but she got side-swiped by a coughing fit. She was definitely coming down with something.

Andy scowled. "You don't sound good."

She waved her hand at him. "Probably the cold that went around. I'll be fine."

"What are you knitting?"

She held up the length of black she'd knit, showing him the gold stripes across one end. "A scarf for Nick for Christmas. In Bruins colors, of course."

"I know you really want a grandkid, Rose, but you should probably let Ryan and Lauren figure out what they're doing before you get too attached to the boy."

Her hands stilled, holding the needles tight. Mostly she wouldn't undo all her work by pulling a knitting needle free of the stitches and sticking it in his leg. "I know that. I'm knitting him a scarf, not writing him into the family Bible."

"I'm just saying—"

"*I'm* just saying that Nick Carpenter works for the lodge now, so I'm knitting him a scarf for Christmas."

"Okay." Andy helped himself to a seat on the sofa, which annoyed her. Shouldn't he be working? "Are you knitting me a scarf, too?"

"No." She'd been knitting him some fisherman's mittens, but now she was considering giving them to somebody else. The mailman, maybe.

"You're a cold woman, Rosie Davis."

While she ignored his statement, she was actually cold. And tired. Rather than go hunting for her sweater, maybe she'd go curl up under her quilts and take a quick nap. But when she dropped the scarf in the basket next to her chair and stood, she had to stop and cough again.

Andy was at her side in an instant, supporting her. "Maybe you should go see the doctor."

She scoffed, which wasn't easy to do when she was so keenly aware of the weight of his arm around her waist. It was Andy Miller, for goodness' sake. She didn't even like him. "I'm fine. I'm going to rest for a little while and then whip up a batch of soup."

After catching her breath, she stepped free of his support—which felt way too much like an embrace—and walked toward the stairs. She managed just fine on her own, but she could swear she felt Andy watching her all the way up.

"GOOD AFTERNOON, DEMAREST Insurance." Lauren glanced at the clock, counting the minutes. It was Friday and she wanted out. "How can I help you today?"

"Lauren, it's your father."

"Hi, Dad." He refused to call her cell phone because he was afraid she'd answer it while driving and hit a tree. Or so he said whenever she asked him why he wouldn't just call her cell. "What's up?"

"Your mother has a cold."

"There's one going around." The silver lining of being too busy to visit her mother recently was not having to feel guilty about being the germ carrier.

"She's out of her cold medicine. You know the one she likes?"

"I know the one." She really didn't have time for this. "I'm leaving here in a few minutes. I'll get her some and run it over to the house."

"You're a good daughter. How's that grandson of mine? Staying out of trouble?"

"He's doing really good, actually. Staying out of trouble and doing well in school."

"If he's keeping his grades up, I can teach him to drive now, no?"

Lauren winced. Since her father refused to acknowledge the existence of his former son-in-law, that meant it was his job—as the man of the family—to teach Nick how to drive. She hadn't yet come up with a believable excuse that would save her son from that horrible fate.

Lauren had had to suffer through it and remembered the experience as being a lot more yelling, cursing in Polish and clutching his chest than driving instruction. She was convinced he was the reason her mother refused to learn how to drive. She'd probably had one lesson from her husband and quit the whole thing.

"I'll think about it," she hedged. "It's only been a little over a month, so I want a little more progress before I commit to spending that kind of money."

"What money? I'll teach him, I said."

"He still has to take a class, Dad. If he doesn't take the class, he can't get his license until he's eighteen."

"That's stupid. He doesn't need a class if I teach him."

No, but he might need medication. Lauren decided it was time to change the subject. "Does Mom need anything besides cold medicine?"

He said she didn't, so Lauren claimed she had a customer waiting and got off the phone.

She'd just found a parking spot near the market when her cell phone rang. It was tempting to ignore it, but she was always afraid if she did that, it would be about Nick. When she saw Ryan's name on the screen, she was glad she'd checked. "Hi."

"Miss me?"

"You've been gone?"

"Funny. You doing anything this weekend?"

Just everything a working mother did on the weekends, which was just about everything. "Nothing I can't be tempted away from by a better offer."

"I borrowed Mitch's bike for the weekend. I was thinking we could take off in the morning and head over to the coast. Cruise down it for a while, then cut across to Brookline. Spend the night at my place, then head back in the morning in plenty of time to get home for Nick."

He wanted to take her to see his house? She wondered for a second if he'd been talking to Rose, but then something else he'd said snagged in her mind. "Bike. Do you mean his Harley? You do know it's the third week of October, right?"

"And I checked the weather forecast. It's going to be in the sixties, which is perfect riding weather if you have a good sweater or a leather jacket. And maybe gloves, just in case we end up out after the sun's gone down."

"That's crazy. *You're* crazy."

"But you're going to go with me, right?"

She sighed. "Yes. I want to see your house. I hear it's very beige."

"Don't let Rosie bullshit you. It's sandstone with cameo trim."

"So it's…a darker shade of beige with a lighter beige trim?"

"Smart-ass. Do you want to go or not?"

"Yeah, I want to go."

"How about I pick you up at eight and we'll have some breakfast before we hit the road?"

"Sounds good." She wanted to invite him to spend the night and they could have breakfast at her place, but she didn't think he'd be shy about inviting himself if that's what he wanted to do.

"Okay, I'll see you at eight. I'd talk longer, but I have two more meetings before I can leave here and I need to look at some prints before the first one."

"See you in the morning then."

He wasn't going to make it back to Whitford until

late, she thought as she shoved her phone back into her purse. She couldn't blame him for not wanting to come over. He'd probably fall face-first into his bed and crash.

By the time she found the cold medicine her mother liked and chatted up Fran for a moment, she knew she wasn't going to be able to spend more than a few minutes with her mom and still make it home before Dean showed up.

Her parents lived eight miles out of town, and almost two of those miles were down a winding dirt road. It was impossible to rush when driving to and from their house.

Usually, no matter when Lauren arrived, her mother would be outside, deadheading flowers or reading in the hammock or sipping tea on the porch. Today, though, she found her mom in the living room. She was on the couch, television remote in hand.

"Hi, Mom. I brought you your medicine."

"Thank you, sweetheart. I told your father I could wait until he got home."

"Maybe, unlike you, he remembers the last time you were sick and he got the wrong kind and had to hear about what an inattentive husband he is for the next week."

Her mother waved her hand, dismissing that subject. "How's Nicky? He doesn't have this cold, does he? It sounds like you did."

"He's good. I had it earlier in the week, but Rose Davis gave me her miracle chicken soup and it worked like magic."

"She gave me that recipe once. The seasonings were ridiculous, though, so I tweaked it." She pulled a tissue out of the box and dabbed at her nose. "It wasn't miraculous at all, in my opinion."

Lauren wanted to point out she hadn't actually made Rosie's soup if she'd changed the recipe, but she didn't have time to argue. "Speaking of Nick, I'm going out of town tomorrow for an overnight and Nick will be with his dad, so if you see Dean's number on the caller ID, you have to pick up, okay?"

"Where are you going?"

She could lie. That would probably be easiest and relatively harmless, like telling her dad she had a customer to get off the phone. But Lauren riding out of town on the back of a Harley was something she could see being casually mentioned at the hardware store. "Ryan's taking me to his house in Brookline. We're going to take Mitch's motorcycle."

"You told me it wasn't serious so you weren't dragging him over here for a family dinner. But you're going away with him overnight?"

"It's complicated."

"What? He doesn't want to have dinner with us?"

"He's not the one who said no. I did. You've known him and his brothers and sister for their whole lives. You knew his parents."

"And his grandfather. He passed away shortly after we bought the store."

"See? This whole meet-the-parents thing is ridiculous and he's too busy for it right now."

"What's going to happen when he's done working on the lodge?"

Lauren dropped into a chair, resigned to finishing the conversation. "I don't know, but I'll find out soon. They're almost done."

"Have you talked about it?"

"No, not yet."

"If it's serious, you need to talk about it."

"I know that, Mom." She took a deep breath, reminding herself grown women didn't snap at their sick mothers. "I don't know how serious *he* is. Maybe he's just having a fling while back in the old hometown."

"Is that what you think?"

She shook her head. "I don't think so. But I think the fact he lives in Massachusetts and we live in Maine is complicated. And then there's Nick and...other stuff. It's just a lot to think about."

"What other stuff?"

"Nothing." She didn't want to talk about it and made a big deal out of checking the time. "I'm barely going to make it back in time to meet Dean. I have to run."

"Talk to him."

Lauren walked over to kiss her mom's forehead. "I will."

Just as soon as she figured out what to say.

## CHAPTER SIXTEEN

IT WAS STILL damp and chilly when Ryan drove into Lauren's driveway the next morning, but he hoped it would burn off and warm up a little by the time they'd eaten breakfast.

Lauren met him at her front door with a smile and a kiss. "You look tired."

He was, but seeing her perked him up. Perked him up a *lot*, actually, but he was afraid if he talked her into a morning quickie, it wouldn't be so quick. They had a good five and a half hours or more on the road in front of them.

She'd packed some overnight things into an oversize purse, which he stowed in one of the bike's side bags, where he'd already stashed the leather jacket he'd borrowed from Josh. It would be too big for Lauren, but he'd rather have it and not need it. For now, the wool sweater she was wearing over a turtleneck would probably be enough. After she'd tucked her phone into her purse, he put that in the side bag, too, and she was ready.

Once he had the big bike balanced, he jerked his head to let her know he was ready. Steadying herself with her hands on his shoulders, she swung her leg over and settled on the padded seat behind him. When she trailed her hands over his back to his waist and her thighs hugged his hips, Ryan made a mental note to go motorcycle shopping.

It didn't take long to get to the diner, but when he helped her off, he saw her cheeks were pink from the cold. "Maybe we should just take the truck."

"No!" Lauren smiled and rubbed her hands on her jeans to warm them up. "This is invigorating. I love it."

He wasn't so sure "invigorating" would be the right word when they were doing fifty, but he had the leather coat and gloves for her if it didn't warm up as much as the forecast claimed it would.

Paige waved when they walked in and gestured toward an empty table near the back. The place was doing one hell of a Saturday-morning business, but she looked as though she had it under control. He wasn't sure how she did it. The ability to carry more than one cup of coffee at a time without sloshing it everywhere was impressive enough, never mind remembering who ordered what.

Ryan slid into the booth across from Lauren, aware that nobody in the diner had given them a second look. Once you stopped attracting curious glances and triggering whispered conversations, he supposed you were a real couple.

Paige barely slowed down as she dropped off their coffees and took their order, but when she brought their food, she managed to stand still for a minute.

"They accepted our offer on the house," she told them, happiness practically pouring off her in waves.

"The one with the barn and the land and the giant shower?" Lauren asked.

"That's the one. Mitch wants to have some remodeling done before we move in, but I don't know if I can wait."

It was on the tip of Ryan's tongue to make the offer. He was a builder and Mitch was his brother, after all, so it was only right he offer to handle the remodeling. And it would give him an excuse to stay in Whitford longer. With Lauren.

But he'd probably lose his business. At the very least, he'd definitely lose Wendi and he couldn't afford that, so he kept his mouth shut.

"I definitely want to try to move in before Thanksgiving though."

Ryan laughed. "I don't think things move that fast."

"You never know. The house is empty, so it's just a matter of paperwork. I wonder if Rosie would mind if I hosted Thanksgiving this year. If she doesn't, you guys will come, right?"

"Sure," he said before Lauren had a chance to reply.

It was only after Paige ran off to deliver an order and Lauren gave him a funny look before digging into her scrambled eggs that he started second-guessing his answer. Had Paige been asking each of them—as one of her best friends and her brother-in-law—over for turkey in her new house, or had the invitation been to them as a couple?

He'd answered for them as a couple, he realized. Like the diners around them who'd stopped taking note of them being together, he'd taken for granted they were in the kind of relationship that assumed they'd spend Thanksgiving together. But, aside from the fact that he had no idea if *she* felt that way, Lauren had a son and a family of her own. He probably shouldn't go around making those kinds of assumptions.

"Will we actually be able to see the ocean from the road?" Lauren asked, and the moment to apologize or even get her take on the situation seemed to have passed.

"Here and there, for a bit. I was thinking once we

get down to the coast, we'd go down as far as Hampton Beach before cutting across to Brookline. We can stop there for a little while if you want."

"I'd like that. I love the ocean in the fall, when the waves are choppy and gray, especially if the sky's a little stormy."

"We don't want *too* stormy," he pointed out, and she laughed.

By the time they'd lingered over third mugs of coffee and chatted with Paige a little more, the sun had put a serious dent in the early-morning autumn chill. Rolling out of Whitford, they headed east and rode for a couple of hours until they hit Route 1. After making a pit stop, they headed south down the coast.

He definitely needed to buy a motorcycle, he thought again. Lauren was having a great time, her body relaxed against his as she pointed things out to him and yelled to him over the wind. Mostly her hands rested casually at his waist and, when they were cruising along, he'd rest his left hand on her knee. There was intimacy to riding that made him feel closer to her than sitting side by side in a pickup.

By the time they rolled into Hampton Beach, he figured her legs and butt must be getting tired of straddling the bike's seat. His certainly were, though he'd be loath to admit it. He found a place to park the motorcycle and gave her a hand off.

"I think I got numb from the waist down about an hour ago," she said with a shaky laugh when her legs wobbled a little.

Once she was steady, he took her hand and led her to the public restrooms and then in search of food. After scarfing down some hot dogs and coffee, they walked out onto the beach. It wasn't stormy, but the ocean was gray and a little whipped up.

"It's so nice to be out of Whitford for a while," she said, turning her face to the ocean breeze.

"When's the last time you went out of town? For fun, I mean."

"Not counting my monthly trek into the city to stock up on groceries, which definitely isn't fun since I take my mother, I can't even remember. Hailey and I did a salon trip the day before the wedding. She talked me into shopping, too, for the dress and at the lingerie store."

"Remind me to thank Hailey."

She gave him a naughty smile. "I'm wearing that bra-and-panty set right now."

He groaned, instantly hard. "I have to spend another hour-plus on that bike."

"And so do I. That thing really vibrates like crazy at certain RPMs."

Yup, he was definitely going motorcycle shopping very, very soon.

They walked the beach for a while, hand in hand, watching the waves and the other people enjoying the warm fall day.

"I want to get home before the temperature starts dropping," he finally said, reluctantly leading her back to where they'd parked.

Once he'd backed the big beast out and she'd climbed on behind him, Lauren leaned forward and ran her hands over his thighs. "Today's been an amazing treat for me. You might just get lucky tonight."

He was already lucky. Taking her to his bed would just be the cherry on top of the lucky-bastard sundae.

Rose was right, Lauren thought, standing in Ryan's living room. His house was very beige. Not that it wasn't gorgeous. She'd been stunned when he pulled into the driveway of a massive, beautiful house surrounded by impeccable landscaping. Sure, it was beige—or sandstone, as he reminded her—but that didn't make it less attractive.

The inside was attractive, too, but looking around, it reminded her of one of the model homes that builders used to sell to customers. They were done up to look like real houses, right down to decorations on the walls, but nobody really lived there. Even cutting him slack because he'd been away a month, the house didn't feel like Ryan's home to her somehow. Despite a few signs of man-debris lying around, it felt more like a hotel.

He gave her the grand tour and everything fell in line with what a show house would look like. His kitchen was gorgeous, though she suspected it was largely wasted on him. The half bath was nice, too. Upstairs, he showed her a massive game room over the garage and then three guest rooms and a very nice full bathroom.

Then he took her hand and led her back downstairs. Off the living room and down a short hallway she'd barely noticed, they came to his bedroom. It was huge, with a massive bed centered on the outside wall. She peeked into the master bath and her eyes widened. Beige tones or not, he'd spared no expense in the master suite.

It was when she turned back toward the door to face him that she smiled. On the wall behind him was a chaotic arrangement of photographs. They were in a variety of wood and metal frames of all shapes and sizes and colors, with no rhyme or reason to how they were hung. With a quick scan, she spotted Rose and Liz and what looked like a Christmas-card photo of Mike and Lisa's boys. They were all there, she was sure.

"There you are," she said softly.

He looked over his shoulder, frowning. "What do you mean?"

"I've been looking for some part of this house that's really *you*. I found it."

She watched his face soften as he looked over the photos. "I have business meetings here sometimes and I like to keep my personal life and business separate and I don't want to keep them in a drawer, so there they hang."

"I like it." She walked to the bed and leaned over it, pressing on the mattress with her hands. "I also like this bed. Mattress is a little on the hard side, though."

"It's not the only thing." She jumped a little when he stepped up behind her, so close she could feel his erection through their clothes.

"Are you serious? I've just started getting the feeling back in the lower half of my body."

He slid his hand between her legs, rubbing the seam of her jeans. "Can you feel that?"

"Mmm-hmm." She pushed against his hand, enjoying the delicious friction.

"Undo your jeans."

She heard his zipper, followed by the rustle of a condom wrapper, and did as she was told.

Ryan grasped the waist of her jeans and tugged them, along with her panties, down over her thighs. Then he pressed one hand against her back, bending her over the bed, while the other guided his hard length into her.

She gasped at the deep penetration, putting one hand on the bed to steady herself. He tangled his fingers in her hair, tugging her head up so her back arched. The rush of heat weakened her knees, but his other hand went to her hip, holding her still so he could drive into her.

"All day long on that damn bike, with your body wrapped around me, I've thought about fucking you." His fingers tugged at her hair while his strokes came faster and harder, driving her thighs against the edge of the mattress. "Then seeing your ass, like that, with you bent over my bed… You are…so…damn…sweet."

He thrust hard with every word and Lauren bunched the covers in her fists, pulling them to her mouth.

"Scream. Nobody will hear you but me."

The orgasm hit hard and strong and fast and she might have screamed. He released her hair and used both hands to rock her hips as he came, driving into her with hard, uneven strokes. Then, when the tremors had passed, he sank to the soft carpeting and, breathless and more than a little weak in the knees, she went down with him.

"Holy shit," he said after a few minutes. "That was…I don't even have a word for it."

"Holy shit sums it up pretty well." She stared up at the ceiling. "Nice carpeting, by the way."

"Thanks. Hardwood's all the rage in bedrooms now. Allergies and asthma and all that. But I like a nice carpet under my feet first thing in the morning."

"That bed sure did look comfy."

He chuckled, groping around for her hand. She laced her fingers through his and he squeezed. "I swear I had every intention of getting you *into* my bed."

"Half-under it's kind of close."

An hour later, they were curled up on the couch, eating pizza delivered to the door. Lauren had to admit she liked that. Whitford didn't have any place that delivered unless Fran was going by your place anyway and happened to be in a good mood. But she didn't cook it for you.

The rosy afterglow of sex and the satisfaction of delicious, extra-cheese takeout were dimmed a little by the big old elephant in the room. Maybe not in the room, exactly, but it was taking up space in her head, anyway. She'd had a lot of time to think on the back of the bike, and her mind wasn't going to rest until she knew what Ryan was thinking.

"So back at the diner," she said, setting her crust on her paper plate, "you told Paige if she was all moved in and Rosie didn't mind, that we'd go to her new house for Thanksgiving."

He paused in midbite, then slowly chewed and swallowed. "Yeah, about that. I probably shouldn't have answered for you."

"I guess the question is, do you see us as…I don't know, the kind of couple who goes to Thanksgiving dinner at the family's together?"

He gave her a grin, which she knew preceded some funny comment meant to deflect the conversation away from becoming too serious. Or to keep her from asking questions he didn't know the answers to. "Well, yeah. I'm your *you know, whatever*, right?"

"Yeah, you are."

"But I know you have Nick and your parents to consider, so I should have put her off and talked to you first."

She nodded, picking some of the crispy melted cheese off the crust to pop into her mouth. "So it's whether or not I already had plans and not our relationship having a question mark?"

"You think our relationship has a question mark?"

"Don't you?" Looking at her pizza crust was easier than looking at him, so she kept picking at it.

"I don't think it has an exclamation point yet, but more than a question mark. Maybe one of those dot-dot-dot things?"

So their relationship had an ellipsis. Like there was more to come, but it was open-ended due to lack of detail. "Okay."

"But you think it has a question mark?"

"I think it has a lot of question marks."

He set his empty paper plate on the coffee table and then leaned back against the couch, his body angled to face her. "There are always question marks."

"But if we're heading toward being the kind of couple who spends family holidays together, I'd like to turn some of those question marks into periods. Or at least into the dot-dot-dots."

"I know you have a son and family and a home and a life in Whitford. I know I have a home and a business in Brookline that I need to get back to. Four and a half hours across state lines is a big question mark, but it's not one that can be answered today."

"And you want kids of your own, Ryan. That's a big one, too."

That widened his eyes. "It's probably a little premature to be talking about having babies."

"No, it's really not, since we're talking about our relationship. Babies are relevant because you want them and I'm not having any more."

"Oh. Did you…you know, have the surgery or whatever?"

"No, but I don't need surgery to know I'm thirty-four years old, I have a sixteen-year-old son and I don't want to start all over again with another baby. Trust me, that clock hasn't ticked in years."

"And you're convinced I want babies?"

"I saw you with your cousins' kids. And look around." She waved a hand in the direction of the stairs. "You built a four-bedroom house."

"And I still barely had enough room for the entire family when I threw Sean's welcome-home party. Now that Mitch and Sean have wives and the babies are going to start coming, I can't fit everybody in. I'll be throwing sleeping bags down in the game room."

"Don't you usually have family get-togethers at the lodge?"

"Yeah. But Sean was going from Boston straight to New Hampshire. Liz was flying in and out of Logan with less than forty-eight hours between flights, and I live here. It made more sense for Josh and Rose to drive down than for all of us to go up."

She wasn't sure if he was being deliberately obtuse or if he didn't get what she was trying to say. "My point is that you didn't build a four-bedroom house on the off chance your family would all show up at the same time."

"No, I built a four-bedroom house with two and a half bathrooms and a bonus room over the garage because it's the ideal meeting of floor plan and price for this neighborhood. I'm a builder, Lauren. Everything I do is about the market and the property's resale value."

It all sounded very logical, but she had a hard time believing it. "I don't think you'd be happy never having kids of your own."

"I'll be honest. I haven't thought that far ahead. But I do know, without a question mark, that being with you makes me happy."

"Being with you makes me happy, too, but—"

"Sometimes, if you stick with something and go with it, those buts have a way of working themselves out."

She wanted to tell him it wasn't that easy for her. She had a son and she had to consider him, too, and whether or not he might get attached to Ryan. But she knew Ryan knew that, and she knew he was too decent a guy to toy with her if he didn't believe those buts would work themselves out.

Besides, she'd had a wonderful day and she didn't want to bring it down any more than she had. "Self-resolving buts, huh?"

"Yeah." He grinned, as though sensing she was ready to put the discussion to bed, if only temporarily. "Besides, you told me I might get lucky tonight."

She laughed. "You did get lucky."

"That was evening. *Now* it's night."

"You're insatiable."

"If that means I can't get enough of you, you're right." He stood up and held out his hand.

It was an offer she couldn't refuse. And maybe he was right, she told herself as he tried to pull her shirt off and walk at the same time. Instead of getting worked up and worrying, she'd go with it and hope those buts resolved themselves.

RYAN CURSED AND slapped the snooze button again. He needed a quieter alarm clock. Preferably one that had a longer snooze time, too.

"You've hit that four times," Lauren muttered from somewhere deep inside the nest of covers she'd made by stealing his.

"It keeps going off."

"And when it does, you're supposed to get up. I swear, you're worse than Nick. At least he keeps his clock on the far side of his room so he has to work for those few extra minutes."

"I notice *you* haven't gotten up yet."

She snuggled deeper under the blankets. They looked warm. Too bad he didn't have any. "I'm waiting for you to go make coffee."

"I have one of those kinds that instantly brews a single cup."

"Good. When my single cup is instantly brewed, I'll get up."

He slapped the lump he thought might be her ass, then swung his feet to the floor and scrubbed at his face. The alarm would go off again in a few minutes and she'd have to leave her cozy nest to deal with it.

After turning on the coffee machine so it could heat up, he put the coffee in it and stuck a cup under the spout. Sure enough, just as he was stirring the milk and sugar into the first mug, he heard the *beep beep* of his alarm, followed a few minutes later by Lauren's bare feet slapping on the polished kitchen floor.

She'd thrown on one of his older T-shirts and brushed her hair into a messy ponytail, but she looked cute as hell anyway, all sleepy-eyed and utterly kissable.

"Coffee."

He set the cup on the marble countertop of the bar and gestured for her to pull up a stool before turning back to the machine to make a cup for himself. About halfway through her cup, Lauren started waking up and even smiled at him.

"How'd you sleep?" he asked, leaning on the opposite side of the bar to drink his coffee. He couldn't look at her face if he sat next to her.

"Good. Your bed's amazing. How about you?"

"Once I got to go to sleep, I crashed. And you call me insatiable."

Her cheeks got a little pink. "Complaining?"

"Hell, no. As a matter of fact—"

"No."

Damn. "I meant after you finish your coffee, of course."

"After I finish this cup of coffee, I'm going to have another cup of coffee." She pointed her finger at him. "And *you* should have shaved a little better. I have stubble burn on my thighs and I have to sit on the back of that bike for hours."

"Could put a little cream on it." She arched an eyebrow at him and he laughed, holding up his hand. "I mean the real stuff, honest. Moisturizing crap."

"I'll definitely put some moisturizing crap on it, thank you."

"You're a little cranky in the morning."

"You should see me on Mondays."

He laughed and got the machine ready to brew her a second cup, but he didn't feel all that amused. It would probably be a long time before he got to wake up next to Lauren on a Monday morning. His brain tried to tack an *if ever* on the end of that thought, but he resisted. He would. It would just take a while to sort out.

It took another hour to get her out the door so they could grab some breakfast. All he had was a package of English muffins and they were in the freezer, so she hadn't been too enthusiastic about those. It was colder than he'd anticipated, so he made her put on Josh's leather coat and the gloves before they hit the highway.

He kept his speed a little lower than he usually would, because of the cold, so Nick was already home when they get there. He waved at them through the window while Ryan rolled the bike to a stop next to Lauren's car.

"I'll just go," he told her once he'd gotten her purse and tote out of the side bag.

"No, come in for a bit. I know you must have to pee as badly as I do, and you can visit with Nick for a few minutes, at least."

He'd planned to pull over and take a leak on the side of the road as soon as he was out of sight of her house, but her plan was probably better. Officer Bob Durgin, the old bastard, hated the Kowalskis and would love to happen by and slap him with an indecent exposure ticket. Come to think of it, Drew Miller would probably get a kick out of it, too.

"Sure, thanks." He carried her bags in and said hi to Nick, who'd sprawled on the couch, while Lauren sprinted for the bathroom.

"Heard you're kicking butt at school lately," he said.

Nick nodded and Ryan could see the pride on his face. "It's actually not that hard if you pay attention and do the homework."

"Keep it up."

"I will. Mom's going to see when the next driver's ed class starts."

"Cool." He almost offered to take him out for practice hours when the time came, but in the nick of time he remembered he wouldn't be around. He'd be in Brookline on the weekdays and Nick would be with Dean on the weekends.

One of those question marks Lauren talked about. A pretty shitty one, too. Not only did he need to build a relationship with her son if the one with Lauren was going to work, but he liked Nick.

Once Lauren was done in the bathroom, Ryan took

his turn and returned to the living room to find them in midconversation.

"The movie was kind of dumb because Alex and Adrienne are little," Nick was saying, "but Jody made popcorn and Dad turned off all the lights and it was kinda cool."

"I told you they wouldn't be upset."

Nick shrugged. "Jody asked if I'd watch the kids one night a month and I said sure. I don't mind doing it. Just not every weekend."

"I'm glad you talked to them."

Ryan felt like a third wheel, standing there watching them talk. It wasn't difficult to figure out what they were talking about, but there was no place in the conversation for him. Especially since it concerned Dean.

When Lauren saw him standing in the junction of the hallway and living room, she smiled. "I was thinking about making some hot chocolate to warm me up. You want some?"

"Hey, the game starts in like ten minutes," Nick said. "You should stay and watch it with us."

Ryan had hoped to make it back to the lodge in time to watch it with Josh, but what the hell? Probably more fun to watch it with Nick anyway. He looked at Lauren and, when she nodded, said, "Sure. Sounds like a plan."

It was a good time, he thought later, when he kissed Lauren goodbye and walked to the bike, even if he was going to freeze his ass off between there and the lodge since the temp had gone down with the sun. He'd spent a few hours yelling at her television and high-fiving her son while she curled up at the other end of the couch and read a book.

"I'll be pretty slammed this week," he told her. "I've got a lot to wrap up before I go back to Brookline next

Sunday. But I'll call you and I'll see you tomorrow when you pick up Nick. Unless you want me to bring him home."

If he brought Nick home after work, maybe she'd invite him to stay for dinner and they could all hang out and watch some television together.

"I'll come get him. I don't want to miss out on Rosie's baked goods du jour."

"Okay." So they'd leave it as it was. "I'll see you then."

She waved to him from the window as he backed the bike out of the driveway, so he gunned the engine a little taking off and saw her laugh.

One more week. Then it was going to start getting harder unless he figured out what the hell he was doing and how to be in two places at once.

## CHAPTER SEVENTEEN

ROSE WAS WORRIED about Ryan. Watching him through the window as he talked and laughed with Lauren and Nick should have warmed her heart. Instead it was adding to the forehead wrinkles and the gray hair.

Since she'd seen it happen on Monday and again on Tuesday when Lauren picked up Nick, Rose was pretty certain she'd see it again today. As soon as Lauren's car disappeared down the road, Ryan's smile would fade. His shoulders would tense, his jaw would clench and she'd have to say his name three times to get his attention.

Her boy was in love and he had no idea what to do about it. The first step would be admitting it to himself, but she wasn't sure he'd gotten that far yet. If Mitch was in town instead of whichever city needed a building imploded this time, she would have seriously considered interfering to the point of asking him to have a heart-to-heart chat with Ryan, but he was out of town until Friday or Saturday.

Coughing, she turned away from the window when Nick started toward the car. She wasn't so nosy she'd spy on Ryan kissing Lauren goodbye.

Five minutes later, he walked into the kitchen. Just as she'd thought, it was as though somebody had turned off his inner light switch.

"I walked around the place with Dill and Matt earlier," he said, going to the sink to wash his hands. "They're done here. They're going to grab their stuff and head out shortly."

"Just like that? I could have made them a special dinner or dessert or something. All I have is a chocolate cake." She was going to miss having those two around. Unlike some men who sometimes took her for granted, Matt and Dill appreciated her fussing over them and made sure she knew it.

"I told you on day one that they're employees, not family. And they're leaving now because I told them they don't have to report in to Wendi until Monday morning, so if they go tonight, they'll have four full days at home."

Normally she would have snapped him with a towel or given him a verbal dressing-down. Not only did she not care for his tone, but she wasn't stupid. She knew Dill and Matt worked for him. But she cut him some slack because she knew he was twisted up inside.

Still, it took a lot of willpower not to get weepy when the two guys passed through the kitchen on their way to pack their things. They'd kept their shared room very neat, probably out of fear of the boss, so it wouldn't take them very long.

"Can I ask you a stupid question?" Ryan asked when their footsteps had faded down the hall.

"You can try, but I don't think you can top Sean wanting to know how much Kool-Aid he'd have to drink to turn his pee blue, especially since he was old enough to shave when he asked it."

That got a brief smile out of him. "If you had met a guy you wanted to marry when Katie was younger and he wanted you to move away from Whitford, would you?"

"I don't know," she said honestly. "It wasn't just Katie. I can't imagine I'd have left you five kids and you weren't mine to take with me. And Katie's dad was gone. Nick's dad gets him every weekend."

Ryan's jaw flexed and he gave a terse nod.

"I'm sorry," she said. "Was I supposed to pretend I don't know this is about Lauren?"

"Yeah."

"Too late, so talk to me."

"That was pretty much it." When she just looked at him, waiting, he leaned against the counter and crossed his arms. "She also thinks I won't be happy long-term because she doesn't want any more kids."

"Some might consider that more important than two hundred miles. How do *you* feel about it?"

He shrugged. "I always thought I'd have kids someday. To be honest, I've never really thought about *not* having kids."

She wasn't sure what to say to that. She'd bandaged their skinned knees and nursed them through colds and teenage melodrama, but making a decision not to be a father was something a man had to do for himself.

"I love her."

That did warm her heart, no matter how twisted up he was because of it. "Does that make it easier or harder?"

"Both."

"I wish there was an easy answer I could give you."

He smiled, looking a little more like his usual self. "I do, too."

"What I *can* do is serve up some slices of that chocolate cake."

"We haven't had dinner yet."

"Sometimes you have to have dessert first. Besides,

I'm not letting Dill and Matt leave here without having some."

"I might have two slices and say screw dinner altogether."

"That's not the worst plan I've ever heard." She started to laugh, but it triggered another damn coughing jag.

"You okay? You've been coughing a lot lately."

"'Tis the season. Grab some plates and let's get that cake cut before those guys escape."

ON WEDNESDAY MORNING, Hailey called Lauren at work. "I'm going to piss everybody off and close the library for an hour lunch today at one. Can you get out of the office? We can go to the diner and harass Paige and eat too many French fries."

"Is something wrong?"

"Nope. I just haven't seen you or Paige hardly at all since her wedding and it looks like this is the only way I can schedule myself into your lives. But let's call it an emergency if it makes Gary feel better."

Lauren's boss had a fleeting moment of panic when she said she was taking off an hour for lunch, but he recovered quickly. She was allowed a lunch break but, more often than not, ate something from home at her desk. He was smart enough not to complain on the rare occasion she actually left the office.

When one o'clock rolled around, she flipped the answering machine to a prerecorded "closed for lunch" message she rarely used but which saved her from having to scour for messages on Gary's desk, and then reminded him she was leaving.

Hailey was already at the diner when Lauren got there and she was surprised to see Paige sitting at a booth with her. Paige rarely even stood still at lunch-time, never mind sat down.

Then Lauren saw a young woman in a Trailside Diner T-shirt step out of the kitchen, and she got more confused. How did she not know Paige had hired some-body new? And it was Whitford. How did she not know the somebody Paige had hired?

Hailey spotted her and slid over on the bench, wav-ing her over. Lauren hung her coat on one of the hooks near the door and joined them.

"Who is that?"

Paige looked over her shoulder. "That's Tori Burns, Jilly's niece. Gavin's cousin."

"Did I know Jilly has a brother?"

Paige laughed at her confusion. "Probably not. Jilly's originally from Portland, remember? Mike met her at college and brought her home. Tori moved here a couple of weeks ago because her parents are divorcing and it's pretty ugly. They keep trying to put her in the middle of it, so she packed up and moved into one of the apart-ments over the bank."

"She looks like she's twelve."

"She's almost twenty-five, actually."

Lauren scowled, feeling old. "So now that you're Mrs. Kowalski, are you becoming a lady of leisure?"

"That's what I asked her, just before you walked in," Hailey said.

"I'd go nuts," Paige said. "Tori's *very* part-time. It'd be nice for me to not get up at four-thirty in the morning every single day, especially when Mitch is home, and there are times Ava wants to do something in the eve-ning. With only two of us, it's really hard to cover each other's shifts without dropping from exhaustion. Tori works from home and just wants to pick up a few hours here and there to get out of the house and meet people."

"What does she do for work?" Lauren asked.

Paige shrugged. "She didn't say."

"And you didn't ask?"

"No."

"Did you have her fill out an application? Did she write down her current job?" Lauren asked.

"No. She's Jilly's niece and she's willing to work odd hours for little money. I had her fill out the IRS forms and that was that."

"It's so sad." Hailey shook her head. "Two years you've lived here and you still haven't figured out how to be all up in everybody's business. Fran needs to give you some lessons."

"The person whose business I want to be all up in is Lauren's."

Lauren looked at Paige and laughed. "Since you're married to a Kowalski and spend a fair amount of time talking to Rose, I'm going to take a wild guess and say you already know more about my business than some people."

"Like me," Hailey grumbled.

"Actually," Paige said, "Ryan's kind of the close-mouthed one of the bunch. A genetic flaw or throwback gene or something. But anyway, I heard that, starting Sunday night when he leaves, he'll be back to only coming up on the weekends."

"He has to run his business. He's been gone a month already."

"And what are you going to do?" Hailey asked.

Lauren felt herself tensing up and tried to force herself to relax. She'd thought she was meeting Hailey for a fun girl's lunch with Paige, so she hadn't expected the Spanish Inquisition.

Tori chose that moment to finally stop by the table, giving Lauren a couple extra minutes to remind herself these were her best friends and of course she was going to tell them everything. That's what best friends were for.

After they'd ordered and she'd put in her own for a grilled cheese and coleslaw, with copious amounts of coffee, she sighed and started folding and refolding her napkin. "I'm going to roll with it and see where it goes."

Both women frowned, but it was Hailey who spoke. "That doesn't sound very...I don't know what word I'm looking for."

"Committed," Paige said. "Serious. Stable. Relationship-ish."

Lauren snorted. "What's not relationship-ish about it? And what, exactly, do you two think I can do about it? He has to go back to work."

"Long-distance relationships suck," Hailey said, even though Lauren knew for a fact she'd never been in one.

"Paige, Mitch travels and you don't get to see him every single day, but that was still relationship-ish enough so you married him."

"But he's away for a few days and then home for a chunk of time. And, unlike Ryan, he has more freedom to work from home, plus he moved home from New York to here. Kowalski Custom Builders can't move to Whitford."

Not and survive, no. "I'd see him on weekends and holidays. And vacations."

"Like parental visitation rights, only not," Hailey pointed out, and Lauren had to bite down on her lip to keep from snapping at her friend.

Then the flash of anger fizzled and she found herself on the brink of bursting into tears. "Stop."

Both women instantly went into consolation mode, but that almost made it worse.

"Just how serious are you?" Paige asked once they were all fairly certain Lauren wasn't going to have a complete emotional breakdown at the table.

"I'm pretty sure I'm in love with him," she confessed for the first time, even to herself.

"But?" Hailey prompted.

"That's the thing. Ryan is convinced the buts will all resolve themselves if we just roll with it."

"But?" This time it was Paige and it made Lauren smile a little.

"How can I build a life with a guy who's only around on weekends? And how often will he get to see Nick? The few holidays he doesn't spend with Dean?"

"Rose is worried about how long he'll be able to keep up with that kind of schedule—working all week, then driving up here Friday night and back on Sunday night to go back to work on Monday morning."

Hailey nodded. "Sometimes he's going to want to chill at home. Mow his lawn or sleep in or go out with the guys."

They weren't telling her anything she hadn't already thought of, but hearing it out loud made it more real somehow. "Maybe it's because I've been a single mom for so long but, if and when I get married, I don't want to keep being a single mom. Know what I mean?"

They both nodded, but Tori appeared with their food and the conversation paused until she'd brought Hailey vinegar for her fries and refilled their coffee mugs.

"So the obvious question," Paige asked when they

were alone again, "is if you've considered moving to Brookline."

"I've thought about it a little. But then I think about having to find a new job down there and selling my house and I have no idea how Nick would take it. He likes Ryan, but enough to move to a new state and a new school? Then there's the fact I'd need Dean's permission to move Nick to Mass. It makes my head hurt and I'm not going to tie myself up in knots when Ryan hasn't even hinted at wanting us there."

"I must be reading the wrong self-help books," Hailey said, "because I have no idea what to tell you."

"Me, either." Paige pointed one of her fries at Lauren. "But I do know one thing. If Ryan loves you, nothing will stop him from being with you."

"He hasn't said he does. Or hinted that he does."

"He may not realize it yet. If he's anything like his brother, it'll take a while to sink in."

"And, in the meantime, I'll get about thirty-six hours of what's left of him after all the working and driving each week."

"You know, this is really awkward," Paige said, staring down at her plate. "I want to ask you if you're going to break it off with him, but I just remembered he's my brother-in-law now, so maybe I don't want to know."

"I should," Lauren said, her heart breaking a little. "I should end it before we get any more involved or he wears himself out or Nick gets any more attached to him. He should find somebody free to step into his life, who wants to give him a horde of kids, which is a whole 'nother can of worms I haven't mentioned. So, yes, I should break it off with him."

"But?" This time they said it in unison.

"I can't. When I'm with him, I can't imagine *not*

being with him, no matter how hard it gets. There's no way I could tell him to leave and not come back. I just have to roll with it, I guess."

RYAN WOULD HAVE preferred to meet Dean in a bar somewhere and maybe buy him a beer, but Whitford didn't have a bar. Plus the guy was working, so he had to settle for a soda at the picnic table in the backyard of the house he was painting.

"Thanks for agreeing to talk to me," was what Ryan opened with, but he wasn't really sure where to go from there.

"Is there a problem with Nick?"

"No. Nick's doing great. It's about Lauren, actually."

Dean gave a dry laugh. "Since I managed to end our marriage so badly that it took a year to rebuild my relationship with my son, I'm probably not the guy to give you advice about her."

"I guess it's about Nick, too." He took a sip of the soda, then decided for direct. "I want to marry Lauren."

"Ah." Dean picked at the edge of the wooden table. "So you want to take my son to Massachusetts."

"That's part of marrying Lauren, yes."

"What does Lauren say about it?"

"I haven't actually asked her yet."

"What?" Dean shook his head. "You haven't talked to her about it, but you're talking to *me* about it? That's not going to make her happy."

Ryan wasn't sure he could explain why he'd felt compelled to come here. "He's your son. I guess I felt a need to…do it right this time. Look you in the eye, totally square, and tell you I want Nick to be my stepson and move to Brookline with his mother and me."

"And what if I tell you to go screw yourself? I've

got a custody agreement and you can't take him out of the state of Maine without my permission. Might even be the county, actually. I'd have to find the paperwork. Would you still ask Lauren to marry you?"

"Yeah." He didn't even have to think about that. "But at least we'd know up front we're going to have problems, and I'd remind you both that, at sixteen, if we all walk into a courtroom, Nick's going to get to make that decision for himself."

"And you think he'd choose you?"

"I don't know, but it's not about me. He'd be choosing between you and his mother and the only thing I know for sure is that it would tear him up inside. I'm hoping it doesn't come to that."

Dean nodded. "Jody and I have talked about this some. Doesn't take a genius to see you and Lauren have been getting serious."

"Since I just figured out how serious myself recently, it's not very comforting everybody could see it but me."

"Nick's gotten into some trouble here."

Ryan wasn't sure where that left turn in the conversation came from. "Nothing bad, though. And, to be fair, there's a good chance he'll get in trouble anywhere. He's sixteen."

"I guess the difference is, when he grows out of it, there's still not much for him in Whitford. Not even crap for jobs around here, whether he goes to college or not. Maybe he could take over the hardware store someday, but you know as well as I do that place is always on the brink. One of those box stores opens within thirty miles and it's gone." He swirled the soda around in his can. "You probably got some good schools down there."

Ryan nodded. "A lot of opportunities for him, too, no matter what field he wants to go into."

"See, there's the difference. You talk about fields, like real careers. Around here, we just hope we can find jobs that pay the bills. He'll have a better future down there."

"He'll have more doors open to him, but he needs the work ethic and the integrity to make the most of those opportunities. You and Lauren already gave him that, no matter where he lives."

Dean was quiet for a few minutes, lost in thought, and Ryan let him be. Brookline wasn't *that* far away, but a nine-hour round-trip meant the ability to easily see each other on a whim would be gone.

"I can't make that drive every weekend," Dean said, as though he'd been reading his mind.

"I'd still be coming up here on the weekends for a while, until we get the lodge sorted out. And maybe we'd have to go to every other weekend, but we'd meet you halfway. And you'd get more school holidays with him."

He probably shouldn't be speaking for Lauren, but he needed to know where Dean stood. The last thing he wanted to do was put Lauren in a position where she felt she had to choose between Nick and Ryan. Nick would win, obviously, but it would hurt Lauren to have to make the decision.

"That sounds fair enough." Dean nodded. "I won't stand in the way, if you can talk her into going with you this time."

"Thank you." He looked at his watch. "She should be getting home soon. She gets home before Nick on Fridays and I want to be there."

Dean snorted. "No fancy dinner and ring in the champagne glass?"

"No. If she says yes, I'd want Nick to know before he comes here for the weekend. Word gets around fast and he doesn't need to hear the news at the market or on the street."

Dean stood when Ryan did and shook his hand. "Good luck."

By the time he pulled his truck in behind Lauren's car, Ryan was what Steph would call a hot mess, but he did his best to hide it as he got out and walked to her door.

"Hey," she said as she opened the door with a smile. "I wasn't expecting to see you until later."

He was supposed to spend the weekend with her. "Are you busy?"

"Just mopping the floor. Are you okay? You look a little flushed."

"I'm okay." He followed her inside and closed the door. "So I have to leave on Sunday."

Some of the light dimmed in her eyes. "Yes, I know."

"I want you and Nick to come to Brookline with me."

She frowned, tilting her head a little. "I don't understand. You know Nick has school Monday. I have to go to work."

"No." Dammit, he was blowing it already, and every line he'd rehearsed in the car had been totally erased from his mind. "Not this Sunday. I mean…I want you to move there. To live with me."

She sat down hard on the couch, looking up at him as if she didn't quite understand what he was saying. "Ryan, I…"

"You what?" he prompted when she drifted into silence. "Let's talk about it."

"I have a job. A home. Nick has school and his friends. And I can't move out of Maine without Dean's permission."

"He gave it."

"What?"

"I just talked to him. He said he wouldn't stand in our way if you and Nick want to move to Brookline."

She didn't look very happy about it. As a matter of fact, red splotches bloomed on her neck and cheeks as he watched, and her jaw tightened. Belatedly, he remembered planning in the car to open with the fact he loved her and wanted to marry her.

"You talked to Dean?"

"Yes. You've thrown so many stumbling blocks into this relationship and that was one of the biggest. I wanted to lay it to rest before I came here so we can focus on us and not Nick."

"Why would you do that? You've done nothing but feed me the 'just roll with it' line, but you go and have a serious sit-down with my ex-husband?"

He really wanted her to understand he hadn't done it to be pushy. "I went behind his back once and it wasn't right. I mean, I *had* to do it because I couldn't leave you and Nick without trying, but it was still wrong. I couldn't do it again."

"I'm not his wife anymore."

He tried to stay calm, but this wasn't going at all the way he'd thought it would. Or hoped it would. "No, but Nick's his son."

"I can't believe you did that, Ryan. My relationships are none of Dean's business."

"Of course they are, because of Nick." He was trying to make her see reason, but as soon as he said the words and saw the flare of temper in her eyes, he knew he made a mistake.

"You thought it was so damn funny being my *you know, whatever*, but Nick called you that because he wasn't comfortable calling you my boyfriend. Now you've told Dean you want us to live with you and, when he says something to Nick, I'm going to feel pressured because you interfered with my family."

The tight leash on his temper slipped. "Dammit, I'm trying to *be* part of your family, Lauren."

"But you're not. You told me we were going to roll with it and then you went behind my back to my ex-husband and had a conversation about my son. Not just about my son, but huge, life-changing events, without even telling me you were considering us moving to Massachusetts. How dare you?"

"I dare because I—"

"It doesn't matter. I don't…I can't believe you did that." She pointed at the door. "You need to go now."

"Lauren, we need to talk this out."

"Go talk to Dean about it. I want you to leave."

His entire body felt hot and shaky. He couldn't believe this was happening. "Lady, I ain't a boomerang. You throw me away again, I'm not coming back."

"You call me lady in that tone again, it's your balls that won't be coming back."

They were done. The conversation had gone so far south a GPS couldn't pull it back now. He turned and went out her front door, resisting the urge to slam it, and got into his truck. That door he did slam.

He sat there for a minute trying to think of something—anything—he could say to make it better, but all he could hear was her voice thundering through his head, telling him he had no right to interfere with her family. Basically telling him he didn't belong there.

So he threw his truck in reverse and left.

## CHAPTER EIGHTEEN

HOW SHE'D MANAGED to keep it together until Nick had gotten home from school and then been picked up by Dean, she didn't know. Willpower. Anger. Shock.

While Nick was grabbing his bag and trying to find the book he'd checked out of the library for a book report he needed to work on over the weekend, she'd walked out to Dean's car.

"Don't say anything to Nick about the conversation you had with Ryan."

He looked up at her through the open window, reading her face. They'd been married so long he didn't miss much. "I told him you wouldn't be happy he'd talked to me first."

"He shouldn't have done that."

"Nick's my son, Lauren. How I feel about my kid going to live in a different state matters."

"I know it does. But *we* hadn't had that conversation yet. He should have talked to me and let me talk to Nick first."

"Maybe. Are you okay?"

"Yeah. I'm fine."

But she wasn't and, once her son was safely out of the emotional fallout zone, the wall of willpower, anger and shock imploded and she crumpled into a sobbing mess. It hurt so much, and all she wanted to do was crawl into her bed and cry until Sunday afternoon.

She might have done just that if the phone hadn't rung. For one heart-stopping, hope-filled moment, she'd thought it was Ryan. But the number on the caller ID was her mother's and she didn't answer it. Her mother would know something was wrong and push until she got the whole story. Then she'd tell her father and there would be yelling and swearing in a mix of English and Polish and Lauren wasn't in the mood for it.

But she also couldn't totally fall apart, so she called Hailey. Hailey would be a good shoulder to lean on until she got her own strength back.

"Are you busy tonight?" she asked when Hailey answered.

"I was going to paint my toenails. You sound stuffy. Have you been crying or are you getting that cold again?"

"Ryan and I are done." Saying the words out loud took her breath away.

"Oh, shit. I'll be right there, okay? Do you want me to call Paige?"

"No. She said it was already awkward because he's her brother-in-law now. And she's always so reasonable. I don't want reasonable. I want you to tell me what an awful bastard Ryan Kowalski is and how lucky I am to be rid of him now instead of later."

Hailey was quiet for a few seconds. "I'll try my best. Give me fifteen or twenty minutes and I'll be there."

It was closer to twenty-five, but since Lauren spent most of them curled up on the couch, sobbing into a massive wad of tissues, she wasn't really counting. Hailey let herself in, holding up a brown paper bag.

"Is that booze?" As crappy as her head felt already, Lauren was pretty sure alcohol was the last thing she needed.

Hailey tipped the paper bag over the coffee table and let the contents spill out. A whole pile of individually wrapped cream-filled chocolate snack cakes. "Tell me everything."

She managed to get through the story with a minimum of tears. Crying would seriously interfere with her ability to console herself with junk food.

"I can't believe he went to Dean like that," Hailey said. "What an awful bastard."

Lauren almost choked on her mouthful of cream and chocolate. "You're not very good at that."

"Sorry. I'm trying because I love you and I'm heartbroken for you, but he's a pretty great guy, so this isn't easy. Although, he should have talked to you first and let you handle Dean."

"He also thinks I can just up and leave everything. This is my home. I have a job."

"I get the home part."

"If I move to Brookline I'll have to find a new job in a strange city in this economy."

"Remembering the part where I said I love you, I have to point out that you're the secretary at a one-man insurance company and Ryan owns a multimillion-dollar construction company."

"So? Does that make him more important than me?"

"Of course not. But in terms of practicality, logic and common sense, it makes his *job* more important than yours."

"If I wanted practicality, logic and common sense, I would have called Paige."

"Fine. He's a horrible bastard. He loves you, wants to marry you, cares about your son and wants to take you both to live in his big, shiny house in a city that has a real mall close enough so you don't have to stop for lunch halfway there."

"Go away." She didn't want to hear it. "He should have told *me* he loves me and wants to marry me, not Dean. It made me mad and now he's gone and I want to feel sorry for myself. If you're going to be the voice of reason, go home."

"If I go home, I'm taking the snack cakes with me."

Lauren looked at the pile on the table. She'd barely put a dent in it. "Fine, you can stay, but you can only refer to him as *that jerk*."

"I'll try." Hailey picked up the television remote and turned the set on. "Now, we're going to find something really hideous to watch. I'm going to spend the night and we're going to eat snack cakes until we puke and feel so tired and shitty tomorrow you don't even care about that jerk anymore."

"You're a true friend, Hailey."

"Always here for you, babe.

TWENTY-FOUR HOURS, RYAN thought. Twenty-four hours since he'd walked out of Lauren's life and he still felt like shit.

He should have gone home. He'd still feel like shit, but at least he wouldn't have a damn audience. But when he got home last night, he'd cracked a beer. Anger, heartbreak and alcohol weren't the way to start a four-and-a-half-hour drive. And today he'd kept hoping some way to fix things would magically occur to him, or that she'd call.

Nothing. All he had was his chair on the porch, a beer that had gone warm and flat some time ago and a younger brother who'd probably been sicced on him by Rose. He knew she was struggling to give him space, but Rose was Rose. If he'd truly wanted to be left alone, he should have skipped the beer and hit the highway.

"Are you really going to just sit there and stare at the trees all day?" he asked Josh, who was parked in a nearby chair.

"I'm just being here if you need me."

"Bullshit. Rosie told you to come talk to me and you don't have the first fucking clue what to say."

"That, too."

Ryan sighed and wished he'd downed the beer when he opened it. He'd taken it out of the fridge, but after opening it, decided he didn't really want it. Now he did. "Tell her I'm fine."

"Yeah, but you're not."

"And none of us have ever fibbed to Rosie. Sure."

Josh sat up straighter in his chair. "It's not all about Rosie. I'm your brother, stupid, and you're hurting. I care and I'm going to sit here until I think of something to say that might help, goddammit."

After about five minutes, Ryan looked over at him. "Anything yet?"

"Nope."

They went back to staring down the driveway.

"Everything that pops into my head would only make you feel worse," Josh said a few minutes later. "But I'm trying."

"Like what, not that I think it's possible for me to feel worse."

"I watched you guys together. Made me a little jealous, to be honest, because it really looked like the real deal."

"Guess not."

"I may not be as very, very old and somewhat wise as you, but even I know couples fight. If two people really never fight, then secretly neither of them give a shit enough to bother."

"Someday, when you grow up and maybe find a girl who likes you, you'll find out that going to ask a woman to marry you and having her throw you out of her house is different from a fight."

"She loves you."

And that was the real kick in the balls. He was pretty sure she did. "Not enough."

"I get why you talked to Dean first, but I can also see why it pissed her off."

Ryan shook his head. "She made my place in her life perfectly clear and it's *not* as part of her family."

"Jesus, no wonder Rosie bakes so much. This support shit is hard."

"Good. Go bake some cookies and leave me alone."

Before Josh could move—assuming he was going to go inside, rather than stay and annoy him some more—a vehicle pulled into the driveway. Ryan groaned. It was Paige's car, but as it drew closer, he could see Mitch was driving it. When he'd parked and gotten out, Ryan could tell by the look on his face his older brother knew the whole story.

"Hey," he said, taking a seat in another porch chair. "Had some free time, so I thought I'd stop by."

"Where's Paige? Is she with Lauren?" As shitty as he felt about the whole mess, he really hoped she'd reached out to her friends. He didn't like to imagine her hurting and upset, alone in the house.

"No. Lauren thought Paige might try to defend you because she's your sister-in-law and she was in the mood for somebody one hundred percent in her corner. Hailey's been with her since last night. Didn't even open the library today, which is going over as well as you can imagine."

"So she and Hailey are sitting around talking about what an asshole I am."

Josh snorted. "And that's what we were doing, too. See how much you guys have in common?"

Mitch managed to get Ryan by the collar before Ryan's fist could make contact with Josh's face, and Mitch hauled Ryan backward into his chair. "Enough. Josh, this isn't really the time for that whole breaking tension with humor thing."

"Why not?" Ryan rested his head back against the chair with a thump. "That's what we do, isn't it? Don't know what to say or how to say it? Be funny and change the subject while they're laughing. That's what I did to her. You're uncertain about the future? Hey, just roll with it. No worries. It's only your entire fucking life I'm asking you to turn upside down, but look into my pretty blue eyes and think about it later."

"Ryan, I—" Josh started to say.

"And you still want to talk about the future? Well, how about I go talk to your ex-husband instead. You know, the guy who treated you like shit and cheated on you in your own goddamned bed, but you still have to deal with for the rest of your life because you have a kid together? Yeah, I'll give that guy more respect than I gave you.

"Son of a bitch." He picked up the warm can of beer and chucked it as hard as he could, but he didn't see where it landed because the tears blurred his vision. "How did I fuck this up so bad?"

"You can fix it," Mitch said. "I fucked up and walked away from Paige, too."

"How the hell am I supposed to get in my truck tomorrow and leave her behind? *Again?* I can't do it."

"Then go tell her that."

"Tomorrow," Josh put in. "You're the emotional equivalent of totally shit-faced right now, and Lauren and Hailey are probably riding high on a Ryan hatefest. Sleep on it. Let her sleep on it, too, and think about where she might have overreacted or screwed up, same as you. Tomorrow, when you're both more sad and regretful than pissed off, then go talk to her. Tell her how you feel straight up."

When Ryan and Mitch both stared at him with almost identical expressions of disbelief, Josh shrugged. "Unlike you two, I've been trapped in this house with Rosie my entire life. You pick up shit along the way."

Mitch nodded. "He's right. Unbelievably."

Ryan knew it, too. As much as he wanted to go over there and make her understand, he was too raw. She would be too, and they'd end up in each other's faces again. Now that he had a plan, maybe he could settle himself. Maybe even sleep a little, which he hadn't done last night.

For now he needed to settle himself and not think about his entire future hinging on one conversation tomorrow. "I bet all this has Rosie baking up a storm. I really need a fucking cookie."

LAUREN HAD THE worst sugar hangover of her life. She'd finally convinced Hailey to go home and had taken a shower, but she didn't feel much better.

It couldn't have been easy for Ryan to go to Dean, given the history between them. And although she really wished Ryan had talked to her first, instead of her ex-husband, time and an unhealthy amount of snack cakes had made her admit to herself he hadn't done it out of disrespect for her. He'd done it because he thought it was the right thing to do. He'd done it because he loved her, and she'd kicked him in the balls for it.

Even though he'd probably meant it when he said he wouldn't come back, she at least had to apologize—to try to make him understand why she'd reacted so badly. She couldn't live with such an ugly ending between them.

Before she could chicken out, she pulled up his number on her phone and hit Call. By the time she heard the third ring, she thought he was going to ignore it, but then she heard his voice—quiet and tense—saying hello.

"I'd like to talk," she said. "I want to apologize and I'd drive over and do it in person, but I don't really want to do it in front of Rose and Josh. Though I will if you don't want to talk on the phone."

He was quiet for so long, any hope he might forgive her started fading, and then he cleared his throat. "I don't want to talk on the phone. I'll drive over to your place if Nick's not home yet."

"He's not."

"Then I'll be right over."

Her stomach was in knots by the time his truck pulled into her driveway and her hands wouldn't stop shaking as she opened the door. He looked almost as rough as she did. His eyes were bruised from lack of sleep and his expression was grim.

"I'm sorry," she told him, and stepped back to let him in.

"You were taking the easy way out," he said in a low voice.

"Oh yeah, because this is so easy. Fun, even."

"It's easier to make me out to be the asshole and walk away, and when I overstepped with Dean, you had your excuse." He stepped inside and kicked the door closed behind him. "It's harder to have a future together, because we'll have to work at it and compromise."

"You're right that I overreacted about you going to Dean, but not about it being easy. I got scared, Ryan. Leaving Whitford and my parents and my friends behind is huge, but you and I hadn't talked about it yet. And it'll be hard on Nick, even though he likes you. It's so much to wrap my head around."

"I'd like to think I'm worth it." He stopped and shook his head. "No, I *know* I'm worth it. I love you, Lauren Carpenter. I want you to marry me. I love you like no other man ever has or ever will and I promise you I'm worth the headache."

"I'm scared." It seemed like there were a million words in her head needing to be said, but those were the only two that came out.

"So am I. We've both tried this before and failed and this time…Don't think I underestimate the impact our relationship has on Nick."

"He's not the only thing, Ryan."

"Let's hear the buts. I won't tell you to roll with it. I won't make jokes or try to charm my way out of answering."

"One thing I can't compromise on is kids. I really don't want any more. It's not something I'll change my mind about."

"Can we sit down? It feels weird and…I don't know, confrontational, standing here like this."

She nodded and sat on the couch. He sat on the couch, too, but further down, and she appreciated the space he left between them. She needed it.

"I've thought about kids since that day at my house," he said with a quiet sincerity she'd never seen in him before. "I've thought about them a lot, actually. Did I always assume I'd have some? Yeah. Did I want some? Maybe. Do I *need* them? No. I need you. It's that simple."

"I'm afraid someday you'll miss having them, though."

"They may not be mine by birth, but I'm not going to suffer a shortage of kids," he said, chuckling a little. "Mike and Lisa will let me borrow theirs in a heartbeat. Emma's pregnant. I'm going to take a wild guess and say Paige will be soon. And before we know it, Nick will get married and give us grandchildren."

Lauren groaned.

"That's a ways down the road," he said quickly. "But the point is, I'll have children in my life. Judging by the way the Kowalski family procreates, probably a lot of them. And we'll love them and play with them and then give them back to their parents so we can go home and have crazy sex with no fear of interruption."

She wanted to believe he meant it. Looking in his eyes, she could see *he* believed it. Tears burned her eyes and she blinked, afraid if they started falling, she wouldn't stop crying for days.

"I want you, Lauren." He reached across the space between them and took her hand. "And I want Nick. I know he's Dean's, but there's room for me, too. I've come to love that kid and I don't want to miss out on his life."

That started the waterworks flowing. "He loves you, too."

"But most importantly, I love *you*." He used his knuckle to brush away her tears. "I don't want to be your *you know, whatever* anymore. I want to be your husband."

With a teenager's impeccable knack for timing, Nick walked through the front door, startling them both. She hadn't even heard Dean's car pull up out front. He looked at them, sitting on the couch, with Ryan holding her hand while she'd obviously been crying. "What's going on?"

Lauren wasn't quite sure what to say, but Ryan cleared his throat and beat her to it. "I'm trying to convince your mother to marry me."

He frowned, his gaze bouncing back and forth between them. "Why?"

"Because I love her and want her to be my wife."

"Yeah, I get that part. I mean, why do you have to convince her?" He looked at Lauren. "Did you say no?"

"I haven't really answered him yet."

"Oh. Well, I think it would be cool."

"So do I," Ryan said. "Very cool."

Two against one wasn't fair. "Nick, you do realize Ryan doesn't *live* at the Northern Star, right? He has a home and a business in Massachusetts."

"So…" Nick sighed and dropped into the chair. "You wouldn't move to Maine?"

Ryan shook his head. "I can't do that. My business is pretty big. I have a lot of contracts and I employ a lot of people. I can't walk away from that to try to make a living being a third wheel at an inn that's barely supporting itself as it is."

"If I marry Ryan, it means you and I would move to Brookline," she said, deciding it was best to spell it out.

He frowned. "I've never moved before. Or gone to a new school."

"We understand that," Ryan said. "You'd spend every

other weekend here with your dad, and some holidays and school vacations. And you could spend summers wherever. Maybe you could stay with your dad and work at the lodge and visit us whenever you want. Especially since you'll be driving."

"What if I hate it?"

"As long as you've given it a fair shot," Ryan said, "then we'll talk about it and figure it out. But you're going to college in two years, so learning to adapt to change now wouldn't be a bad thing."

"If it really, really sucked, I could move back and live with Dad."

"Yeah, you could," Ryan said. "Though I'd like to think living with me wouldn't really, really suck."

Nick blushed, giving a nervous laugh. "That's not really what I meant. Just that… Mom, like he said, I'm going to college in two years. I have my dad so I can visit him and Whitford when I want and if I really hate it in Brookline, I can stay with Dad and Jody. You can't make a decision for the whole rest of your life based on, like, less than two years of mine. I'm a kid. I'm resilient."

Lauren made a hiccupping sound, trying really hard not to bawl, and she groped at the coffee table for the tissue box.

"Wow," Ryan said. "That's really wise and insightful for your age."

Nick flashed him a grin. "I think I heard it on TV. Maybe one of those Lifetime or Hallmark movies Mom watches."

"And they say watching television doesn't teach kids anything." Ryan looked him in the eye. "Nick, would you like to be my stepson and come live in Brookline with me?"

After only a couple of seconds, Nick nodded. "Yeah. That would be cool."

Ryan turned back to Lauren. "See, that's how it's done. I proposed to your son and he said yes."

"I've never moved out of Whitford, either. What if *I* hate Brookline?"

"You sure as hell can't go live with Dean."

The laughter that bubbled up surprised her and eased some of the tension that had been threatening to suffocate her.

"I think you'll both love it there," he said. "But if you don't—if we can't be a strong, happy family there—then we'll do what we have to do. I don't want to sell my company and it's not just about contracts and employees. It's mine. I built it and I'm damn proud of it. But if it comes down to Kowalski Custom Builders or us, I'll choose us. I will *always* choose the three of us."

She liked that. The three of them. "I love you."

"I love you, too. Marry me, Lauren. I had to walk away from you once, but I can't do it again. I don't have the strength for that."

And, this time, she couldn't watch him go. "I choose us, too. I choose you. It's that simple."

He blew out a breath as though he'd been holding it for a lifetime, before leaning in to kiss her. "Thank you. I loved being your *you know, whatever*, but I can't wait to be your husband."

"I think we should celebrate with pizza," Nick contributed to the moment.

"I've had chili in the slow cooker all day," she said. Then she watched her future husband and her son share a look and knew she was doomed.

"Chili's always better reheated the second day," Ryan said. "If we get pizza now, you guys can have even better chili for supper tomorrow. And I can take some in a container to heat up, too."

She laughed, unable to resist that look in his eyes. "Fine. But I want mushrooms on it."

Ryan leaned in and kissed her again. "For you, and only for you, I'll pick off the mushrooms."

\* \* \* \* \*

*If you love the Kowalskis,*
*turn the page for a sneak peek at*
*Shannon Stacey's* BE MINE *anthology,*
*also featuring bestselling authors*
*Jennifer Crusie and Victoria Dahl.*

**Available now from Harlequin HQN.**

*SIZZLE*
Jennifer Crusie

# CHAPTER ONE

"BUT, I DON'T WANT A partner," Emily Tate said through her teeth. "I like working alone." She clenched her fists to pound them on the desk in front of her and then unclenched them and smoothed down the jacket of her business suit, instead. "I don't need a partner, George."

Her boss looked exasperated, and she automatically put her hand to her hair to make sure every strand was in place, that no dark curls had escaped from her tight French twist. Be cool, calm and detached, she told herself. *I want to kill him for this.*

"Look, Em." George tossed a folder across the table to her. "Those are the cost estimates from your Paradise project and the final costs after you brought the project in."

Emily winced and clasped her hands in front of her. "I know. I went way over. But we still showed a mammoth profit. In fact, Paradise was the biggest money-maker Evadne Inc. has ever had. The bottom line, George, is that we made money for the company." I *made money for the company,* she thought, *but I can't say that. Be modest and cooperative, Emily.*

"Yeah, we did." George Bartlett leaned back in his chair, looking up at her.

*I hate it when he does that,* Emily thought. *He's short, fat and balding, and he doesn't have a quarter of my brains, but he's the one leaning back in the chair while I stand at attention. I want to be the one leaning back in the chair. Except I wouldn't. It would be rude.* She sighed.

"Listen to me, Emily," George said. "You almost lost your job over this last project."

"You got a promotion because of this last project," Emily said.

"Yeah, because of the profit. If it hadn't made a profit, we'd have both been canned. Henry wasn't happy."

Henry Evadne was never happy, Emily thought. It didn't have anything to do with her.

George leaned forward. "I don't want to lose you, Emily. You're smart, and you have a sixth sense about marketing that I'd kill to have. But you screw up the financial side on this next deal, and no profit is going to save you, no matter how big."

Emily swallowed. "I'll bring it in under budget."

"You're damn right you will, because you'll be working with Richard Parker."

"Who is Richard Parker?"

"He's a whiz kid from the Coast," George said. "He did an analysis of the Paradise project. It's in the folder, too. You ought to read it. He wasn't too complimentary."

"George, how much have we made on Paradise?" Emily demanded.

George looked smug. "Close to four million as of last month."

"Then why am I getting whiz kids from the Coast and nasty reviews in my project folders? Where's the champagne?"

George shook his head. "You could have flopped."

"I never flop."

"Well, someday you will," George said philosophically. "And when you do, you better flop under budget. Which is exactly what Richard Parker is here to guarantee. You're meeting him at eleven in his office."

"His office?"

"Next floor up," George said with a grin. "Two doors from the president. Nice view from up there, I'm told."

"Why not my office?"

"Emily, please."

"Is he in charge of this project? Because if so, I quit."

"No, no." George waved his hands at her. "Just the financial end. And you're not the only one he's working with. He's financial adviser for all our projects. It's still your baby, Em. He just watches the spending." He looked at her closely. She'd made her face a blank, but she knew the anger was still in her eyes. "Emily, please cooperate."

"His office at eleven," she said, clamping down on her rage.

"That's it," George said, relieved.

EMILY SLAMMED HER OFFICE door and slumped into her rolling desk chair. Jane, her secretary, followed her in more sedately and sat in the chair across from her. She broke a frozen almond Hershey bar in half and tossed the larger piece to her boss.

"I keep this in the coffee-room freezer for emergencies," she said. "And I've given you the biggest half. Greater love hath no friend."

"How do you keep people from stealing it?" Emily asked, pulling off the foil.

"They know I work for you," Jane said. "They know I could send you after them."

"No, really, how do you do it?"

"I keep it in a freezer container marked 'Asparagus,'" Jane said, sucking on the chocolate.

"And nobody asks what you're doing with asparagus at work?" Emily broke off a small piece of the chocolate and put it on her tongue. The richness spread through her mouth, and she sighed and sat back in her chair.

"They probably figure I keep it for you—you're the type who looks like you only put fruits and vegetables in your body." Jane studied her. "How come you never gain weight? We eat the same stuff, but I'm fighting ten extra pounds while you look like you're losing. And you've got nothing to lose."

"Frustration," Emily said, breaking off another tiny piece. "I'm working for narrow-minded patriarchal creeps."

"In the plural?" Jane finished her half and checked the foil for crumbs. "Did George clone himself?"

"Evidently," Emily said. "I now have a budget adviser to answer to. Some suit named Richard Parker."

"Ooooh," Jane said. "Him I've seen. Things are looking up."

"Not a suit?"

"Oh, yeah, but what a suit. Too bad I'm happily married." Jane sighed. "Tall. Dark. Handsome. Cheekbones. Chiseled lips. Blue eyes to die for. Never smiles. The secretaries are lining up to be seduced and so are the female junior execs, but it's not happening."

"No?" Emily broke off another piece of chocolate.

"He's a workhorse. All he thinks about is finance. Karen says he's always still here working when she leaves."

"Karen?"

"That tiny little blonde on the twelfth floor. She's his secretary now."

"Make good friends with Karen. We need a spy in the enemy camp."

"No problem," Jane said, licking her fingers to get the last of her chocolate. "She loooves to talk about the boss."

"Good, good," Emily said. "He could be a real problem for us."

"How so?"

"He's controlling the money."

"And we're not good with money." Jane nodded wisely. "Good thing Paradise took off like it did. It's been fun rising to the top with you, but I wasn't looking forward to hitting the bottom together when we went sailing over the budget."

"You wouldn't have hit bottom," Emily said. "George isn't dumb. He'd steal you as his own secretary."

"I'm not dumb, either," Jane said. "You and I stay together. I knew when I met you in high school that you were going places and taking me with you. President and secretary of the senior class. President and secretary of student council. President and secretary of our sorority in college. I'm hanging around until you make president of this dump." She threw her foil away and smiled smugly. "I've already made secretary."

"You're every bit as smart as I am," Emily said. "Why don't you let me get you into an executive-training program?"

"Because I'm smarter than you are," Jane said. "I'm making more than most executives here right now, and I don't have to kiss up to the boss. Are you going to eat the rest of that chocolate?"

"Yes," Emily said.

"So I gather you slammed the door in honor of Richard Parker?"

"Yes."

"I know how you can handle Richard Parker."

"How?" Emily broke off another piece of chocolate. She wasn't interested in handling Richard Parker. She wanted, in fact, to eliminate him, but she was always interested in Jane. She didn't insist that the company pay Jane a lavish salary just because they were friends; she insisted because Jane had a lot of ideas and none of them were dumb. If Emily did get to be president, it would be due as much to Jane's brains as to Emily's.

"I think you should seduce him," Jane said.

Emily reconsidered her thoughts about Jane not having dumb ideas. This seemed to be one.

"Why?"

"Because you need to get out more. You live in the office. You only stop by your apartment to shower and change. You don't even have a pet, for crying out loud. I'm your only companionship."

"I like it that way."

"Well, it's not natural. And it sounds like Parker is the same way. You could save each other. He'll be grateful and fall in love with you, you'll get married, and I'll get to buy baby gifts, instead of accepting them from you. You're not going to eat that chocolate, are you?"

"Yes," Emily said, breaking off another piece. "How will marrying Richard Parker help me?"

"Sex always helps," Jane said. "It's like chocolate."

"I need help at the office," Emily said. "This guy is going to tie my hands."

"Kinky."

"Be nice to Karen," Emily said. "This could get very dirty. Now go get Parker on the phone. I have an eleven-o'clock meeting with him, and I want to hear what he sounds like first."

"A meeting, huh? Why don't you change your look? Let that long dark hair down. Take off your suit jacket. Especially take off your glasses. You look like a bug."

"I want to look like a bug. I have a hard enough time getting respect around here looking like a bug. If I start taking off my clothes, no one will pay attention."

"Want to bet?" Jane looked at her boss. "If I had your body, I'd take off my clothes all the time."

"You do take off your clothes all the time," Emily pointed out. "Has Ben ever seen you clothed?"

"Certainly," Jane said. "I was dressed for my wedding. You were there. You slapped the best man at the reception."

"You never forget, do you?"

Jane got up and headed for the door. "I'll get Parker. Don't slap him. I'll make friends with Karen, but we'll get further if you seduce the guy."

"Feel free to sacrifice my body for your ambitions," Emily said as Jane went through the door.

"Our ambitions," Jane said. "And I've seen him. It would be no sacrifice."


"MR. PARKER ON LINE TWO," Jane said in her secretary voice.

Emily picked up the phone. "Mr. Parker?"

"Yes?"

"This is Emily Tate. I understand we have a meeting at eleven."

"Yes, Ms. Tate, we do." He sounded bored but patient. She'd been expecting the high tight tones of a monomaniac; his voice was deep with a little bit of New York rhythm in it.

"Is there anything you'd like me to bring to the meeting?"

"No, Ms. Tate, I have everything I need. Is there anything else?"

*Sorry,* Emily thought. *Taking up your time, am I?* "No, Mr. Parker, there's nothing else."

"Eleven, then," he said, and hung up.

Not good, Emily thought. Efficient and not impressed with her in spite of her terrific track record. Which must mean he was still hung up on the budget overruns.

Jane poked her head in. "Okay, so he's not a charmer. But I still say go for it. Maybe he loosens up in bed."

"Not a chance." Emily hung up the phone. "He probably doesn't go to bed. He probably sleeps standing up in a corner of his office."

"Do you need me in the meeting to take notes?"

"No. Do you want to take notes?"

"Yes."

"Then come along, sweetie, and we'll have lunch at the Celestial afterward. We can discuss the situation."

"Good idea."

"And, Jane, try to pretend you're really a secretary in there. He doesn't need to know you're the brains of our outfit."

"I'll stick a pencil through my bun and borrow your glasses," Jane said.

"What bun?"

"I'll have one by eleven."

"This I've got to see."

WHEN EMILY LEFT THE OFFICE at five to eleven, Jane really had pulled her hair into a bun. It was a terrible bun, with wisps of hair escaping and two pencils jabbed through it, but it was indisputably a bun.

"That's really disgusting," Emily said as they waited for the elevator.

"Wait." Jane lifted Emily's glasses off her nose and put them on. "How do I look?"

"You look like a bug with a very bad hairdo," Emily said. "You look like Norman Bates's mother as a young mental patient. You look like—"

The elevator doors opened, and they got on with several other executives. Emily glanced sideways at Jane and tried not to laugh. If things got really bad, she'd just look at Jane and feel better.

"It's a good thing there's only going to be the three of us in this meeting," Emily whispered. "Anybody else would know you were up to something."

Jane pushed the glasses up the bridge of her nose, sniffed and said loudly and nasally, "I just want you to know, Ms. Tate, that it is an honor and a privilege to work for you, and I really mean that from the bottom of my heart."

"Thank you, Mrs. Frobish," Emily said. "Your loyalty is heartwarming."

"Do you have any of your chocolate left?"

"No."

Jane sniffed.

The conference room was across from the elevator. Once inside, Emily realized she'd made a mistake. It wasn't going to be just the three of them. There were six other executives in there, four of whom had brought their secretaries.

"What is this?" Emily whispered to Jane, frowning.

"I don't know," Jane whispered, "but I'm glad I'm here."

"I am, too," Emily whispered. "Guard my back."

The door at the other end of the conference room

opened, and Richard Parker came in, tall, dark and serious. And indisputably the best-looking man Emily had ever seen. Distinguished. Beautifully dressed. Powerful. And sexy, Emily thought. Definitely sexy. Every executive there except Emily stiffened in his or her seat. Every secretary there except Jane smiled warmly. For everyone there, Richard Parker radiated power and authority. For the secretaries and female execs, he also radiated sex appeal. The power and the authority were conscious, Emily decided; the sex appeal wasn't.

*He really is extraordinarily good-looking,* Emily thought. *Except for his height and that jaw, he's almost pretty. Those electric blue eyes and long dark lashes. Not businesslike. How can I make that work against him? If he was female, it'd work against him.*

His eyes swept the room and caught hers. She was the only one not looking at him with fear or lust. She met his eyes coolly and stared back at him, calculating. He was the enemy.

He raised his eyebrows at her and moved his gaze on. Jane made a note. Emily looked at her pad. "He's not stupid," Jane had written, "but you can take him."

Emily shook her head. Jane's one weakness was overestimating her.

George leaned over to Emily. "What's wrong with Jane? She looks funny."

"PMS," Emily whispered back, and George nodded solemnly.

Richard Parker looked up and frowned at them.

George blushed.

Emily raised her eyebrows at Parker.

He looked startled, and then his lips twitched.

*Almost smiled there, didn't we?* Emily thought. *You're not so tough. Maybe I can take you.*

"I've asked you to meet with me today to discuss your past performance in budgeting your marketing campaigns," Parker began. "It's abysmal."

Several of the executives tittered and then fell silent. A few colored and looked away. Emily yawned and checked her watch.

"Am I boring you, Ms. Tate?" Parker asked.

"Not at all." Emily smiled back politely. "I'm sure you'll make your point soon."

George closed his eyes.

"The point, Ms. Tate," Parker said without raising his voice, "is that you all regularly exceed your budgets, thereby cutting into the profits this company could be making. You alone went over your budget on the Paradise account by almost thirty percent. That's a lot of money, Ms. Tate. You may have thought there was no price too great to pay for Paradise, but I don't agree. You could have cost this company a fortune."

Emily smiled at him again.

"I could have, but I didn't, Mr. Parker," Emily said. "I made four million dollars for this company by having the guts to go thirty percent over budget."

"That doesn't take guts, Ms. Tate. That just takes lack of control. That's where I come in. I'm your control." Parker's eyes swept the room. "From now on all budgets go through me. So do all purchase orders, all payments. I'm the money pipeline. I'll make sure you get the money you need for your projects. And I'll make certain you stay within your budgets. Now, I'm sure you have questions about how this new procedure will operate, so let's get started."

He sat down and leaned back in his chair while the others began a process of hemming and hawing and assuring Parker that they appreciated his help and were anxious to work with him.

Jane wrote on her pad, "Don't antagonize him."

Emily fumed, although she kept her face a mask. No price too great to pay for Paradise. *Don't get snide with me, buddy,* she thought. *I didn't get where I am today taking that from anybody.*

And then she thought, *yes, I did. I'm modest, cooperative and polite, and I regularly back down. I back down in front of George, who is an idiot, all the time. Then Jane and I sneak around behind his back and get things done the way we want. What am I doing confronting this guy?*

She watched him listening to Croswell from Research and Development. He was listening politely and nodding, and she wanted to throw something.

*He patronized me,* she thought. *He assumed he was right, and he didn't listen, and he patronized me. He thinks I'm insignificant.*

*Boy, is he going to pay for that.*

*I don't care how good-looking he is.*

Without realizing it, she'd let her eyes narrow as she looked at him, so that when he gazed idly around while he listened to Croswell's drivel, he saw her look of undiluted antagonism. His eyes widened slightly, and then he grinned at her as if he was seeing her for the first time, a real smile that accepted her challenge and recognized her as an equal, sharing the absurdity of the moment and of his own new-kid-on-the-block power play.

It was a killer smile.

Emily narrowed her eyes even more. *It's going to take more than a smile, buddy boy. Hit me with another line like "no price too great for Paradise," and*

*I'll wipe that smile off your face so fast you won't know what hit you.*

Jane nudged her and she looked down at the pad. It said, "Why is he smiling?"

Emily took the pad languidly and wrote, "Because he knows I'm angry, and he thinks it's amusing."

Jane took the pad back and wrote, "Then he's not as smart as I thought."

Emily nodded and turned her attention politely back to the group.

"Any other questions?" Parker surveyed the table before turning to Emily. "Ms. Tate, you've been very quiet. Do you have any questions?"

"No, I've found out all I need to know," she said calmly.

"Good. Do you have time to meet with me now?"

"Now?" Emily raised her eyebrows. "I have a lunch meeting. I could possibly meet with you at two."

"Let me check my appointments," he said. "I'll have my secretary call yours." He looked at Jane for the first time and stopped.

What is she doing? Emily thought, not daring to look. She's probably blacked out a couple of teeth and is now grinning maniacally at him.

"Fine." Emily stood so that she blocked Jane. "Anything else?"

He stayed seated, watching her. "No. There's nothing else."

"Thank you," Emily said, and left with Jane clumping in her wake.

When the door closed behind them, Jane stopped clumping and took off her glasses. "That was dumb," she said flatly. "We get nothing by antagonizing him. What's wrong with you?"

"He's arrogant," Emily said, punching the elevator button.

"Everybody in that room's arrogant," Jane said. "The only difference is that he has reason to be."

"What? You've fallen for that 'hello, I'm God' presentation he just did?"

"He's right," Jane said. "We were over budget. We could have done the campaign for less. He could help you here."

"Whose side are you on?"

"Ours," Jane said. "First, last and always. I'm just not sure he's not on our side, too."

They got on the elevator, and Jane handed the glasses back to Emily. "He likes you."

"Please."

"He likes you. I saw his eyes. Which are incredible, by the way. He likes watching you. He thought you were cute."

"Cute!" Emily exploded. "Cute!"

"Make it work for you," Jane said.

"The hell I will. I'll give him cute." Emily stormed off the elevator and down the hall to her office, slamming the door behind her. A minute later, Jane came in with her coat.

"Your lunch meeting is here," she said. "You promised me Chinese."

"YOU'D HAVE TO DO THE new campaign for less, anyway," Jane said later over potstickers and sizzling rice soup. "The new stuff's not as expensive as Paradise. Your profit margin's lower."

"Not necessarily." Emily spooned the hot soup carefully into her mouth. "We'll sell more—to the younger woman who uses perfume more frequently. We'll be fine. *If* I'm not forced to under budget."

"Give him a chance," Jane said. "There's no point in firing the first shot."

"I haven't," Emily said. "I've just made it clear that I'll return fire."

Jane gave up for the time being. "Garlic chicken?"

"Not if I'm meeting with Attila the Budget Hun this afternoon. Did Karen call?"

"Yep. Two o'clock. His office."

"Of course." Emily sighed. "I'd prefer neutral ground. From now on let's make it the conference room. On our floor, not his."

"I'll try," Jane said. "Prawns?"

"Yes," Emily said. "I'm in the mood to crunch little backbones."

"Then we'll go shopping," Jane said. "I found this incredible pink lace bra and bikini—" She stopped and looked past Emily.

"Ladies."

It was the Hun with George in tow. George *would* bring him here, Emily thought. Showing the new boss the best place to eat. I'll bet he offers to pick up his dry cleaning later. She looked up and smiled tightly. "Mr. Parker. How nice to see you."

"George assures me this is an excellent place to have a lunch meeting." He looked at Jane.

"It is." Emily turned her back and began spooning soup again.

Jane grinned at him. "Lovely meeting you again."

"Oh, yes. You're Ms. Tate's secretary. Mrs. Frobish, isn't it? I didn't recognize you at first."

"Well, that's the lot of the secretary," Jane said cheerfully. "Unrecognized, unrewarded, underpaid…"

"Hardly underpaid," Parker said. "Your salary is part of the budget, you know. It's very generous."

"Actually," Emily said, staring straight ahead, "she is underpaid. And I shall fight tooth and nail to stop any attempt to reduce her salary or to curtail her future raises." She raised her eyes to Parker's, and the steel in her voice was also in her eyes.

"I have no intention of interfering with Mrs. Frobish's salary," Parker said, calmly. "A good secretary is worth her weight in gold."

"Good idea," Jane said. "I'll take that as a basis for my next raise. Let's have two orders of prawns now that I have a reason to gain weight."

Emily thought about stabbing Parker with her fork but decided it would be too overt. Subtlety is the key here, she thought.

"I'll see you at two, Ms. Tate," Parker said, and moved on to the table the waiter was patiently holding for him, George toddling along in his wake.

"I thought you were going to stab him with your fork," Jane said. "Bad move, careerwise, although as your friend I would have been touched."

"I've got to stop hating him." Emily stabbed an egg roll instead. "I've got to work with this overbearing, egotistical control freak."

"See?" Jane said. "Already you're speaking of him with warmth."

THE UNDERWEAR WAS made of hot-pink lace embroidered with silver thread, and Jane bought it. The bra was just two large pink lace roses stitched into demi-cups, held in place with tiny pink satin ribbons, and the bikini was a strip of the same roses and ribbons. It was silly and luxurious and sexy and fun.

"Ben is going to love this," Jane said. "Why don't you get some and try it on Richard?"

"Richard who?"

"Parker," Jane said patiently.

"He'd never go for it." Emily looked at the price tag. "It's not cost-effective. There are small countries that don't spend this much for defense."

"Defense is not what I have in mind." Jane looked at herself in the mirror. "I'm planning on surrendering almost immediately and being invaded shortly thereafter."

Emily sighed. "Sounds like fun."

Jane pounced. "You buy some, too."

"Why? There's no one interested in invading."

"Wrong. Croswell down in R & D still speaks of you with passion."

"Croswell was a mistake." Emily picked up a pink-and-silver lace bra and looked at it longingly. "If he tries to invade, I'm defending."

"Then go back to plan A. Richard."

Emily looked at the pink-and-silver lace and thought of Richard Parker. *If he'd just keep his mouth shut,* she thought, *I could stand it. In fact, I'd be very interested. That long lovely body. Those crazy blue eyes. That classic, chiseled, supple mouth.*

That mouth. The one that kept opening and accepting his expensively shod foot. "No price too great to pay for Paradise."

"Hardly underpaid."

"Not even if he was unconscious." Emily put the underwear back. "Let's go. I have a meeting at two."

"I'VE LOOKED AT YOUR preliminary ideas," Richard the Hun said. "You're not being cost-effective."

"Already?" Emily tried to stay calm. "I've barely started."

"Rubies." He tossed a folder across the table to her.

"Look, we marketed Paradise with diamonds. Very classy stone. But this new stuff is for a younger hotter market. So rubies. Still classy, but hotter."

"Fine." He shrugged. "Use paste."

"This is for photographs." Emily folded her hands calmly and clenched them until her knuckles went white. "We're not studding the bottles with them."

"Can you rent them?"

"Loose stones? I don't know." Emily tried to consider it, but she was against it. "We might be able to buy and resell. I don't know much about gemstones."

"Well, I know a little, and what you're suggesting would tie up half your budget."

"Gems are a good investment." Emily deliberately unclenched her hands. "We wouldn't lose money."

He shook his head. "We're not in the gem-investment business. Rent them."

Emily shook her head. "We might need the same stones back again for later pictures. We couldn't be sure we'd get them. Plus, we often use them in special displays at openings and benefits. We did this with Paradise, and it was very successful."

He leaned back in his desk chair and looked at her steadily.

"Are you really serious about this, or is this just something you're going to fight me on?"

*Hasn't he been listening to me?* Emily thought. *Do I sound like I'm playing games?* "I'm serious. And I never fight just for the sake of fighting."

"That was a business lunch today?"

"Jane knows more about this company than you or

I do." Emily clenched her hands again. "When you've been here a little longer, you'll know that. I consult with her often, and I value her opinions highly. So, yes, that really was a business lunch."

"Pink lace underwear?" He smiled at her dryly.

He would overhear that comment, she thought. Emily smiled back sweetly. "I told her you wouldn't think it was cost-effective."

"I don't look at everything in terms of cost, Ms. Tate." His eyes dropped almost involuntarily to the open collar of her blouse.

Emily raised her eyebrows at him, and he flushed. He looked good flushed. *What do you know,* she thought. *He's human. There may be hope.* "I'm sure you don't, Mr. Parker. And I'm hoping you'll see that in the case of the rubies, cost-effectiveness simply doesn't apply. We're selling emotions here, the sizzle not the steak." She leaned across the desk to him, suddenly earnest, trying to convince him. "You can't sizzle with paste, Richard. You need the real thing."

His eyes had widened a little at her use of his name.

"All right." He cleared his throat. "I'll take it under consideration. Now, the next item…"

Emily worked with him for another hour, politely agreeing on a few things she didn't care about, anyway, leaving the others open for further discussion, trying to build a foundation of compromise so that when she came back for real money, for rubies and whatever else she wanted, he'd be used to negotiating with her, not flatly dismissing her. From the look in his eyes, he had a fairly good idea of what she was doing, but he was patient with her. Toward the end, Emily realized her plan wasn't working; any compromising had been done by her, not him. Richard liked saying no or yes and moving on.

When she stood up to go, Richard pushed back his chair and stood, too. "We'll have to meet again. We haven't accomplished much."

"I wouldn't say that." Emily tried to smile warmly but her lips were tight. "I think we've established a very creditable working relationship." She held out her hand. "Please call Jane if you need any information. She knows exactly what's going on."

He took her hand and held it for a moment, and she tried to ignore the warmth he generated there. "I'd rather talk to you. I like to go straight to the person in charge."

"Then definitely talk to Jane." Emily pulled her hand away. "She's been running my life since high school."

"I thought I sensed a lot more there than just boss-and-secretary." He came around the desk and walked her to the door.

"We're partners."

"I envy you. I've always worked alone." He stopped by the door. "Would you consider having dinner with me tonight? To go over some of these points again? Maybe in a…warmer atmosphere, we could get closer on some of these disagreements."

He smiled down at her, and Emily was caught off guard, her knees going to jelly while she frantically tried to gather her thoughts under the wattage of that suddenly sweet, boyishly endearing, sexy smile.

*He's a Hun,* she told herself. *Unless you want to be invaded, turn back now.*

"Sorry," she croaked. "I have a dinner engagement."

"Jane again?"

"Oh, no. Jane goes home to a husband and three lovely children."

"And you?"

"I go home to cost-effectiveness reports." Emily opened the door. "I have a very tough budget adviser."

She didn't turn around as she walked down the hall, but she could feel him watching her all the way to the elevator.

"How did it go?" Jane asked, following her into the office.

"Not well, but not badly, either." Emily kicked off her shoes. "I really hate panty hose. They itch."

"Back to Richard," Jane said firmly. "What happened?"

"I tried to compromise. He told me what to do. He likes telling people what to do. He listened part of the time. At one point, he looked down my blouse and blushed. He asked me to dinner."

"Wear something sexy."

"I'm not going. I told him I had a previous engagement. He thought it was with you, but I told him you were happily married. That's about it."

"Go out with him." Jane sat down and folded her arms on Emily's desk. "Sleep with him."

"Sell my body for a perfume campaign?" Emily shook her head. "Not likely."

"No." Jane leaned back, disgusted with her. "The hell with the perfume campaign. Share your body for a wonderful experience. He looks like a wonderful experience. Did you see his hands?"

Emily frowned. "I must have, but I didn't pay attention."

"He has great hands. And he's really very charming. He's a little obsessive about getting his own way, but he's not a Hun."

"No."

"Listen, Em." Jane leaned over the desk again and caught Emily's hand. "I'm worried about you. You haven't had a serious relationship since you dumped that fool Croswell in R & D. That was two years ago. You're not getting any younger. You're obsessive about your work, and that's not going to change. You've just met a truly beautiful man who is also obsessive about his work, but who has focused his eyes on you long enough to ask you to dinner. You could build a life as obsessive executives together. You could have great obsessive sex together. You could have little obsessive children in suits together. This is the man for you. Go buy that pink lace bra and seduce this guy before you're too old to wear pink lace."

"I will never be too old to wear pink lace," Emily said.

"Are you wearing any now?"

"What do you mean?"

"Do you have anything sexy or fun in your whole wardrobe?"

"I have some white lace. Sort of."

"You may already be too old to wear pink lace. Mentally you're already in gray flannel long johns."

Emily sighed and thought about what Jane was saying because she always thought about what Jane was saying. Then she shook her head. "I could never be serious about somebody who told me what to do all the time. Telling people what to do is this guy's reason for living."

"So change him." Jane leaned back again. "He has one tiny fault and the rest of him is perfect. Teach him not to boss you around."

"Maybe." Emily thought about it.

"That's a start." Jane got up to go. "Keep an open mind. I bet he can make love like crazy."

*Change him*, Emily thought. *No, better yet, change me. I'm in this position because I'm modest, cooperative and polite. Because I'm modest, cooperative and polite, I'm working for a vain, obstructive, rude man like George. And as if George wasn't enough, now I have Richard Parker, the Budget Hun.*

*A Hun who can make my knees go weak when he smiles, dammit.*

*Well, no more of that,* she told herself. *I'm tired of being told what to do. Starting tomorrow, Richard Parker treats me like a partner, not a slave. Starting tomorrow, I am going to make that man listen to me.*

*And starting tomorrow, my knees are going to stiffen up, too.*

*TOO FAST TO FALL*
Victoria Dahl

# CHAPTER ONE

THE COP GREW larger in Jenny's side mirror as he approached, his sunglasses glinting ominous light as she considered whether or not to make a run for it.

She might be able to escape. The highway was a nice, straight run here, and a gorgeous 350 V-8 engine purred beneath the hood of her 1978 Camaro, just waiting for her to punch the accelerator. The deputy would have to get all the way back to his SUV before he could even consider chasing her down. By then, she'd be a speck of bright yellow a mile down the asphalt. And hell, with the snow still five feet deep on either side of the road, she could just pull off onto any old trail and he might pass right by her.

Jenny flexed her fingers against the thin circle of the steering wheel. She was tempted. She knew how to run. It had always been her first instinct, and she'd pulled it off many times. But as she watched the cop's hard-hewn jaw begin to tic in anger, she sighed and slumped in her seat. Deputy Hendricks knew very well where she lived. He'd written her address down on three separate speeding tickets, not to mention two terse warnings.

"Good Morning, Deputy Hendricks!" she said brightly, as if she weren't easing her foot from a tempted hover above the gas pedal.

He didn't return her greeting. He didn't say anything at all. He just...*loomed,* his sharp cheekbones and hard-edged jaw a warning of danger. His lean body a threat of strength. The mountains looked small behind him.

Jenny made a valiant attempt not to squirm. "I thought I had a few more days on my tags."

His hands were loose by his sides in a pose she recognized from the other five times he'd pulled her over. One hand near his gun. One near his baton. He'd never reached for either, thank God, but this time, both his hands spasmed into brief fists before relaxing into readiness again.

"End of the month, right?" she squeaked. She'd found him pretty cute on previous stops. Now she only felt nervous.

His hands closed one more time, and then he eased them open with deliberate slowness. "Ms. Stone," he said, grinding out her name.

She aimed a big smile up at him, though her lips felt stiff. "That's me."

"Unfortunately, I'm well aware of that."

"I—"

"Just as I assume you're well aware of why I've stopped you today."

"Is it—?"

"And *no*," he barked. "It has nothing to do with your damn tags."

She flinched at the way his voice filled her car.

In response, he cleared his throat and rolled his neck. "Excuse me," he said in a much quieter tone, though the ends of the words were clipped enough to sound razor-sharp. "While I run your information to see if you've acquired any warrants for your arrest since the last time I stopped you."

His heel scraped against the asphalt. Jenny leaned out. "Don't you need my license and—?"

He threw a hand up to stop her words and muttered something she didn't quite catch. Apparently he had no trouble recalling her name and birth date.

"Shit," she groaned as she ducked back into her seat. He'd been lenient in the past, but last time he'd clocked her going eighty in a fifty-five, he'd been clear that his tolerance had worn thin.

*One more ticket, Ms. Stone, and you'll be called before a judge. You'll lose your license for thirty days, at best. At worst, you'll be charged with reckless endangerment.*

"Of what?" she muttered to her steering wheel. "Chipmunks?" It had been November. Too cold for Yellowstone tourists and not snowy enough for skiers. She rolled her eyes as she heard the door of his truck open, but immediately after he slammed it, his footsteps sounded again. She watched him approach in her mirror, just as he had a few minutes before, but this time, she sank down a little in defense.

"Do you know how dangerous this is?" he growled before he even reached her window. "It's the middle of winter, damn it! You could hit a patch of ice! You could—"

"It hasn't snowed in two weeks," she argued. "The roads have been bone-dry for days!"

"Are you kidding me? There's snowmelt streaming across the road everywhere! And what if you'd suddenly come up on an elk? Or some stupid tourist stopped in the road to take a picture of a stupid elk? Are you… just…are you…?"

"Stupid?" she volunteered, hunching farther down in her seat. If she lost her license, she'd go mad. She couldn't live without her car. Or rather, she couldn't live without driving. It felt like flying to her. It felt like freedom. And it had been, three times now.

"Yes!" Deputy Hendricks yelled. "Stupid!"

"I'm sorry," she whispered. He'd never, ever lost his temper before.

He was silent for a long moment. A gas tanker drove past them, sucking the air through her open window, then hurling it back in.

Jenny shook her head. "I'm really sorry." She meant it. He'd been kind to her and she'd promised not to speed again. And now here she was.

He took a deep breath. His clenched teeth looked very white against his tan skin. "Jenny," he said, the only time he'd used her first name since she'd invited him to three tickets ago. She glanced up but couldn't puzzle out his expression behind his sunglasses. She'd never seen him with his glasses off. She worked at the saloon at night, so all her joyrides occurred during day-light hours. All she knew of him was his dark skin and sculpted jaw and wide mouth. Under his hat, his hair looked deep brown. The wide shoulders beneath his uniform jacket eased the insult of the tickets, and the cheekbones didn't hurt, either, but for all she knew he had bug eyes that wandered in different directions and brows like a twitchy mad scientist.

But probably not.

He stared steadily down at her. Jenny's heart fell. "It's okay," she said softly. "Just write the ticket. It's my own fault, and I know you've tried to help."

He watched her for a long moment, then cleared his throat and shifted. "Ms. Stone, you're not some eigh-teen-year-old punk with too much testosterone and too little intelligence. Why can't you just go the speed limit and save us both some pain? Why is that so hard? Even five miles per hour over and I'd be able to shrug it off. Just…why?"

She couldn't tell him, because she had no idea. Driving made her happy. The feel of the power at her fingertips. The rush of the wind past her open window when the weather cooperated. And the faster she drove, the freer she felt. Fifty-five miles per hour wasn't happiness. It was just more constriction. "I don't know," she said honestly. "But it makes me feel better that giving me tickets is painful for you. After all this time, we're practically friends now, aren't we?"

His flat mouth didn't budge in the slightest. "I meant that writing another ticket will be painful for me because I'll lose a whole morning in court testifying against you."

Her heart sank and bleated an ugly curse on its way down. She was mad at herself, and terrified about the consequences, and just a tiny bit hurt that Deputy Hendricks didn't feel some small affection for her. She'd always been polite to him. Cheerful, even as he wrote her a ticket. She wasn't a bad person.

"I warned you last time."

"I know." She felt tears prick her eyes, and blinked them furiously away. If he was going to be mean, she didn't want him to see her cry. "It's okay," she said again.

He walked away, thank God, because a tear had managed to escape and slip down her cheek. She swiped at her jaw and sniffed hard. She wouldn't cry. It was her own fault, and even if Deputy Hendricks was being particularly hard-nosed, she wouldn't cry. She wouldn't. She deserved this, and he'd cut her enough slack. She sniffed again and scrubbed at her eyes.

The deputy cleared his throat from right beside her.

She froze in horror. He'd walked away to write her a ticket. What was he doing back so quickly?

When she snuck a glance out the window, she saw him holding out a business card instead of the thin paper of a ticket. "What's that?" she asked, thinking it was a card for the attorney she was going to need.

"Take it," he said gruffly.

She took it gingerly, barely touching the edges of the card.

"It's information about a local driving class. I want you to promise to sign up. One, you need it. And two, it'll help your case the next time I pull you over. Because I will give you a ticket next time, Ms. Stone. No questions. No leniency."

"What?" she breathed.

"I'm serious. This is getting ridiculous. You're too old for this crap, and you make a fool out of me every time I let you off."

"I don't mean to! I'm sorry! It's not like I drive away thinking, 'Yeah! I fooled the Man!' I mean… Um…" She felt her face flame. His sunglasses stared down at her in unwavering judgment. Her attempt at a smile felt like a grimace as she held up the card. "I'll take the class. I really appreciate this. I do every time."

"Every time," he muttered. "Right."

"Each time," she tried. "Both times. Well, this is maybe the third…"

"Yes," he said. "It is the third. The third warning. The *sixth* stop."

"I just get lost in thought. I don't realize I'm going so fast. It's kind of hard to keep her under sixty."

His head turned slightly toward the hood of the car. "Maybe it's time to buy a nice sedan."

A tiny, horrified whimper escaped from her mouth.

"I bet you'd save a hell of a lot of money on gas. And it would have airbags."

"I'll slow down," she croaked.

"You'd better. Or you'll find out how easy it is to keep her under sixty when you're not allowed out of the garage."

"Yes, sir."

His face tipped toward her again at her hoarse whisper. He stared for a moment. She could see her own tiny face looking pitiful and pale in the black lenses.

"Go on," he finally said. "I'm not giving you an official warning because I don't want any record of this. It's an embarrassment. Drive safely, Ms. Stone. And *slowly.* Please? For the love of whatever it is you value?"

"Yes, sir," she whispered again.

He stepped back. She waited, but he finally shook his head. "Just go before I change my mind."

Jenny started the car, wincing at the roar of the engine. Normally, she loved that sound, but right now it seemed a little much. "Thank you," she said again. "Really. Come in for a free beer sometime, okay?"

Maybe not the right thing to say to a deputy who seemed obsessed with road safety. Shoot. Jenny released the brake and pulled away. In her nervousness, she hit the gas too hard and as she pulled off the shoulder, the tires squealed. Just a little. Just enough to make her wish she was dead.

"Oh, God," she groaned, eyes flashing to the rearview mirror as she left Deputy Hendricks behind in an unfortunate cloud of dust. Well, not a cloud. More like a tiny, harmless puff.

Heart pounding hard, Jenny drove back to town safely. And very slowly, keeping her eye on the speed-

ometer the whole way. It didn't feel very much like flying, but it was better than being grounded.

It might be time to make a run for it, after all.


NATE PULLED INTO THE lot of the Crooked R Saloon, and
his gaze was immediately drawn to the yellow Camaro
parked in the far corner. He felt his left eye twitch at
the sight. That woman and her damned menace of a car.

He should've given her the ticket. He'd sworn to himself that he would. After issuing that last warning, he'd
ordered himself to have a steel will the next time she
flew past him.

In fact, each time he stopped her, each time she drove
away, he told himself that was it. He wouldn't be lenient
again. If she deserved jail time, the judge would give it
to her. It wasn't Nate's responsibility to decide. She was
a repeat offender. She deserved whatever she got, even
if she was always cheerful and sweet and apologetic.

But yesterday he'd seen her flying by again, a bright
flash of yellow that shot adrenaline straight into his
heart, and despite his rage and frustration and impa-
tience, his resolve had been as weak as paper. She'd
flashed that slightly crooked smile and called him "Deputy Hendricks" as if it were a private joke they shared,
and…

"Fuck," he growled as he made himself turn away
from her car and walk toward the front porch of the
saloon.

What the hell was he doing here?

His brain had snuck up on him to issue a reminder
that whatever excuse he had to be at the Crooked R,
it was flimsy as hell. But he *did* have an excuse. His
cousin had needed to meet with him, so why not here? It
had been thirty-two hours since Nate had pulled Jenny

Stone over, so it was time for a reminder about that driving class.

Sure, she'd promised. She'd even shed grateful tears. But he didn't think for one minute that she'd called about the class yet. Why would she, when she had yet another chance to push him toward insanity? Instead of doing what he'd ordered, she'd probably attach floating neon lights to the undercarriage of her car and get her windows tinted before adding a sticker about pigs to taunt him the next time she flashed her bumper.

He was just another cop fooled by a pretty face. Hardly a rare breed. And now here he was, at her workplace like a hormone-addled fool.

Nate slid off his sunglasses and walked into the saloon, cursing himself every step of the way.

The place was packed. Five-dollar pitcher night, he realized belatedly. Not the ideal place to have a serious talk with his cousin. Then again, considering how worried Luis had sounded, maybe he'd appreciate the roar of background noise. Whatever it was, he'd made it clear that he couldn't invite Nate over to his own house.

Nate glanced around, meaning to look for his cousin, but somehow searching out a blond ponytail at the same time. And there she was, out from behind the bar, delivering a tray of pitchers. He'd never seen her outside her car. He'd never made her walk the shoulder to check for any telltale signs of inebriation. Reckless as her speeds were, her car always followed every curve of the road perfectly. Even when she spotted his lights, she eased into the stop, edging just far enough over to be safe, and never far enough to veer too deeply into the soft slope next to the highway. Jenny Stone was dangerous, but not in that way.

No, her danger lay in an entirely different set of curves.

"Damn," he cursed as his eyes roamed down her body. He'd gotten several nice glimpses of cleavage before, and had even wondered whether she'd purposefully set free a button or two as he approached. But he'd had no idea she'd been hiding a perfect ass the whole time. He almost cringed at the sight of it. Beautiful and plump and not at all good for his tenuous hold on sanity when it came to her.

And then she dealt another blow. His gaze traveled back up her body just as her eyes moved over the room. They paused on him for a moment, then moved on, no spark of recognition flashing. Not even a hint of it.

She had no idea who he was. He was just another cop when he was in his uniform, and nothing but a stranger in street clothes tonight.

"Perfect," he murmured, vowing right then that he'd talk to his cousin and then get the hell out of this place before his pride was permanently damaged by his sex drive.

Looking away from Jenny Stone, he caught sight of Luis raising a hand from a back table and headed gratefully in that direction.

"Cousin," he said as Luis flashed a tense smile and stood to give Nate a quick hug.

"Hey, Nate."

Nate had hoped to start off on a positive note, but Luis didn't look good. "You look like you haven't slept in a week."

Luis's tense smile disappeared in a flash, replaced by a pained grimace that even his goatee couldn't hide. "Shit, man. I don't know what to do."

"Is it James?" Nate asked, his thoughts immediately

going to Luis's fifteen-year-old son. A ripe age for trouble, even for good kids.

"Yes… No!" Luis said. Then his head dropped. "I don't know. I'm really worried. I don't think he's gotten mixed up in it, but…he might have."

"Mixed up in what? Please tell me you haven't done anything stupid. I know the concrete business has been slow lately, but—"

"No, it's not me. It's… You know Teresa's cousin Victor came to live with us last year?"

Nate frowned. He'd met the kid once, and had his suspicions, but he'd never said a word. Teresa was a wonderful woman, quiet and strong with a will of steel. If a family member needed help, she wasn't going to ask more of him than clean language in the house and scrubbed hands when he came to dinner. "I remember," he finally said carefully.

"Everything seemed fine at first. He wasn't exactly a hard worker, but he's nineteen, you know? He took the job I offered and showed up every day. Okay, almost every day. Maybe he was a little lazy, but I kept my mouth shut about it to Teresa, because…"

Nate nodded. Teresa was as traditional a wife and mother as they came, and if she'd taken Victor in as one of her kids, that was that.

"Well, he quit a couple of months ago. Said he'd found other work. He wasn't specific, but he was paying his rent. Even bought an old car to get around in. Frankly, I was too relieved to ask any questions. I should have, though."

Nate's gut tightened in dread. He had a feeling he knew where this was headed, and it was nowhere good.

Running a hand through his hair, Luis met Nate's gaze for a moment, then let his chin drop. "Teresa let him borrow my truck one day. When I got home, I asked what had happened to it. It was muddy as hell, like it'd gotten stuck somewhere. The kid just smiled and said he'd been helping a friend move. I let it go. Teresa said he'd probably been out joyriding on a trail somewhere, but it felt off to me. He's been cocky as hell about something lately. Two days ago, I followed him when he was supposed to be going to work. He ended up out at the cabin."

For a moment, Nate had no idea what he was talking about. "What cabin? The family cabin?"

"Yeah."

It was a run-down cabin down near South Park that had been in his dad's family for years. Forty years ago, when his father had been newly married to Nate's mom, her brother had come up from Mexico with nothing but a wife and hope for a better life. Nate's dad had rented them the cabin for a few years, and eventually they'd bought it from him. Nate had spent countless summer days there, playing with Luis and his other cousins. But these days the place was vacant and falling in on itself.

"So he's getting into trouble down there? Drinking, having sex?" But even as he said it, he knew that wasn't what had Luis glancing over his shoulder. Nate looked around himself, and caught sight of Jenny, grinning from ear to ear as she set a pitcher down a few tables away, then passed out mugs to the cowboys who smiled back at her.

Nate pulled his eyes away and leaned closer to Luis. "Listen, if he's cooking meth, I can—"

"That's not it. He's growing pot. That little bastard has a whole greenhouse set up out back."

"Are you kidding?"

"No. It's a shit job, made out of two-by-fours and

plastic sheeting. I can't believe it hasn't collapsed under the snow yet, but I guess the heaters and lamps are melting it off. It's full of plants. And he's clearing out more land, like he plans to expand during the summer. That's why the truck is so muddy. He was trying to pull stumps out of half-frozen ground, because he apparently doesn't have even half a brain."

"Okay, listen. I'm glad you came to me. You're not responsible for it just because it's being grown on your land. This happens all the time these days. Somebody picks a secluded area, and—"

"It's not just on my land," Luis interrupted. "That damn greenhouse is sitting half on my land and half on federal forest. And that's not the worst of it."

Nate took a deep breath. "Do I want to know?"

"I have no idea, but I don't know who else to turn to. I need your help, Nate. It's…"

"Shit. Is James involved? Tell me the truth."

Luis slumped. "I don't know. He's a good boy, but he loves his cousin. Looks up to him. And I found out he skipped school last week. The same day Victor borrowed the truck. Regardless of what Teresa wants, if I was sure James wasn't involved I would've just called you and had your guys go out and shut it down and arrest that little shit. But if he's pulled James into it…"

"Listen. Even if James is marginally involved, he's a good kid, like you said. He's only fifteen. He won't—"

"He's fifteen, yeah. And he's almost six feet tall, and he's got brown skin and the last name Hernandez, just like me. To a lot of people around here, he doesn't look like a good, harmless kid. He looks like an ad trying to scare people about dangerous illegals."

"Come on, Luis. People around here know you and your family."

"Yeah. And some of them probably remember when I was a kid and got up to no good."

Nate sighed. He'd forgotten about that. Luis had gone through a rebellious stage, and rebelled himself right out of school a couple of times. And into jail once after stealing beer from a local gas station. The same kind of trouble lots of kids got up to, but it was different when you were one of the few brown-skinned kids in the school.

"I'm scared, Nate. If my boy's involved and it's on my land, it's going to look like a whole damn Mexican family operation."

"You're as American as I am," Nate snapped. "I shouldn't even have to say that. We were both born right here."

Luis raised an eyebrow, and Nate didn't bother arguing further. Sure, Nate bore the Hernandez name, as well, but it was his middle name, not his last. And he had his father's gray eyes and lighter skin than his cousins. He knew it wasn't the same for him.

He cursed and ran a hand over his jaw. "All right. Listen. Is there anywhere you can send James for a few days? Maybe a week? Doesn't Teresa's family live in Colorado?"

"Yeah. Maybe I can arrange something. But I'd have to pull him out of school. Teresa won't like that at all."

"You're going to tell her, though, right?"

Luis's eyes shifted away.

"Come on, man. You have to tell her."

"She won't like it. Better to lie. If I tell her, she'll want to let—"

A sudden shadow cut off Luis's words. "Hello, boys! You're not conspiring to lie to an innocent woman, are you?"

Luis flashed wide, panicked eyes up at Jenny, whose ponytail was still swaying from her abrupt appearance. "What?" he yelped.

She waved off his alarm. "I'm a bartender. Believe me, I see it every day. Just be kind to her, okay?" Smiling, she tipped her head toward Nate to include him in her advice, but still didn't seem to recognize him. "You gentlemen want a pitcher?"

Luis shook his head, but Nate said, "Sure."

Her eyes flickered down his body. "Light?"

Nate was suddenly damn glad for all the hours he put in at the gym to keep in shape over the winter. "Bring us the real thing. We'll indulge."

She flashed that smile again. Wide and open enough that it shouldn't have felt intimate, but did. He'd thought that smile was something secret for him. But no. It was just her. She offered it to everyone in the crowd.

Good to know.

Nate laughed at himself as she turned away, already moving toward the bar to get their pitcher. But while he was still shaking his head at his own foolishness, Jenny jerked to a stop, frozen midstep.

Luis was leaning toward him, but Nate held up a hand and kept his eyes on Jenny as she slowly pivoted.

She frowned and cocked her head. Her eyes narrowed at him. And then her face broke into a grin wider than any she'd ever given to him.

"Deputy Hendricks?" she asked.

He tried not to feel thrilled. "Yes, ma'am."

She laughed, her blond hair swinging as her chin tipped up. "Oh, my God! I didn't recognize you without the shades!"

"Yeah, I noticed," he said dryly.

"It's not my fault! You look totally different. Not nearly so scary."

"Still a little scary, though, I gather?"

Instead of answering, she just stood there looking at him for a few long seconds. "My God," she finally said. "Look at you. You're a real person."

"That's just a rumor."

"Okay," she said, still smiling. Then she shook her head. "Okay. Well, the beer's on the house, Deputy."

"It's Nate," he responded.

Her eyebrows rose. "I like that."

She liked that. Thank God she finally turned away, because Nate knew he looked far too pleased with her opinion of his name.

"Hey," his cousin said, the worry in his voice making it clear he'd already dismissed any idea of the cute server. "What the hell am I going to do, man?"

Nate kept his eye on Jenny Stone's swinging hips until she was swallowed by the crowd at the bar before he gave up the vigil and met Luis's eyes. "No kidding around, are you asking me as a cousin or a cop?"

"Hell, I don't know. Both?"

"We've got two options, but whichever way we do this, I don't want James around. If you want me to handle this as your cousin, I'll do that. We send James away to keep him out of the fight, we tear down the greenhouse, burn the plants and put the fear of God in Victor. But that means he's got to go. You have to be sure Teresa understands that. I can do this on the quiet, but he has to leave."

"Okay. Yeah. We could do that."

"But," Nate added, letting the word hang there.

Luis gave him a weary look. "But what?"

"Are you sure he's working alone? If he doesn't have

a truck, how did he get all this set up in the first place? And where did he get the money? The plants, the heaters, the lamps. Do you really think he built that greenhouse and started clearing that land on his own?"

Luis had gone pale. "If James...but he doesn't have any money, and he's only missed one day of school!"

"I don't mean James. But that's the other reason I want him gone. I want to watch the place. See who's coming and going. And I don't want to see James. If Victor isn't the only one involved, if he's not the money and the brains, I'm going to have to handle this as a cop, and I can't have any reason to mention James in the reports."

Luis looked grimmer than ever.

"How do you want to handle it, Luis?"

"Christ. Victor isn't a great guy, but he's not a criminal mastermind, either. He's working for someone. Some guy who uses kids to do the dirty work, I'm sure. Will you check it out for me?"

"Yeah. You'll send James away?"

"He's going to be out of school for a day or two next week for Presidents' Day, anyway. I'll tell Teresa that John Lopez needs help with calving over in Casper. She's always liked that guy and she keeps complaining that James needs to learn how to work harder."

"Has calving started yet?"

"Hell if I know."

Jenny arrived with the pitcher, and she paused as if she'd say something, but someone called her name from another table and she flitted away with an apologetic smile.

Nate poured two beers and slid one toward his cousin. "Teresa's going to find out about all this, you know. You can't hide it for long."

"I know." Luis closed his eyes for moment. "But I don't want to tell her until I know the extent of it. Otherwise she'll convince herself it's nothing and we should sweep it under the rug."

"It's big money these days, cousin. People get shot over it. Remember that. You could've been killed just going out to the cabin if the wrong person was waiting. There was that case up in Gallatin Forest last year. A hiker ran across a crop in a federal forest and someone shot him to keep him from talking. Luckily, the shooter had bad aim."

Luis nodded. "Yeah. I know. Damn it. That little shit Victor has put my family and my livelihood in danger. And if he's involved James…" He took a deep breath. "I can't just let it go. I'll call you when James is on his way, all right?"

"Perfect."

Luis only drank half his beer before he blew out a deep breath and stood. "I've got to get going."

Nate stood and gave him a tight hug.

"Thank you, man. I don't know what I would've done about this if you weren't around."

"Does that mean you'll stop calling me The Fuzz behind my back?"

Luis slapped his shoulder and stepped away. "Hell, Nate. You know that was because of that mustache you tried to grow to be more like me in high school. I figured you became a cop just to try to live down the nickname."

"If you want my help, you'll keep that quiet."

"Got it." Luis's smile faded. "I'll call you."

Nate sank back into his seat and topped off his beer. He wasn't going to take any unofficial law enforcement action, but he could poke around the cabin a little without stepping too far outside the rules. There might be some personal danger, but Nate was willing to risk a lot for the sake of Luis and his family. Luis was more like a brother than a cousin. Nate had a sister, but she was a few years older and had always been more of a second mother than a playmate. But Luis…if he needed help, Nate would step up any day.

"Hey!" Jenny suddenly appeared, her head tilted toward the front door of the saloon. "I hope your friend's coming back. I can't let you drive if you drink that whole pitcher on your own. I'm sure you understand. The cops around here are real uptight."

Nate raised one eyebrow and refused to meet her smile.

"Right. Ha! So, anyway…" she drawled.

"Luis isn't coming back, but I promise not to finish the pitcher by myself."

"Are you waiting for someone?"

"No. I'm on my own."

"I could…" Her eyes slid to the chair Luis had vacated, but then she just flashed a wide smile. "I'll check back on you later."

Nate looked from the chair to her. "I wanted to talk to you, actually. Care for a drink?"

"Yes! I was just about to take my break. I'll be right back."

He watched her ponytail bounce as she hurried toward the bar. If someone had asked him an hour before, and if he'd allowed himself to be completely honest, he would've said that sitting down for a drink with Jenny Stone was the goal of the evening. But at this point, he had no idea if he should be satisfied or just embarrassed that he was so damn easy for her.

*ALONE WITH YOU*
Shannon Stacey

# CHAPTER ONE

"ASHGABAT." THE SEXY stranger's breath blew warm over her neck as he whispered the word near her ear, and Darcy Vaughn chased a full-body shiver with a big gulp of martini.

"Ashgabat," she repeated for the trivia host, since he hadn't been wrong yet.

"That's correct!" The other teams around the bar all groaned, and Darcy smiled sweetly at Kent and Vanessa, formerly the reigning know-it-alls of Tuesday-night trivia.

She and her sexy fountain of random facts were kicking butt tonight.

Her regular partner hadn't called to cancel until after Darcy had ordered her margarita and nachos, so she'd left it to the waitress serving as trivia host to pair her with another customer flying solo. She hadn't expected the guy rocking the scruffy, blue-collar look to raise his hand and join the academic fun, but figured he'd contribute on the sports questions. Despite working at a sports bar, Darcy wasn't much of a fan.

But now she knew a few things about her trivia partner. His name was Jake. He had brown eyes the same shade as his close-cut hair, smelled delicious and had a body made for selling charity calendars. He also knew a little something about which capital city sat between the Kara-Kum Desert and the Kopet Dag Mountains.

Being able to cough up Turkmenistan trivia was almost as sexy as the way he rested his arm across the back of her bar stool every time he leaned in to whisper an answer in her ear.

"Ten-minute break," the host announced.

After hitting the restrooms, the teams eventually settled back on their bar stools to wait for the host, who'd disappeared into the kitchen. When the silence stretched toward awkward, Darcy turned to Jake. "So, let me guess. You're taking a break from exploring the world after an expedition to Turkmenistan to find an ancient, possibly cursed relic went bad."

His smile should've been illegal. "And that must make you the Russian spy sent to charm the relic's location out of me with your knowledge of U.S. presidents and the Periodic Table of Elements."

"I have ways of making you talk," she joked, though it came out a little more suggestively than she'd intended.

"I bet you do."

Darcy realized, with the way they were gradually leaning in closer to each other and the innuendo, they were in heavy flirting territory and she panicked a little. Guys didn't usually come on to her in bars. At Jasper's Bar & Grille, where she waited tables and occasionally worked the bar, most of the guys were looking at Paulie, who managed the place. She was tall, had a killer body—including great breasts—and knew everything and anything about sports.

Darcy was on the short side of average. Her breasts were on the small side of average. She pretty much ran just left of average overall. Her hair was nice, though. Dark and thick, with just enough wave to keep it cute in a ponytail.

"So, Darcy, what do you really do when you're not answering trivia questions or charming Indiana Jones types out of their relics?"

"I wait tables." She shrugged. "It's a good cover. Lots of eavesdropping opportunities. What do you do when you're not sifting through ancient ruins?"

"Some business consulting. Boring stuff."

"Do you get to travel a lot?"

He shook his head. "Honestly, I don't fly, so a few sledding trips to Canada and a really misguided summer in Florida during my youth are the extent of my travel. Not trusting airplanes to stay in the sky killed my dreams of being Indiana Jones when I grew up."

"Yeah, well, my Russian accent sucks." They were laughing as the trivia host stepped back into the horseshoe center of the bar and poured them all another round before continuing the game.

After Kent and Vanessa got an economics history question right and the next couple blew it on geography, the host turned to them. "What famous player, inducted into the Baseball Hall of Fame in 1972, was known for the phrase 'It ain't over till it's over'?"

As Jake leaned in to whisper in her ear, Darcy blocked him with her hand. "Wait. I know this one, dammit. Finally a sports question I know the answer to."

"We should talk about it."

"Why? Don't you think women can answer sports questions?"

His mouth brushed her ear as his arm pressed against her back. "I just like having an excuse to whisper in your ear."

"Yogi Berra," she told the trivia host in a surprisingly normal voice, considering how on the inside she was a shivery, breathless mess.

A couple of drinks and a few rounds later, Jake and Darcy were declared the winners. The grand prize was nothing more than bragging rights and the his-and-hers puckered looks Kent and Vanessa sported as they went out the door.

"How are you getting home?" Jake asked as he held Darcy's sweater so she could slip her arms in. Such a gentleman.

It was an innocent enough question, but Darcy's overheated, alcohol-fueled imagination added a pronounced ungentlemanly slant to his words. "I'm walking."

"Alone?"

"It's not far."

"You've had a bit to drink." A bit more than she usually did, actually. "I'd feel a lot better if you let me walk you home."

He didn't know it yet but, unless she'd totally misread his signals, he'd feel a *lot* better because if he got as far as her front door, she was going to drag him inside and have her way with him. She wasn't in the habit of bringing men home after the first date—and random trivia partnership was stretching the definition of date—but she was going to roll the dice on this sexy, smart guy with a sense of humor. They were rare. Plus, she just really, really wanted him.

JAKE HELD THE DOOR for Darcy, cursing himself the entire time. Now wasn't the time to be romancing a woman, even if she was smoking hot and correctly guessed that painite was considered the rarest mineral gem.

But he couldn't let her walk home alone in the dark. And after watching that mouth smile at him all night and her teeth catching on her bottom lip when she wasn't sure of an answer and her tongue flicking out to grab a stray dab of nacho cheese, he wanted a goodnight kiss. Maybe it wasn't the most traditional first date, but it counted. Sort of.

Translating a woman's body language didn't come as naturally to him as it did to other guys, but he was pretty sure he was reading Darcy right. She walked really slow, as if she was lingering to make the walk last longer, and she stayed close enough to him so their arms occasionally brushed. After the third time, he threw caution to the wind and captured her hand in his. She didn't pull away.

"Do you do that every Tuesday night?" he asked after a few minutes of comfortable silence.

"As often as I can. My usual partner couldn't make it, so I was lucky you showed up tonight." Her usual partner? He didn't like the idea of her sharing random facts and sexy smiles with anybody else. "Her youngest was sick and her husband does diapers and homework help, but no puke buckets."

So not a boyfriend, then. "I'm sorry your friend's kid is sick, but I'm glad I got to be your partner tonight."

On the well-lit street, he had no trouble seeing the blush on her cheeks. "And I talk to you about puke buckets. That's so sexy."

"Puke buckets might not be sexy, but a woman as pretty as you who knows the Treaty of Paris ended the Seven Years' War is hot as hell."

The blush got brighter and he squeezed her hand. It wasn't a line, either. Brains and beauty were like peanut butter and chocolate—each good on its own, but downright delicious together.

Leave it to him to find a potentially right woman at the totally wrong time. And in the wrong place. The city was a quick stopover between the life in Connecticut he'd grown bored with and the exciting, new restaurant venture with an old friend. When he'd seen a flyer at the auto shop for trivia night, he'd decided to scope out how it was run and the turnout in case it was something he might want to try in the future. He hadn't expected to meet a woman he'd be reluctant to walk away from.

"This might sound pushy, but I'm only passing through here and I'm leaving tomorrow for business and I really want to ask for your number, so...what's your romantic situation?"

"No boyfriend. No husband, though there was one once. No kids and we went our separate ways years ago. How long will you be gone?"

"It'll be an extended trip, but I'll be traveling back and forth a lot and I'd like to maybe see you when I'm in the city. You know, if you want." Which was probably a dumb thing to say considering she was holding his hand.

"I'd like that." Her voice was soft and warm and his mind jumped ahead to the possibility of a good-night kiss. "This is my building."

He was so busy imagining how her mouth would feel, he barely registered that they'd stopped walking. Would her lips taste like margaritas? He started to reach for his phone, intending to program her number into it.

"If you come up, I'll write my number down for you."

Some of the blood left his brain and headed south, but he was no fool. He left the phone in its holster. "Sounds great."

Darcy unlocked the glass door tucked between two business entrances and led him up the stairs to a very small hallway somebody had tried to make nice with a few potted plants and a bright throw rug. There was a door on either side of the hall and she unlocked the one on the left, reaching in to turn on the light.

Her apartment was small and pretty, just like her. The walls were a plain beige, but she'd hung colorful pictures on them and she had a bunch of those little pillows on the couch that matched the curtains and throw rugs that matched the one in the hall. He wasn't surprised to see several bookshelves taking up space.

He watched her tear a sheet of paper off a memo pad stuck to the fridge and then rummage in a drawer for a pen. After jotting something down, she held it out to him. *Darcy, from trivia night.* And her number.

It made him chuckle. "How many Darcys do you think I know?"

"I thought it might help you remember me when you fish that out of your pocket later."

In the light of the bar, he'd thought her eyes were a hazel color, but now—standing close enough to her to touch—he realized they were more green, with flecks of brown and gold. "I'm not going to forget you that easily."

When she blushed again and shifted her weight from one foot to the other, and then back again, he realized she either wanted him to make a graceful exit with a promise to call her later or make his move. The problem was deciphering which she was looking for.

Then she stood on her tiptoes and leaned forward, so he took the hint and moved in for the kiss.

DARCY HAD NEVER BEEN SO thoroughly kissed in her life. When Jake first touched his mouth to hers, he'd been tentative, maybe even a little shy. Now she was backed up to her fridge, her nails digging into his shirt as his tongue danced over hers.

His hands slid from her waist up to her breasts and she moaned when his thumbs brushed over the taut nipples. Just the lightest touch, but it ignited a need in her stronger than any she'd felt in a long time. And then his lips left her mouth and blazed a trail down her neck.

"All I thought about tonight was kissing you," he said, his breath warm against her skin.

"And yet you still almost always knew the right answer."

"Well, I tried to pay attention when it was our turn, but when it wasn't, all I could do was think about touching you."

Darcy took a deep breath and said the words. "I'd like for you to stay. You know, if you want to."

He straightened and looked down into her face. "You're sure?"

"Very sure."

"Then I want to." He kissed her and, when she curled her arms around his neck, he lifted her off the floor.

It startled her and she wrapped her legs around his waist, really hoping he wouldn't drop her. But she wouldn't have fallen, anyway, with her back against the fridge and Jake between her thighs, his denim-clad erection putting a little pressure in just the right spot.

Once he'd kissed her until she could barely breathe, she felt him shift his arms to hold her more securely and then they were crossing the living room. She'd never been carried before and she buried her face in his neck, hoping nothing mood-killing happened, like running into a wall or hitting her head on the doorjamb.

When he leaned forward, she clutched at his shoulders for a second, until she felt the mattress under her. He went down with her, kissing her and nibbling at her ear, with short interruptions to pull her shirt off, then his shirt and then her bra.

The feel of his warm, naked skin against hers sent shivers through Darcy and she wanted more. She reached for the fly of his jeans, but was momentarily distracted when his mouth closed over her nipple. Gentle suction, then a little bit harder, and when he slid his hand between her legs, she lifted her hips, desperate for the touch, even through the jeans she still wore.

"Remember how I told you I spent the whole night thinking about touching you?" She made an *mm-hmm* noise. "It's even better than I imagined."

They lost the jeans and socks and underwear then, and he lifted her so he could lay her down higher on the bed. She heard the rustling of a condom packet and then he covered her body with his.

Closing her eyes, she moaned as he filled her, moving with slow, even strokes that felt so good, but weren't enough at the same time. "Faster."

"In a hurry?"

She opened her eyes to find him smiling down at her. "It's been a while."

"Good." But he didn't seem inclined to obey her demand. If anything, he slowed his pace, drawing almost completely out of her and then pushing deep. She moved her hips, trying to urge him on, but his fingers pressed into her thighs, holding her still. "Not yet."

"Who made you the boss?"

He drove into her, and her back arched off the bed as she bit down on the side of her hand, trying not to scream and wake her neighbor. Again and again he did it until she was almost at the brink…and then he stopped moving.

"More," she whispered. One small, lazy circle of his hips was all she got. "You're making me crazy."

"Good." He bent to her breast, sucking one nipple just hard enough to make her squirm. "I want you to be crazy about me."

Then he kissed her mouth while his hips moved faster and harder and she gasped against his lips. This time when she lifted her hips, he didn't stop her. Each thrust came faster and deeper until the orgasm rocked her.

With her ankles crossed behind him, she used her legs to hold him to her as the tremors faded. He groaned her name against her neck as he pushed into her in the deep, jerky rhythm of his own orgasm.

Darcy ran her hands over his back, trying to catch her breath. After a minute, Jake disappeared to the bathroom for a minute, but then he slid back into bed and pulled the covers up over them.

She'd rolled onto her left side when he got up because that was how she lay in bed and she was going to turn to face him, but Jake curled his body around hers before she got the chance. With his right arm thrown over her, he pulled her tight against him and kissed the top of her head.

"That was incredible," he whispered, and she could already feel the relaxing of his muscles as he started nodding off.

The next thing Darcy knew, sunlight was streaming through her bedroom window and her trivia partner was leaning against the doorjamb, cursing and rubbing his toe. She winced, having kicked the cedar hope chest at the foot of her bed more than once herself.

"Sorry," he said when he realized she was awake. "I was trying to be quiet."

"Were you going to sneak out without saying goodbye?"

"No, I was going to let you sleep until the last possible second and then kiss you goodbye on my way out so you could maybe nod back off."

Sweet, if it was true. He already had his jeans on, sadly, but she watched him pull on the rest of his clothes. He had an amazing body and it was such a shame to cover it up.

When he was done, he disappeared into the other room and then came back holding the paper with her name and number on it. He folded it before shoving it into his pocket, and then he leaned over the bed.

"I have a full day today, with a lot of travel and a meeting with a contractor, but I'll call you tomorrow."

Lounging in bed—her body happy and lazy from a night of lovemaking—and looking up into his dark eyes, she almost believed him. "I have tomorrow off, so whenever you get the chance is good."

He kissed her goodbye and then got halfway across the bedroom before he came back and kissed her again. She laughed and wrapped her arms around his neck, but didn't miss the fact that he was sneaking a peek at his watch.

"If I didn't have a meeting with a contractor, I'd crawl back into bed with you," he muttered against her lips. "And I already called a cab."

"When will you be back in the city?"

"As soon as I can." He kissed her one more time and then made it to the bedroom door. "I'll call you tomorrow."

She heard the front door close and then snuggled under her covers, grinning like an idiot. Jake just might be the keeper she'd been looking for.

USA TODAY bestselling author

# CHRISTIE RIDGWAY

**introduces a sizzling new series set in
Crescent Cove, California, where the
magic of summer can last forever....**

Combat medic Vance Smith made a
promise to a fallen officer: to treat
the man's young daughter to an idyllic
vacation at Beach House No. 9.
One month, some sun and surf, a
"helmet list" of activities to check
off, and Vance will move on. But the
"little girl" he's expecting turns out
to be a full-grown woman. With silky
hair, big brown eyes and smelling
sweetly of the cupcakes she makes
for her mobile bakery, Layla Parker is
irresistible. And Vance shouldn't lay a
finger on her. Honor—and one heck
of a scarred heart—says so.

To Layla, Vance is a hero who was
injured trying to save her father's life.
She intends to spend their month of
lazy days and warm nights taking very good care of the gorgeous soldier—
inside and out….

### Available wherever books are sold!

### Be sure to connect with us at:

Harlequin.com/Newsletters

Facebook.com/HarlequinBooks

Twitter.com/HarlequinBooks

**HARLEQUIN®** HQN™
™ www.Harlequin.com

PHCR745

**Sometimes the best man
is the one you least expect....**

*New York Times* **Bestselling Author**

# KRISTAN HIGGINS

Faith Holland left her hometown after being jilted at the altar. Now a little older and wiser, she's ready to return to the Blue Heron Winery, her family's vineyard, to confront the ghosts of her past, and maybe enjoy a glass of red. After all, there's some great scenery there....

Like Levi Cooper, the local police chief—and best friend of her former fiancé. There's a lot about Levi that Faith never noticed, and it's not just those deep green eyes. The only catch is she's having a hard time forgetting that he helped ruin her wedding all those years ago. If she can find a minute amid all her family drama to stop and smell the rosé, she just might find a reason to stay at Blue Heron, and finish that walk down the aisle.

## Available wherever books are sold!

**Be sure to connect with us at:**

Harlequin.com/Newsletters

Facebook.com/HarlequinBooks

Twitter.com/HarlequinBooks

www.Harlequin.com

PHKH792

# Harlequin More Than Words
## Where Dreams Begin

### *Three bestselling authors*
### *Three real-life heroines*

Each of us can effect change. In our own unique ways, we can all make the world a better place. We need only to take that first step, do that first good deed and the ripple effect will be life-changing to so many. Three extraordinary women who were compelled to take that first leap and make a difference have been chosen as recipients of **Harlequin's More Than Words** award. To celebrate their accomplishments, three bestselling authors have written short stories inspired by these real-life heroines.

SHERRYL WOODS captures the magic of pretty dresses and first dances in **Black Tie and Promises.**

CHRISTINA SKYE's **Safely Home** is the story of a woman determined to help the elderly in her newly adopted community.

PAMELA MORSI explores how literacy and the love of reading can enrich and indeed change lives in **Daffodils in Spring.**

*Thank you... Net proceeds from the sale of this book will be reinvested into the* **Harlequin More Than Words** *program to support causes that are of concern to women.*

**Available wherever books are sold!**

www.Harlequin.com

PHSWCKPM784

# REQUEST YOUR
# FREE BOOKS!

## 2 FREE NOVELS
## FROM THE ROMANCE COLLECTION
## PLUS 2 FREE GIFTS!

**YES!** Please send me 2 FREE novels from the Romance Collection and my 2 FREE gifts (gifts are worth about $10). After receiving them, if I don't wish to receive any more books, I can return the shipping statement marked "cancel." If I don't cancel, I will receive 4 brand-new novels every month and be billed just $5.99 per book in the U.S. or $6.49 per book in Canada. That's a savings of at least 25% off the cover price. It's quite a bargain! Shipping and handling is just 50¢ per book in the U.S. and 75¢ per book in Canada.* I understand that accepting the 2 free books and gifts places me under no obligation to buy anything. I can always return a shipment and cancel at any time. Even if I never buy another book, the two free books and gifts are mine to keep forever.

194/394 MDN FVU7

| | |
|---|---|
| Name | (PLEASE PRINT) |

| | |
|---|---|
| Address | Apt. # |

| | | |
|---|---|---|
| City | State/Prov. | Zip/Postal Code |

Signature (if under 18, a parent or guardian must sign)

Mail to the **Harlequin® Reader Service:**
**IN U.S.A.:** P.O. Box 1867, Buffalo, NY 14240-1867
**IN CANADA:** P.O. Box 609, Fort Erie, Ontario L2A 5X3

**Want to try two free books from another line?**
**Call 1-800-873-8635 or visit www.ReaderService.com.**

* Terms and prices subject to change without notice. Prices do not include applicable taxes. Sales tax applicable in N.Y. Canadian residents will be charged applicable taxes. Offer not valid in Quebec. This offer is limited to one order per household. Not valid for current subscribers to the Romance Collection or the Romance/Suspense Collection. All orders subject to credit approval. Credit or debit balances in a customer's account(s) may be offset by any other outstanding balance owed by or to the customer. Please allow 4 to 6 weeks for delivery. Offer available while quantities last.

**Your Privacy**—The Harlequin® Reader Service is committed to protecting your privacy. Our Privacy Policy is available online at www.ReaderService.com or upon request from the Harlequin Reader Service.

We make a portion of our mailing list available to reputable third parties that offer products we believe may interest you. If you prefer that we not exchange your name with third parties, or if you wish to clarify or modify your communication preferences, please visit us at www.ReaderService.com/consumerschoice or write to us at Harlequin Reader Service Preference Service, P.O. Box 9062, Buffalo, NY 14269. Include your complete name and address.

# shannon stacey

| | | | |
|---|---|---|---|
| 77686 | YOURS TO KEEP | ___ $7.99 U.S. | ___ $9.99 CAN. |
| 77685 | UNDENIABLY YOURS | ___ $7.99 U.S. | ___ $9.99 CAN. |
| 77678 | EXCLUSIVELY YOURS | ___ $7.99 U.S. | ___ $9.99 CAN. |

*(limited quantities available)*

| | |
|---|---|
| TOTAL AMOUNT | $ _____ |
| POSTAGE & HANDLING | $ _____ |
| ($1.00 FOR 1 BOOK, 50¢ for each additional) | |
| APPLICABLE TAXES* | $ _____ |
| TOTAL PAYABLE | $ _____ |

*(check or money order—please do not send cash)*

To order, complete this form and send it, along with a check or money order for the total above, payable to HQN Books, to: **In the U.S.:** 3010 Walden Avenue, P.O. Box 9077, Buffalo, NY 14269-9077; **In Canada:** P.O. Box 636, Fort Erie, Ontario, L2A 5X3.

Name: _____
Address: _____ City: _____
State/Prov.: _____ Zip/Postal Code: _____
Account Number (if applicable): _____

075 CSAS

*New York residents remit applicable sales taxes.
*Canadian residents remit applicable GST and provincial taxes.

**HARLEQUIN**® HQN™
™ www.Harlequin.com

PHSS0113BL